Checks and Balances

The Three Branches of the American Government

Checks and Balances

volume 1

executive

The Three Branches of the American Government

Daniel E. Brannen Jr.

Lawrence W. Baker, *Project Editor*

U·X·L
An imprint of Thomson Gale,
a part of The Thomson Corporation

THOMSON
™
GALE

Detroit • New York • San Francisco • San Diego • New Haven, Conn. • Waterville, Maine • London • Munich

Checks and Balances:
The Three Branches of the American Government

Daniel E. Brannen Jr.

Project Editor
Lawrence W. Baker

Editorial
Michael Lesniak

Rights Acquisition and Management
Jacqueline Key, Ronald Montgomery,
Sheila Spencer

Imaging and Multimedia
Randy Bassett, Lezlie Light, Denay
Wilding

Product Design
Kate Scheible

Composition and Electronic Prepress
Evi Seoud

Manufacturing
Rita Wimberley

LIBRARY OF CONGRESS CATALOGING-IN-PUBLICATION DATA

Brannen, Daniel E., 1968–
  Checks and balances : the three branches of the American government / Daniel E.
Brannen, Jr. ; Lawrence W. Baker, project editor.
     p. cm.
  Includes bibliographical references and index.
  ISBN 0-7876-5409-4 (set hardcover : alk. paper) — ISBN 0-7876-5410-8 (v. 1) —
ISBN 0-7876-5411-6 (v. 2) — ISBN 0-7876-5412-4 (v. 3)
  1. United States—Politics and government. I. Baker, Lawrence W. II. Title.
     JK271.B6496 2005
     320.473—dc22
                                                                                     2005009975

This title is also available as an e-book.
ISBN 1-4144-0468-9
Contact your Thomson Gale sales representative for ordering information.

Printed in the United States of America
10 9 8 7 6 5 4 3 2 1

Contents

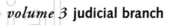

volume 3 judicial branch

Reader's Guide

Checks and Balances: The Three Branches of the American Government offers relevant, easy-to-understand information on the inner workings of the American federal government, from its earliest beginnings to its current structure. The eight chapters of each volume focus on the American government and a particular branch: Volume 1, executive; Volume 2, legislative; and Volume 3, judicial. The first chapter of each volume begins with an identical overview of the American government. The other seven chapters focus on the following aspects of the specific branch:

★ Historic roots

★ Constitutional role

★ Changes through the years

★ Key positions

★ Daily operations

★ Checks and balances with each of the other two branches (two chapters)

Each of the "checks and balances" chapters appears twice in the set. For instance, the "Executive-Legislative Checks and Balances" chapter in the executive branch volume is duplicated as the "Legislative-Executive Checks and Balances" chapter in the legislative branch volume. Illustrations and sidebars vary in those chapters, however.

All chapters include "Words to Know" boxes that provide definitions of important words and concepts within the text. Other sidebars highlight significant facts and describe other related governmental information. A timeline of events, a general glossary, reprints of the U.S. Constitution and the Constitutional Amendments, a general bibliography, and a cumulative index are included in each volume. Approximately 150 black-and-white photos help illustrate *Checks and Balances.*

Acknowledgments

Many thanks go to copyeditor Rebecca Valentine, proofreader Amy Marcaccio Keyzer, indexer Dan Brannen, and the folks at Integra Software Services for their fine work.

Comments and suggestions

We welcome your comments on *Checks and Balances* and suggestions for other topics to consider. Please write: Editors, *Checks and Balances,* UXL, 27500 Drake Rd., Farmington Hills, Michigan 48331-3535; call toll free: 800-877-4253; fax to 248-699-8097; or send e-mail via http://www.gale.com.

Timeline of Events

6th century • Emperor Justinian I of the Byzantine Empire oversees the compilation of the *Corpus Juris Civilis,* or Body of Civil Law. This enormous collection and organization of the laws and legal opinions from emperors and jurists of the Roman Empire affects the development of legal systems in Europe after the Dark Ages (476–1000), and eventually affects the development of American legal systems.

1100s–1200s • England establishes three permanent courts to hear cases that affect the interests of the monarch. The courts, called superior common law courts, influence the development of law in America.

June 1215 • King John of England signs the Magna Carta, a document that proclaims and protects the political and civil liberties of English citizens.

1300s • Political philosopher Niccolò Machiavelli writes *Discourses on the First Ten Books of Titus Livius.* Machiavelli champions the Roman Republic system of government, which influences the convention delegates in Philadelphia, Pennsylvania, nearly five hundred years later.

1648 • British Parliament member Clement Walker writes of a British government that divides its power into three branches.

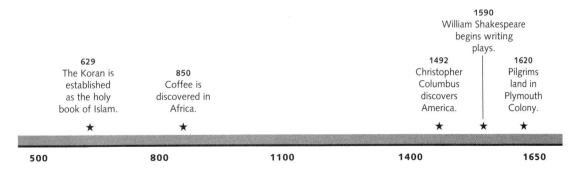

629	850		1492	1590	1620
The Koran is established as the holy book of Islam.	Coffee is discovered in Africa.		Christopher Columbus discovers America.	William Shakespeare begins writing plays.	Pilgrims land in Plymouth Colony.
★	★		★	★	★

500	800	1100	1400	1650

1689 • British Parliament adopts the English Bill of Rights, strengthening Parliament's power in the constitutional monarchy.

1689 • English philosopher John Locke publishes *Two Treatises of Government.* In it, he argues that the legislative branch of government should be separate from the executive branch.

1696 • British Parliament establishes the Board of Trade to oversee Great Britain's commercial interests worldwide. The Board of Trade has the power to review and strike down colonial laws that violate British law. In this way, the Board of Trade resembles the U.S. Supreme Court.

1748 • French philosopher Charles Montesquieu publishes *The Spirit of Laws,* influencing the authors of the U.S. Constitution four decades later.

1765–69 • English legal scholar Sir William Blackstone publishes *Commentaries on the Laws of England,* a thorough description of English law at the time. In it, he celebrates the checks and balances of the British system. Most of the men who write the U.S. Constitution two decades later were familiar with Blackstone's work.

1773 • American colonists express their displeasure over taxes by dumping tea into the harbor during the famous Boston Tea Party.

1774 • The thirteen American colonies first send delegates to the Continental Congress.

1775 • The American Revolutionary War begins.

1776 • Revolutionary figure Thomas Paine criticizes the British system of checks and balances in his pamphlet *Common Sense.*

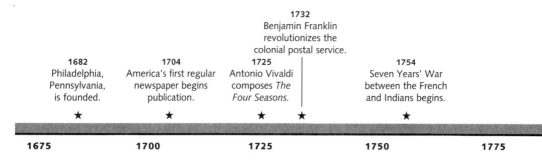

1682 Philadelphia, Pennsylvania, is founded.	1704 America's first regular newspaper begins publication.	1725 Antonio Vivaldi composes *The Four Seasons.*	1732 Benjamin Franklin revolutionizes the colonial postal service.	1754 Seven Years' War between the French and Indians begins.
★	★	★	★	★

| 1675 | 1700 | 1725 | 1750 | 1775 |

July 1776 • The United States of America is born when representatives from the thirteen American colonies join together to break from English rule by signing the Declaration of Independence.

1777 • Delegates serving in the Continental Congress write the Articles of Confederation, one year after America declared independence from Great Britain.

1777 • Pennsylvania physician and political leader Benjamin Rush publishes *Observations on the Government of Pennsylvania,* in which he alludes to a checks and balances form of government. He supports men of moderate wealth having representation in one chamber and men of great wealth having representation in another chamber.

1781 • The states adopt a new form of government with the Articles of Confederation. The articles provide for only a Congress, with no president or judiciary.

1783 • The American Revolutionary War ends.

1786 • Farmers protest debtor laws in Massachusetts in Shays's Rebellion.

1787 • Fifty-five state delegates meet at the Constitutional Convention to frame a Constitution for a federal government.

1787 • In the draft of the Constitution, delegates James Madison and Elbridge Gerry suggest changing Congress's power to "make war" to "declare war."

1787 • The Constitution is presented to the states for approval.

May–June 1787 • Virginia delegate Edmund Randolph proposes that the free men of the states elect members to the

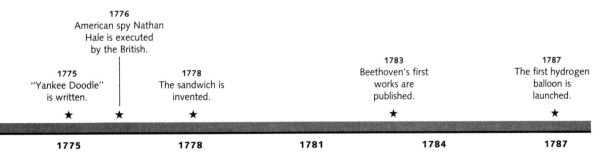

1776
American spy Nathan Hale is executed by the British.

1775
"Yankee Doodle" is written.

1778
The sandwich is invented.

1783
Beethoven's first works are published.

1787
The first hydrogen balloon is launched.

1775   1778   1781   1784   1787

House of Representatives. In turn, members of the House would choose the members of the Senate from nominations made by the state legislatures. Most of the large states, however, want free men to control elections to Congress. They also want state population to be the basis for determining how many members each state would have in each chamber. Most of the small states want at least one chamber of Congress to be elected by the states, and they want that chamber to provide equal representation to each state. A set of compromises leads to the delegates agreeing that free men will elect the members of the House and state legislatures will elect the members of the Senate; also, representation in the House will be based on population, while representation in the Senate will be equal for each state.

1787–88 • New York politician Alexander Hamilton and Secretary of Foreign Affairs John Jay write a series of essays called "The Federalist," an attempt to convince Americans to adopt the U.S. Constitution.

1788 • Virginia delegate and future U.S. president James Monroe writes *Observations upon the Proposed Plan of Federal Government,* in which he states that a preamble would be an important part of the Constitution.

June 1788 • The Constitution becomes law in the United States following ratification.

1789 • The new federal government begins to operate under the Constitution, with George Washington as the country's first president.

1789 • The Judiciary Act of 1789 creates a federal judiciary with trial courts (district and circuit courts) and appellate courts to serve under the Supreme Court, as well as the position of attorney general, who is the lead attorney for the United States, and U.S. attorneys to assist the attorney general with the government's caseload. Congress sets the number of

1787 The dollar currency is introduced in the United States.	1788 New York City becomes the temporary U.S. capital.	1789 The U.S. Army is established.
★	★	★
1787	**1788**	**1789**

Supreme Court justices at six, a number that is raised and lowered seven times until 1869, when it settles on nine justices.

1789 • Congress creates four departments to oversee certain aspects of the government: State, Treasury, War, and Navy.

1789 • President George Washington signs the first appropriations law for the United States. He approves of $568,000 to fund the Departments of War and Treasury, as well as to fund government salaries and pensions.

January 1790 • President George Washington delivers the nation's first annual message, as required by the Constitution.

1790 • Maryland donates land to the U.S. government to be used as the location for the federal capital. The new city is called Washington, D.C., or the District of Columbia.

1791 • The states approve the first ten constitutional amendments, often called the Bill of Rights.

1794 • President George Washington helps end the Whiskey Rebellion by granting a full pardon to rebels involved in the skirmish. The rebellion was a protest by grain farmers against a tax on whiskey.

1797 • The House of Representatives impeaches U.S. senator William Blount of Tennessee, the only time in U.S. history a member of Congress has been impeached. Blount is accused of conspiring to conduct military activities for the king of England; the Senate opts not to conduct an impeachment trial, reasoning that it does not have power under the Constitution to conduct an impeachment trial of a senator.

1798 • Congress passes and President John Adams signs into law the Sedition Act. The new law makes it a crime to say or write anything "false, scandalous and malicious" against the government.

1792	1794	1796
Farmer's Almanac is first published.	The cotton gin is patented.	Edward Jenner introduces the smallpox vaccination.
★	★	★

1789	1792	1794	1796	1798

1798 • The Eleventh Amendment is officially declared part of the Constitution, nearly three years after it was ratified. The amendment decrees that a citizen of one state (or foreign country) may not use the federal court system to sue the government of another state.

1800 • Congress creates the Library of Congress; one year later, it receives its first collection of materials.

1800 • Vice President Thomas Jefferson and New York politician Aaron Burr receive the same number of electoral votes in the presidential election, forcing the House of Representatives to break the tie vote, as required by the Constitution (even though the electors clearly intended Jefferson to be president and Burr to be vice president). Jefferson wins on the thirty-sixth ballot.

1801 • President Thomas Jefferson begins the tradition of delivering his messages to Congress in written form. This form of communication between president and Congress continues for 112 years.

1801 • President Thomas Jefferson repeals the Sedition Act.

1801 • The Federalist-controlled Congress lowers the number of Supreme Court seats from six to five so that the new president, Democratic-Republican Thomas Jefferson, would be unable to appoint a replacement if Justice William Cushing, who was ill at the time, died.

1802 • The Democratic-Republican Party gains control of Congress, and raises the number of justices back to six.

1802 • Congress assigns one Supreme Court justice to travel to each circuit to hear trials.

1803 • In *Marbury v. Madison,* the U.S. Supreme Court rules that a federal law giving the Supreme Court the power to hear cases for compelling government action is unconstitutional.

1799	1800	1803
The Rosetta Stone is found in Egypt.	John Adams is the first president to live in the White House.	The United States nearly doubles, following the Louisiana Purchase.
★	★	★

1798	1799	1800	1801	1803

Under the Constitution, such cases must begin in a lower federal court, with the Supreme Court permitted to review them only on appeal.

1803 • Federal district court judge John Pickering is the first judge to be impeached. He is convicted of drunkenness and removed from office.

1803 • Judicial review becomes a permanent part of the federal judiciary after the U.S. Supreme Court announces its power to strike down congressional laws that violate the U.S. Constitution.

1804 • The House of Representatives impeaches Supreme Court justice Samuel Chase; the Senate, however, votes not to convict him.

1804 • The Twelfth Amendment to the Constitution is adopted, requiring that electors label their two votes: one for president and the other for vice president. Previously, electors voted for their top two choices, with the leading vote-getter becoming president and the runner-up being elected vice president. In 1800, this flawed system resulted in a tie vote between two members of the same party.

1812 • Congress uses its constitutional right by declaring war (the War of 1812).

1824 • None of the presidential candidates receives a majority of electoral votes, forcing the U.S. House of Representatives to choose between the leading three vote-getters. Secretary of State John Quincy Adams wins the election after the candidate who was no longer eligible, Speaker of the House Henry Clay, convinces the states that had voted for him to support Adams. Later, Clay becomes Adams's secretary of state, leading many to believe that Adams had promised Clay the position in exchange for his votes.

1804	1806	1814	1825	1834
apoléon Bonaparte is crowned emperor of France.	*Webster's Dictionary* is first published.	Francis Scott Key writes the "Star Spangled Banner."	The New York Stock Exchange opens.	The Braille system for the blind is invented.
★	★	★	★	★
1803	**1810**	**1817**	**1824**	**1837**

April 1841 • President William Henry Harrison dies after only a month in office. His vice president, John Tyler, insists that the Constitution allows him to fill the office of the presidency for the remainder of Harrison's term. Evidence to the contrary does not exist, so Tyler stays on as president, establishing a line-of-succession tradition.

1846 • Congress uses its constitutional right by declaring war (the Mexican War).

1857 • In *Scott v. Sandford,* the U.S. Supreme Court rules that former slave Dred Scott is not a citizen of the United States because African Americans could not be citizens under the U.S. Constitution.

1860 • Congress creates the Government Printing Office, which serves as a printer for Congress and collects and publishes information about the federal government for all three of its branches.

1861 • The American Civil War begins.

1862 • U.S. district judge West H. Humphreys of Tennessee is impeached by the U.S. House of Representatives and removed by the Senate, on charges of joining the Confederacy without resigning his judgeship.

1862 • President Abraham Lincoln creates the U.S. Department of Agriculture.

1863 • Congress raises the number of justices on the U.S. Supreme Court to ten. This allows President Abraham Lincoln to appoint a new justice at a time when he is stretching his constitutional powers to conduct the American Civil War.

1865 • The Thirteenth Amendment bans slavery.

1865 • The American Civil War ends.

1844 Samuel F. B. Morse transmits the first telegraph message.	1852 The Otis safety elevator is invented.	1856 Neanderthal man fossils are found.	1862 Jefferson Davis becomes president of the Confederacy.	1865 President Abraham Lincoln is assassinated.
★	★	★	★	★

| 1841 | 1847 | 1853 | 1859 | 1865 |

1866 • Congress reduces the number of U.S. Supreme Court seats from ten to seven. Congress fears that President Andrew Johnson, who is against many of Congress's Reconstruction Acts for rebuilding the country after the American Civil War, will appoint justices who will strike down the acts as unconstitutional.

1868 • The states adopt the Fourteenth Amendment, which declares that all people born or naturalized in the United States are citizens of the country and of the state in which they live.

1868 • Andrew Johnson is the first U.S. president to be impeached. He escapes removal from office by a single vote in the U.S. Senate.

1869 • Congress raises the number of Supreme Court seats from seven to nine, shortly after the inauguration of Ulysses S. Grant. The number has been fixed there ever since.

1870 • The Fifteenth Amendment makes it illegal to deny a person the right to vote based on race or color.

1870 • The attorney general becomes head of the U.S. Department of Justice.

1873 • England combines common law and equity courts into one court. U.S. federal courts would later do the same thing.

1875 • Congress passes the Civil Rights Act of 1875, making discrimination illegal in places of public accommodation, such as inns and theaters.

1875 • Congress reorganizes the judiciary by passing the Judiciary Act of 1875. It shifts some kinds of trials from the circuit courts to the district courts and gives the circuit courts more responsibility for hearing appeals.

1866	1868	1870	1874	1876
The first U.S. oil pipeline is completed.	Louisa May Alcott publishes *Little Women*.	The first African American congressmen take office.	The first American zoo opens in Philadelphia.	Alexander Graham Bell invents the telephone.
★	★	★	★	★
1866	1869	1872	1875	1878

1883 • The U.S. Supreme Court strikes down the Civil Rights Act of 1875, saying the Fourteenth Amendment only made discrimination by states illegal, not by private persons in their businesses.

1891 • Congress passes the Circuit Courts of Appeals Act, finishing the judicial branch reorganization that began in 1875. The act transfers most federal trials to the district courts, creates nine new circuit courts of appeals, and requires the Supreme Court to hear only certain kinds of appeals from the district and circuit courts and from the circuit courts of appeals.

1896 • The U.S. Supreme Court decides in *Plessy v. Ferguson* that the Fourteenth Amendment does not prevent states from requiring whites and blacks to use separate railway cars. The Court rules that "separate but equal" facilities satisfy the "equal protection" requirements of the Fourteenth Amendment.

1898 • Congress uses its constitutional right by declaring war (the Spanish-American War).

1899 • The U.S. House of Representatives names its first official whip.

1912 • The number of members of the U.S. House of Representatives reaches 435, a total that has not changed in subsequent years.

1913 • President Woodrow Wilson revives the practice of delivering his annual address to Congress orally.

February 1913 • The Sixteenth Amendment is ratified, giving Congress the power to collect an income tax.

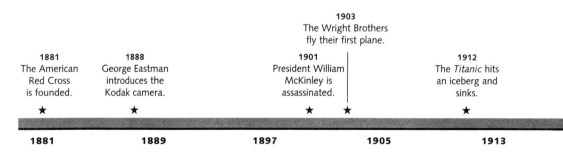

1903
The Wright Brothers
fly their first plane.

1881
The American
Red Cross
is founded.

1888
George Eastman
introduces the
Kodak camera.

1901
President William
McKinley is
assassinated.

1912
The *Titanic* hits
an iceberg and
sinks.

1881   1889   1897   1905   1913

May 1913 • The Seventeenth Amendment is ratified, which changes the way U.S. senators are elected to office. Instead of state legislatures electing them, citizens vote them in.

1917 • Congress uses its constitutional right by declaring war (World War I).

January 1919 • The Eighteenth Amendment is ratified, making the manufacture, sale, and transportation of alcoholic beverages illegal.

1920s • U.S. senators of both the Republican and Democratic parties began to elect official majority and minority leaders.

August 1920 • The Nineteenth Amendment is ratified, giving women the right to vote.

1921 • Congress passes the Budgeting and Accounting Act. The act gives the president the job of preparing an initial budget plan each year, and also creates the Bureau of the Budget (later renamed the Office of Management and Budget), a governmental office for helping the president prepare the budget.

1923 • President Calvin Coolidge is the first president to broadcast his annual address to Congress on the radio.

1933 • The Twentieth Amendment is ratified, changing the dates the president, vice president, and members of Congress take office, following the November election. The amendment also states that the vice president–elect becomes president in the event of the death of the president-elect.

1933 • The Twenty-first Amendment is ratified, ending nationwide prohibition by repealing the Eighteenth Amendment.

1937 • President Franklin D. Roosevelt tries to change the philosophical makeup of the Supreme Court by asking Congress to increase the number of seats on the Supreme Court from nine to fifteen and allow Roosevelt to fill the new seats

1913 The first Charlie Chaplin silent movie is released.	1920 Joan of Arc is canonized a saint.	1923 Edwin Hubble identifies galaxies beyond the Milky Way.	1929 The Great Depression begins.	1933 German Nazis build the first concentration camps.
★	★	★	★	★
1913	1919	1925	1931	1937

whenever a justice over seventy years of age does not resign. (Four justices who regularly voted against Roosevelt's New Deal program were already over seventy, and the president wanted to appoint new justices who would support his New Deal.) The plan is controversial, and is proved to be unnecessary; the Court winds up approving much of Roosevelt's New Deal legislation and the president names five replacement justices through 1940 as a result of three retirements and two deaths. Congress does not approve of Roosevelt's "court-packing."

1939 • President Franklin D. Roosevelt creates the Executive Office of the President to help the president manage the executive branch. Four of the most important positions in the department are the chief of staff, director of the Office of Management and Budget, director of the National Economic Council, and national security advisor.

1940 • President Franklin D. Roosevelt tells Democratic Party officials he will not run for a third term unless they select Secretary of Agriculture Henry A. Wallace as his vice presidential running mate. The party grants Roosevelt's wish, thus beginning the tradition of presidential candidates choosing their running mates.

1941 • Congress uses its constitutional right by declaring war (World War II).

1947 • President Harry S. Truman is the first president to broadcast his annual address to Congress on television.

1947 • The War Department, Navy Department, and Department of the Air Force combine to form the Department of Defense.

1947 • The National Security Council is created to advise the president on national security affairs.

1939	1942	1945	1948
The Baseball Hall of Fame is established.	Humphrey Bogart stars in *Casablanca*.	The United States drops two atomic bombs on Japan.	Jews in Palestine form the State of Israel.
★	★	★	★

1937	1940	1943	1946	1949

1949 • Congress passes a law making the vice president an official member of the National Security Council.

March 1951 • The Twenty-second Amendment is ratified, limiting presidents to a maximum of two terms, or two terms and two years if the president was finishing no more than half of his predecessor's term.

1954 • The U.S. Supreme Court unanimously decides in *Brown v. Board of Education of Topeka* that separate public services are not equal under the Fourteenth Amendment. This is an example of an amendment not changing but the Supreme Court's *interpretation* of it changing.

1961 • The Twenty-third Amendment is ratified, allowing Washington, D.C., to select a number of electors equal to the number of senators and representatives it would have if it were a state, but no more than the number of electors allowed for the least populous state. This gives electors from Washington, D.C., the chance to vote in a presidential election.

January 1964 • The Twenty-fourth Amendment is ratified, making it illegal for the United States or any state to charge a poll tax for participating in presidential and congressional elections.

July 1964 • President Lyndon B. Johnson signs into law the Civil Rights Act, making discrimination illegal in public places, such as motels and restaurants. Congress says it passed the act using its power under the Interstate Commerce Clause. Later, in *Heart of Atlanta Motel v. United States* and *Katzenbach v. McClung,* the U.S. Supreme Court rules that the Civil Rights Act is lawful under the Constitution because Congress can outlaw private discrimination under its power to regulate interstate commerce, but not under the equal rights provisions of the Fourteenth Amendment.

1951 Color television is introduced in the United States.	1954 Elvis Presley makes his first commercial recording.	1955 Jonas Salk invents the polio vaccine.	1959 Fidel Castro becomes premier of Cuba.	1963 President John F. Kennedy is assassinated.
★	★	★	★	★

| 1949 | 1953 | 1957 | 1961 | 1965 |

1967 • The Twenty-fifth Amendment is ratified, officially providing for the vice president to become president "in case of the removal of the president from office or his death or resignation." Prior to the adoption of this amendment, the vice president's swearing-in to office—which had happened seven times before—was by tradition only.

1967 • The Department of Transportation is established.

1968 • Congress passes the Federal Magistrates Act, giving district courts the power to appoint magistrate judges to help district court judges do their jobs.

July 1971 • The Twenty-sixth Amendment is ratified, lowering the voting age to eighteen.

1972 • The U.S. Supreme Court rules in *Roe v. Wade* that states cannot ban abortions completely because women have a constitutional right to have abortions in some cases. After that decision, some states rewrite their abortion laws to ban abortions in situations allowed under the Supreme Court's ruling. This is an example of a legislative check on judicial power.

1973 • Congress passes the War Powers Resolution to try to strengthen the constitutional separation of military powers. President Richard Nixon vetoes the bill, but both chambers of Congress vote to override the veto. The resolution says presidents should commit troops only with congressional consultation and authorization.

1973 • President Richard Nixon tries to use executive privilege to hide information about the Watergate scandal from Senate investigators.

October 1973 • Spiro T. Agnew resigns as vice president after it is divulged that he failed to report almost $30,000 on his federal income tax return in 1967 while he was governor of

1967	1969	1970	1972	1973
The first human heart transplant takes place.	Neil Armstrong is the first astronaut to walk on the moon.	Four Vietnam War protesters are killed at Kent State University.	The United States reestablishes relations with the People's Republic of China.	U.S. troops pull out of Vietnam.
★	★	★	★	★
1967	**1969**	**1970**	**1972**	**1973**

Maryland. He is also accused of taking bribes while serving as a county official in Maryland.

December 1973 • The Twenty-fifth Amendment is invoked for the first time when U.S. representative Gerald Ford is approved by Congress as the new vice president.

1974 • Congress passes the Budget and Impoundment Control Act, which creates the Congressional Budget Office and standing budget committees in both chambers of Congress.

August 1974 • President Richard M. Nixon resigns from office, the first president in history to do so. The House was almost certainly about to impeach him for his role in covering up a 1972 burglary of the offices of the Democratic National Committee by members of the Republican Party, a scandal known as Watergate. Gerald Ford succeeds him, becoming the only person to serve as both president and vice president without being elected to either office.

September 1974 • President Gerald Ford pardons former president Richard Nixon for any involvement he had in the Watergate scandal. Ford reasons that a long trial involving Nixon would not allow the country to move beyond the scandal.

1980 • Congress creates the Department of Education.

1981 • Sandra Day O'Connor becomes the first female U.S. Supreme Court justice.

1983 • The U.S. Supreme Court decides in *INS v. Chadha* that the legislative veto violates the Constitution. The Constitution says the only way Congress can pass a bill or resolution is when both chambers approve it and present it to the president for executive veto consideration. Legislative vetoes violate this by giving either one or both chambers of

1974 Hank Aaron passes Babe Ruth as baseball's all-time home run hitter.	1976 The United States celebrates its bicentennial.	1978 John Paul II begins his reign as pope.	1982 The compact disc (CD) is introduced.
★	★	★	★

1973	1976	1978	1981	1983

Congress the power to take official action that the president cannot veto. Despite the Court's ruling, Congress continues to include the legislative veto power in the nation's laws.

1984 • U.S. congresswoman Geraldine Ferraro of New York becomes the first female vice presidential candidate on a major party ticket, running unsuccessfully with the Democratic presidential contender, former vice president Walter Mondale.

1992 • More than two hundred years after it was first proposed by Congress, the Twenty-seventh Amendment is ratified. It says that if Congress passes a law changing the salaries for senators or representatives, the law cannot take effect until after at least one House election passes. This prevents representatives from giving themselves pay raises while in office.

1993 • The National Economic Council is created to help the president develop and implement economic policies, both domestic and international.

1996 • Congress passes the Line Item Veto Act, allowing the president to strike specific dollar amounts and tax benefits from appropriations bills passed by Congress. Congress can override the line item veto only by passing another bill containing the portions the president has stricken.

1997 • Madeleine Albright becomes the first female secretary of state.

1998 • The U.S. Supreme Court strikes down the 1996 Line Item Veto Act. The Court rules that it violates the Constitution, which states that the president may use his veto power to veto only an *entire* bill.

1998 • President Bill Clinton becomes the second president to be impeached. He is charged with perjury and obstruction of justice relating to an Arkansas real estate deal, a sexual

1985 Microsoft introduces Windows to the market.	1989 The Berlin Wall is torn down.	1993 Toni Morrison becomes the first African American to win the Nobel Prize for literature.	1994 Nelson Mandela becomes the first black president of South Africa.	1999 The euro is accepted as legal tender in Europe.
★	★	★ ★		★

| 1984 | 1988 | 1992 | 1996 | 2000 |

harassment case, and a relationship with a White House intern. The U.S. Senate vote leaves him in office, however.

2000 • In the extremely tight presidential election of 2000 between Texas governor George W. Bush and Vice President Al Gore, a narrow victory for Bush in Florida leads Gore to sue to have votes in certain counties recounted. Bush appeals one of the cases from the Florida Supreme Court to the U.S. Supreme Court. The U.S. Supreme Court issues a decision in December, stopping the recounts in Florida, giving Bush Florida's twenty-five electoral votes and, therefore, making him the presidential victor.

September 2001 • President George W. Bush delivers a special message to Congress following the terrorist attacks of September 11, 2001. Aside from their annual addresses to Congress, it is rare for presidents to speak to the complete Congress.

October 2001 • The Office of Homeland Security is created following the terrorist attacks of September 11, 2001. A year later, it becomes a full department in the executive branch.

2001	2002	2003	2004	2005
Terrorists attack the World Trade Center and the Pentagon.	Washington, D.C., snipers kill ten, wound others.	The United States declares war on Iraq.	A powerful tsunami in the Indian Ocean kills hundreds of thousands.	George W. Bush begins his second term as president.
★	★	★	★	★
2001	2002	2003	2004	2005

Words to Know

appropriations bill: A bill, or law, that assigns money to a government department or agency.

Articles of Confederation: The document that established the federal government for the United States of America from 1781 to 1789.

bicameralism: The practice of dividing the legislative, or law-making, power of government into two chambers.

Bill of Rights: The first ten amendments to the U.S. Constitution, proposed in 1789 and adopted in 1791. The Bill of Rights contains some of the rights of citizens of the United States of America.

cabinet: A group of executive officials who advise the president on important policy matters and decisions. By law, the cabinet includes the heads of the executive departments. Presidents can also include other important executive officials in their cabinets, such as the vice president.

casework: Work that a member of Congress does to help a voter with a personal governmental problem.

checks and balances: The specific powers in one branch of government that allow it to limit the powers of the other branches.

circuit court of appeals: A court in the federal judicial system that handles appeals from the trial courts, called federal district courts. The United States is divided into twelve geographic areas called circuits, and each circuit has one court of appeals that handles appeals from the federal district courts in its circuit. A party who loses in a circuit court of appeals may ask the Supreme Court to review the case.

civil case: A case that involves a dispute between private parties or a noncriminal dispute between a private party and a government.

cloture rule: A rule that allows senators to end a filibuster, or prolonged speech, by a vote of three-fifths of the Senate.

common law: A law developed by judges in England and America on a case-by-case basis for governing relationships between private parties. Examples of common law include contract law and tort law.

Congress: The legislative, or lawmaking, branch of the federal government. Congress has two chambers, the Senate and the House of Representatives.

constituents: The voters who are in a representative's district or a senator's state.

Constitution of the United States of America: The document written in 1787 that established the federal government under which the United States of America has operated since 1789. Article I covers the legislative branch, Article II covers the executive branch, and Article III covers the judicial branch.

Constitutional Convention of 1787: Convention held in Philadelphia, Pennsylvania, from May to September 1787, during which delegates from twelve of the thirteen American states wrote a new Constitution for the United States.

Continental Congress: The main body of American government from 1774 until 1779.

courts of appeals: Federal appellate courts that review district court trials to correct serious errors made by judges and juries.

criminal case: A case in which a person is charged with violating a criminal law.

district courts: The courts in the federal judicial system that handle trials in civil and criminal cases. Each state is divided into one or more federal judicial districts, and each district has one or more federal district courts. A party who loses in a federal district court may appeal to have the case reviewed by a circuit court of appeals.

executive branch: The branch of the federal government that enforces the nation's laws. The executive branch includes the president, the vice president, and many executive departments, agencies, and offices.

executive departments: Departments in the executive branch responsible for large areas of the federal government. As of 2005, there are fifteen departments: Agriculture, Commerce, Defense, Education, Energy, Health and Human Services, Homeland Security, Housing and Urban Development, Interior, Justice, Labor, State, Transportation, Treasury, and Veterans Affairs. The heads of the departments, called secretaries, make up the president's cabinet.

executive privilege: A privilege that allows the president to keep information secret, even if Congress, federal investigators, the Supreme Court, or the people want the president to release the information. The privilege is designed to protect information related to national security, or public safety.

federalism: A principle of government under which independent states join to form a central government to serve their collective needs.

filibuster: A tactic used by one or more senators who speak for a prolonged period of time so that the time for considering a bill runs out before a vote can be taken on the Senate floor.

Founding Fathers: General term for the men who founded the United States of America and designed its government. The term includes the men who signed the Declaration of Independence in 1776 and the Constitution of the United States in 1787.

impoundment: The presidential practice of refusing to spend money that Congress appropriates for an executive department, agency, or program.

income tax: A tax on the money and property that a person earns during the year.

Interstate Commerce Clause: The clause in Article I, Section 8, of the Constitution that gives Congress the power "to regulate commerce ... among the several states."

iron triangle: The three-way relationship between congressional committees, executive agencies, and private interest groups that all specialize in the same area of government.

judge: A public official who presides over a court and who often decides questions brought before him or her.

judicial interpretation: The process by which federal courts interpret the meaning of laws passed by Congress.

judicial review: The process by which federal courts review laws to determine whether they violate the U.S. Constitution. If a court finds that a law violates the Constitution, it declares the law unconstitutional, which means the executive branch is not supposed to enforce it anymore. Congress can correct such a defect by passing a new law that does not violate the Constitution.

judiciary: The branch of the federal government that decides cases that arise under the nation's law. The federal judiciary includes the Supreme Court of the United States, circuit courts of appeals, and federal district courts.

justice: One of nine jurists who serve on the U.S. Supreme Court. The chief justice serves as the head of the Supreme Court; the other eight are called associate justices.

legislative courts: Courts created by Congress to handle some of its lawmaking powers under Article I of the U.S. Constitution.

lobbying: Meeting with members of Congress to convince them to pass laws that will benefit businesses, citizen's groups, or other organizations.

monarchy: A government under which power is held by a monarch, such as a king or queen, who inherits power by birth or takes it by force.

natural law: The idea that human laws must conform to a higher law—one of nature, often believed to come from God.

Necessary and Proper Clause: The clause in Article I, Section 8, of the Constitution that gives Congress the power "to make all laws which shall be necessary and proper" for exercising the other powers of the federal government.

personnel floor: A congressional minimum on the number of employees a governmental department, agency, or program must employ.

plutocracy: A government under which power is held by the wealthy class of society.

president: The highest officer in the executive branch of the federal government, with primary responsibility for enforcing the nation's laws.

quorum: The number of members of Congress who must be present for Congress to conduct business, such as voting on bills. The U.S. Constitution says a chamber has a quorum when a simple majority of its members is present.

ratification: The process of formally approving something, such as a treaty, constitution, or constitutional amendment.

reception provisions: Laws passed by some of the new American states around 1776 to define which parts of the common law, English statutes, and colonial statutes continued to apply in the states after they separated from Great Britain.

reprogramming: The practice of using money that Congress appropriates to one governmental program for a different program.

republicanism: Theory of government under which power is held by the people, who elect public servants to represent them in the bodies of government.

separation of powers: Division of the powers of government into different branches to prevent one branch from having too much power.

suffrage: The right to vote.

Supreme Court: The highest court in the federal judiciary. The judiciary is the branch of government responsible for resolving legal disputes and interpreting laws on a case-by-case basis.

unicameralism: The practice of placing the legislative, or law-making, power of government in one chamber.

veto: Rejection of a bill, or proposed law, by the president of the United States. If the president vetoes a bill, it does not become law unless two-thirds of both chambers of Congress vote to override the veto.

vice president: The second highest officer in the executive branch of the federal government. The vice president replaces the president if the president dies or becomes unable to serve. The vice president also serves as president of the Senate, with power to break tie votes when the whole Senate is equally divided on an issue.

Checks and Balances

The Three Branches of the American Government

American Government: An Overview

The Constitution is the framework for the federal government of the United States of America. Written in 1787 and adopted in 1788, it carves the federal government into three branches. Generally, the legislative branch makes America's laws, the executive branch enforces the laws, and the judicial branch decides cases under the laws. The Constitution also gives the three branches duties outside the realm of the nation's laws.

The division of government into branches is what political scientists call the separation of powers. The separation of powers prevents the same person or branch of government from having full power to make, enforce, and interpret the nation's laws. The separation set up by the Constitution, however, is not absolute. Each branch has powers that allow it to affect the affairs of the other branches. These checks and balances prevent the branches of government from being completely separate. Indeed, some observers believe the checks and balances make the federal government one of shared powers, not separate powers.

The legislative branch: Congress

The Constitution contains six parts called articles and, as of 2005, twenty-seven parts called amendments. Amendments are changes made since the original six articles were adopted in 1788. The first three articles cover the three branches of government, and the very first article covers the legislative branch. It begins, "All legislative Powers herein granted shall be vested in a Congress of the United States, which shall consist of a Senate and House of Representatives."

Words to Know

checks and balances: The specific powers in one branch of government that allow it to limit the powers of the other branches.

Congress: The legislative, or lawmaking, branch of the federal government. Congress has two chambers, the Senate and the House of Representatives.

judicial interpretation: The process by which federal courts interpret the meaning of laws passed by Congress.

judicial review: The process by which federal courts review laws to determine whether they violate the U.S. Constitution. If a court finds that a law violates the Constitution, it declares the law unconstitutional, which means the executive branch is not supposed to enforce it anymore. Congress can correct such a defect by passing a new law that does not violate the Constitution.

president: The highest officer in the executive branch of the federal government, with primary responsibility for enforcing the nation's laws.

separation of powers: Division of the powers of government into different branches to prevent one branch from having too much power.

Supreme Court: The highest court in the federal judiciary. The judiciary is the branch of government responsible for resolving legal disputes and interpreting laws on a case-by-case basis.

The powers of Congress The legislative power is the power to make laws, so Congress is the nation's main lawmaker. Article I, Section 8, lists Congress's lawmaking power, including the power to:

★ collect taxes and other money for paying the nation's debts and providing for its common defense and general welfare

★ regulate commerce, or business, that crosses the boundaries of states, Indian lands, and foreign nations

★ establish rules for naturalization, which is the process by which people from other countries can become citizens of the United States

★ create money and punish counterfeiters (people who make fake money to be used as real money)

★ raise and support armies and navies and provide rules for regulating them

In the Constitution, this list ends with a general clause that says Congress has the power "to make all Laws which shall be necessary and proper for carrying into Execution the foregoing

Powers, and all other Powers vested by this Constitution in the Government of the United States, or in any Department or Officer thereof. " In other words, Congress has the general power to make all laws the government needs to exercise its specific powers.

The chambers of Congress The very same section of the Constitution that makes Congress the lawmaker divides it into two chambers, the Senate and the House of Representatives. The Senate contains two senators from each state of the United States, for a total of one hundred as of 2005. Delegates from small states, such as New Jersey and New Hampshire, insisted on this arrangement when they met to write the Constitution in steamy Philadelphia, Pennsylvania, in the summer of 1787. The delegates from small states feared that the large states would control the federal government without a legislative chamber that gave each state equal representation. Two senators from each state—regardless of geographic size or population—means each state has equal power in the Senate.

As of 2005, the House of Representatives contains 435 members, a total that has not changed since 1912. This number comes from a law passed by Congress, not from the Constitution. The Constitution only says that each state must have at least one member in the House, and may have no more than one member for every thirty thousand people in the state.

Under the Constitution, the total number of members in the House must be divided among the states once every ten years based on the population of each state. Roughly speaking, then, each state has control in the House in proportion to the size of its population. States then divide themselves into districts, with one House member representing each district. Redistricting is the process of dividing the total number of House members for a state among its districts based on the population census taken every ten years. The most recent redistricting happened after publication of the 2000 federal census.

The Senate and the House of Representatives share most of the powers of Congress equally. Both chambers can propose changes to the Constitution, called amendments, although three-fourths of the states must approve an amendment before it becomes law. Action by both chambers is necessary to admit new states to the United States, a topic that occasionally arises concerning the District of Columbia and Puerto Rico, which are

Birth of a Government

The U.S. Constitution, written in 1787, created a federal government that has lasted into the twenty-first century. The Constitution was signed by representatives, then called delegates, from twelve of the thirteen states that made up the United States in 1787: Connecticut, Delaware, Georgia, Maryland, Massachusetts, New Hampshire, New Jersey, New York, North Carolina, Pennsylvania, South Carolina, and Virginia. (Rhode Island sent no delegates to the Constitutional Convention of 1787. Its population of mostly farmers rejected the Convention's goal of creating a strong central government, which would be hard for the people to control from their communities, far away from the capital.)

The Constitution became law in the United States in June 1788 after ten of the thirteen states ratified, or approved, it. The new federal government began to operate under the Constitution in 1789.

The Constitution, however, did not create the United States of America, and was not the blueprint for its first government. The country was born on July 4, 1776, when representatives from the thirteen American colonies joined together to break from English rule by signing the Declaration of Independence.

At the time of independence in 1776, the new American states operated together as a nation in the Continental Congress. In 1781, the states adopted a new form of government with the Articles of Confederation. American government under the Articles of Confederation had only a Congress, with no president or judiciary. The weakness of this government led the men who wanted a powerful federal government to call for writing the U.S. Constitution in 1787.

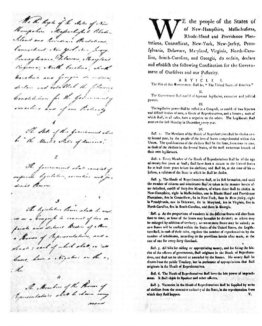

Manuscript draft and only known copy of first printing of the U.S. Constitution. Getty Images.

not states as of 2005. Congress as a whole shares the power to make rules and regulations for territories of the United States, which are lands that the United States controls without making them states. Examples of territories are Puerto Rico and the U.S. Virgin Islands in the Caribbean Sea, and Guam and the Northern Mariana Islands in the Pacific Ocean.

Each chamber of Congress must pass a bill for the bill to become law. Both chambers can pass bills for raising money, such as through taxes, but such bills must start in the House. If the president vetoes, or rejects, a bill, the bill dies unless two-thirds of the members of each chamber of Congress vote to override the veto. In this case, the bill becomes law despite the president's veto.

Only the House can impeach the president, vice president, and other civil officers of the United States, including judges. Impeachment is a formal accusation that someone has committed treason, bribery, or other high crimes or misdemeanors. The Constitution defines treason as levying war against America or giving aid and comfort to its enemies. Bribery is an illegal payment to influence official action. U.S. district judge West H. Humphreys (1806–1882) of Tennessee was impeached in 1862, and removed by the Senate, on charges of joining the Confederacy without resigning his judgeship, but nobody has been impeached specifically for treason. Additionally, nobody has been impeached for bribery, but six of the seventeen impeachments in history to date have involved accusations that an official used his office for improper personal gain. The Constitution does not define "high crimes" or "misdemeanors." The House has interpreted the phrase loosely to mean any conduct that makes a person unfit to continue in office. The two highest-profile impeachments were presidents: Andrew Johnson (1808–1875; served 1865–69) in 1868 and Bill Clinton (1946–; served 1993–2001) in 1998.

Once accused by impeachment in the House, a civil officer stands trial in the Senate. The Senate alone can convict the officer. To convict an impeached officer, two-thirds of the senators at an impeachment trial must vote for conviction. Following their impeachment, neither President Johnson nor President Clinton were voted out of office, though Johnson missed conviction by only a single vote.

In addition to conducting impeachment trials, the Senate has two other powers that the House does not. If the president makes a treaty, or formal agreement, with another country, the treaty becomes law in America only if two-thirds of the senators present approve it. Similarly, a simple majority of senators must approve the president's selection of Supreme Court justices, ambassadors, and other important government officers, including the heads of the departments in the executive branch, such as the Justice Department.

Limits on congressional power The Constitution limits the powers given to Congress. Section 9 of Article I says Congress may not eliminate the writ of habeas corpus. A writ is a judicial order, and habeas corpus is a Latin term meaning "to have the body." The writ of habeas corpus is a procedure that prisoners can use to get released if they are being held in violation of the law. The writ requires a jailer to bring the prisoner before a court, where a judge can set the prisoner free if he or she is being held in violation of constitutional rights.

The Constitution also says Congress may not pass bills of attainder or ex post facto laws. A bill of attainder is a law that convicts a person of treason or other serious crime without a trial. An ex post facto law is one that punishes a person for doing something that was not illegal when done.

Amendments adopted since 1789, when the federal government began to operate under the Constitution, also limit the power of Congress. The states approved the first ten of these amendments, often called the Bill of Rights, in 1791. The Bill of Rights limits but does not eliminate Congress's power to restrict the freedoms of religion, speech, and assembly (First Amendment) and the right to bear arms (Second Amendment). The Eighth Amendment prevents Congress from passing a law that would impose cruel and unusual punishment on convicted criminals.

In addition to limits imposed by the Constitution, the system of checks and balances limits congressional power, too. As chief executive of the United States, the president enforces the laws made by Congress. A president who thinks a particular law is unwise or unimportant can ignore it by devoting people and money to enforcing other laws. As commander in chief of the U.S. Army and Navy, the president controls the military that Congress establishes.

The judiciary also checks the power of Congress. The primary judicial check is judicial review, which is the power to review congressional laws to determine if they violate any of the limitations in the Constitution. Judicial review is a controversial part of the system of checks and balances, because the Constitution does not specifically say the judiciary has this power. Many of the men who wrote the Constitution, however, presumed the judiciary would exercise this power. The Supreme Court confirmed this presumption in the 1803 case of

Marbury v. Madison. In that case, the Supreme Court decided that a federal law giving the Supreme Court the power to hear cases for compelling government action was unconstitutional. Under the Constitution, such cases must begin in a lower federal court. The Supreme Court may only review them on appeal.

The executive branch: the president

The second Article of the Constitution begins, "The executive power shall be vested in a President of the United States of America." The executive power is the power to enforce the laws made by Congress.

The president's duties Only four paragraphs in the Constitution say what the president's duties are. The power to enforce the nation's laws comes from the clause that says, "he shall take care that the laws be faithfully executed."

Making sure the laws are enforced would be impossible for one person, even in 1789. The Constitution says the president "may require the Opinion, in writing, of the principal Officer in each of the Executive Departments." This clause is a seed that has grown to give the executive branch fifteen major departments plus many more agencies. As of 2005, the fifteen departments are: Agriculture, Commerce, Defense, Education, Energy, Health and Human Services, Homeland Security, Housing and Urban Development, Interior, Justice, Labor, State, Transportation, Treasury, and Veterans Affairs. Some of the agencies are the Central Intelligence Agency (CIA), the Environmental Protection Agency (EPA), the National Aeronautics and Space Administration (NASA), the Peace Corps, and the U.S. Postal Service.

Many of the departments and agencies make and enforce laws, called regulations, that relate to their area of service. For example, under power given to it by Congress, the EPA makes rules concerning the nation's air, land, and water. Executive departments and agencies also administer government programs. The Department of Agriculture, for instance, gives money to industrial farming operations that qualify for financial help under congressional laws.

The head of each of the fifteen executive departments is called the secretary (except for the head of the Department of Justice, who is called the attorney general). The fifteen department heads make up the core of the president's cabinet. Presidents also may include other officials in their cabinet, such as the vice president, the chief of staff (the person who manages the president's staff), and important directors from executive agencies, such as the Central Intelligence Agency or the Office of Management and Budget. Presidents rely on their cabinet not only to run the departments, but also to give the president information and advice for making important decisions.

Besides enforcing the nation's laws, the president is commander in chief of the U.S. Army and Navy. This means the military is ultimately controlled by a civilian, a person who is not part of the military. Putting a civilian in control of the military is

Cabinet members of President George W. Bush's first term. Front row (left to right): Donald Evans, Gale Norton, Donald Rumsfeld, Colin Powell, President Bush, Vice President Dick Cheney, Paul O'Neill, John Ashcroft, Ann Veneman, and Elaine Chao. Back row (left to right): Robert Zoellick, Christine Todd Whitman, Roderick Paige, Norman Mineta, Tommy Thompson, Mel Martinez, Spencer Abraham, Anthony Principi, Mitch Daniels, and Andrew Card. Cabinet members are the president's top advisors. Photograph by Paul Morse. Copyright © AP/Wide World Photos. Reproduced by permission.

supposed to prevent the military from using its power against civilians.

The Constitution requires the president to give Congress "information of the State of the Union" and to recommend "such Measures as he shall judge necessary and expedient [proper]." President George Washington (1732–1799; served 1789–97) delivered the nation's first annual message on January 8, 1790. Washington read his written speech to Congress. President Thomas Jefferson (1743–1826; served 1801–9) thought this practice was too formal, so he simply delivered a written copy of his messages to Congress. President Woodrow Wilson (1856–1924; served 1913–21) revived the practice of delivering the address orally in person in 1913. President Calvin Coolidge's (1872–1933; served 1923–29) message of 1923 was the first to be broadcast by radio, and President Harry S. Truman's (1884–1972; served 1945–53) 1947 speech was the first to be televised.

Each year in January, the president delivers a televised State of the Union address to both chambers of Congress, with

President Woodrow Wilson delivers his State of the Union address to a joint session of Congress on December 2, 1918. © Corbis.

President Ronald Reagan delivers his State of the Union address on February 4, 1986 (delayed that year due to the Challenger explosion). Vice President George Bush (left) and Speaker of the House Tip O'Neill applaud behind him. The Constitution requires the president to give Congress "information of the State of the Union." © Bettmann/Corbis.

Supreme Court justices attending, too. The address gives Congress the president's view on how the country is doing, what is working, and what needs to be changed. On rare occasions, presidents appear before Congress to deliver special messages, such as when President George W. Bush (1946–) addressed Congress to explain his plan for responding to the terrorist attacks of September 11, 2001.

The president recommends "Measures" by proposing an annual budget for the federal government, which outlines how the government plans to raise and spend money. The president also recommends new laws, or changes to old laws, for Congress to consider. Because the president can veto, or reject, a law passed by Congress, Congress pays close attention to the president's recommendations. It is not, however, required to do what the president wants.

Another major role for the president under the Constitution is receiving "ambassadors and other public ministers." This makes the president the head of America's relations with foreign nations.

Limits on presidential power One of the major limitations on the power of the executive branch is Congress's power to override a presidential veto by a two-thirds vote. Without this congressional power, the president would have full control over what bills become law. For example, in 1995, Congress passed a bill called the Private Securities Litigation Reform Act. The bill made it more difficult to sue private companies for misleading their investors, the people who invest money in a company. President Bill Clinton vetoed the bill in December 1995. Both chambers of Congress voted to override the veto, making the bill law.

The president can make treaties with other nations only when two-thirds of the senators approve. On May 24, 2002, for example, President George W. Bush and President Vladimir Putin (1952–) of Russia signed the Moscow Treaty on Strategic Offensive Reductions. The Moscow Treaty was an agreement to reduce the number of strategic nuclear warhead arsenals in America and Russia to between 1,700 and 2,200 each by December 2012. The U.S. Senate ratified the treaty unanimously in March 2003.

The Senate also must approve the president's selection of federal judges, ambassadors to other countries, executive department heads, and other important officers. This approval, however, need only be by a simple majority.

Both chambers of Congress check the president by playing a role in impeachment and conviction for treason, bribery, and other high crimes and misdemeanors. The House has the power

The U.S. Supreme Court building.
AP/Wide World Photos.

to impeach, or formally accuse, a president of such misconduct. The Senate then has the power to try (put on trial) and convict a president accused of impeachable offenses.

The federal judiciary also checks the president's power, mostly by hearing and deciding cases under the nation's criminal laws. In these cases, federal courts determine whether an accused person is guilty of breaking the law. Many of these cases also involve questions of whether the executive branch has violated the accused person's constitutional rights.

The judicial branch: the Supreme Court and lower federal courts

Article III of the Constitution says, "The judicial power of the United States, shall be vested in one supreme Court, and in such inferior Courts as the Congress may from time to time ordain and establish." This means the Supreme Court is the only federal court created by the Constitution. Congress has sole authority to create federal courts underneath the Supreme Court.

Congress has used that power to create a vast federal judicial system. At the lowest level are federal district courts, the courts that hold trials. Criminal trials deal with people and businesses accused of violating the nation's criminal laws. A criminal law is a law that makes it unlawful to do something that is harmful to society, such as making illegal drugs or committing murder. Civil trials typically involve people or businesses that have private disputes to resolve, such as when one person breaks a contract, or agreement, that he or she has with another person.

As of 2005, the United States has ninety-four federal district courts. The districts cover either a portion of a state or an entire state, the District of Columbia, the Commonwealth of Puerto Rico, and the territories of the U.S. Virgin Islands, Guam, and the Northern Mariana Islands.

The next level of the federal judiciary is the circuit courts of appeals. There are twelve circuit courts of appeals, each of which covers a geographic region containing federal district courts. When a party loses a trial in federal district court, the party usually can appeal to the court of appeals in that district's circuit. The job of the courts of appeals is to review cases from the federal district courts to make sure the judges and juries there have not made significant errors.

If a party loses in the circuit court of appeals, the last place to go is to the Supreme Court of the United States, often called the court of last resort. As with the courts of appeals, the Supreme Court's job is to make sure the courts below did not make any major errors in a case.

The U.S. Supreme Court does not only hear appeals from the federal courts. It also hears appeals from the state judicial systems. Generally speaking, each state has trial courts similar to the federal district courts, courts of appeals similar to the federal circuit courts, and supreme courts similar to the U.S. Supreme Court. If a case that reaches a state supreme court involves federal laws or rights, the losing party can ask the U.S. Supreme Court to review the decision of the state supreme court. In the tight presidential election of 2000 between Texas governor George W. Bush and Vice President Al Gore (1948–), for example, an extremely narrow victory for Bush in Florida led Gore to sue to have votes in certain counties recounted. Bush appealed one of the cases from the Florida Supreme Court to the U.S. Supreme Court. The U.S. Supreme Court issued a decision in December

2000, stopping the recounts in Florida, giving Bush the victory. Florida's twenty-five electoral votes put Bush over the top and made him the presidential victor.

There is a limited amount of work the Supreme Court can do in one year, so it has a procedure for deciding which cases to review. The losing party in a federal circuit court of appeals or in a state supreme court can begin the process by filing a document called a petition for a writ of certiorari. (A writ is a court order, and *certiorari* is a Latin word that means "to certify a court case for review.") In the petition, the party asks the Supreme Court to review the case, explaining why the case is important enough to deserve the Supreme Court's attention. If four of the nine Supreme Court justices agree to review the case, the Supreme Court issues a writ of certiorari, which allows the losing party to present its appeal to the Supreme Court. Out of the tens of thousands of petitions that the Supreme Court receives each year, it agrees to hear around one hundred of them.

Cases and controversies: the lifeblood of the courts The federal judiciary at all levels (district courts, circuit courts of appeals, and Supreme Court) only has power to hear cases and controversies listed in the Constitution:

★ cases arising under the Constitution, laws, and treaties of the United States

★ cases affecting ambassadors and other public ministers

★ cases concerning the use of navigable waters

★ controversies in which the United States is a party

★ controversies between two or more states, between citizens of different states, and between citizens of the same state claiming lands under grants from different states

★ controversies between a state (or its citizens) and a foreign state or nation (or its citizens or subjects)

Most of the time, a case or controversy that falls into one of these categories must be brought in a federal court. State courts cannot handle these cases. One exception is cases between citizens of different states. If their dispute does not involve a federal law, they may resolve it in a state court, or they may choose to go to federal court anyway if their dispute involves an amount of money that exceeds (as of 2005) $75,000.

In cases involving ambassadors or in which a state is a party, the Supreme Court acts like a trial court and hears the case originally. In all other federal cases, the Supreme Court has appellate jurisdiction. This means the trial must first be handled by a federal district court and then might be appealed to the circuit court of appeals and, finally, to the Supreme Court by petition for certiorari.

Judicial interpretation and judicial review The plain language of Article III of the Constitution says the judiciary hears "cases and controversies." Some scholars and citizens believe that the sole power of the federal judiciary is to decide cases—that is, determine guilt or innocence in a criminal trial, and resolve a legal disagreement in a civil trial. Criminal and civil cases can both require the courts to interpret what a congressional law means, because the meaning is not always clear from the way Congress writes the laws. Such interpretation is one of the most important duties of the courts.

Federal courts, however, also exercise a power called judicial review. This is the power to review congressional and state laws that are involved in a case to decide whether the laws violate the U.S. Constitution. Some people think judicial review is necessary to prevent Congress and the president (who approves Congress's laws) from being too powerful. In other words, judicial review is part of the system of checks and balances set up by the Constitution. Others think that because the Constitution does not mention the power of judicial review, the federal judiciary should not exercise that power.

Judicial review, for example, was an important part of the case of *Elk Grove Unified School District v. Newdow.* In that case, a father named Michael Newdow sued the school district where his daughter attended public school. Newdow wanted the school to stop saying the Pledge of Allegiance because the Pledge says America is a nation "under God." Newdow, who is an atheist (a person who does not believe in God), argued that the Pledge is a religious prayer that violates the First Amendment, which prevents government from favoring one religion over others. The Ninth Circuit Court of Appeals agreed with Newdow, banning public schools in western states from using the Pledge. On Flag

Day in June 2004, the U.S. Supreme Court reversed the ruling on a technicality. It said Newdow, who was never married to his daughter's mother and did not have custody of the child, had no power to file the lawsuit. The case, however, illustrated the controversy that arises when the Supreme Court is asked to use judicial review to strike down a widely accepted government practice based on an important constitutional right.

Because of judicial review, the federal judiciary is perhaps the branch most responsible for protecting civil liberties. These are rights that people have to be free from unreasonable governmental power. Civil liberties come primarily from the Constitution. As previously noted, the First Amendment in the Bill of Rights protects the freedoms of speech, religion, and assembly. The Fourth Amendment says the federal government may not search or arrest a person in an unreasonable fashion. The Sixth Amendment says accused criminals have a right to trial by jury and to face the witnesses against them with assistance from counsel, or a lawyer. The Eighth Amendment prevents cruel and unusual punishment. Criminal cases often require the courts to decide whether the government has violated a defendant's civil liberties.

Limiting judicial power Just as with Congress and the president, the Supreme Court and lower courts have checks on their power. One of these comes not from the Constitution, but from the makeup of the Supreme Court. Under federal law, the Supreme Court contains up to nine justices. (Nine is the accepted total, but the Court continues to function with less than nine in the event of a justice's retirement or death.) Four out of the nine must vote to hear a case by issuing a writ of certiorari in order to review it. When the justices vote on how to decide a case, five must agree in order to change the result from the courts below. This means that, in theory, one justice alone has little power, and so not much ability to abuse it.

The biggest check on judicial power is the power of Congress. If senators and representatives disagree with how the Supreme Court is interpreting a law, they can amend, or change, the law to clarify it so the Court can alter its interpretation. Congress can also pass a new law to correct a constitutional defect when the Supreme Court strikes a law down as unconstitutional. For example, in *Roe v. Wade* in 1972, the Supreme Court ruled that states cannot ban abortions completely because women have a constitutional right to have abortions in some cases. After that decision, states rewrote their abortion laws to ban abortions in situations allowed under the Supreme Court's ruling. For example, most states ban abortions during the last three months of pregnancy unless the abortion is necessary for the health of the mother. In addition to its lawmaking power, Congress has the power to propose constitutional amendments, which change the Constitution if approved by the legislatures or conventions in three-fourths of the states.

As for the president, when a Supreme Court justice or lower court judge retires or dies, the president gets to appoint a replacement, and the Senate confirms or rejects the president's selection. Presidents use these opportunities to fill the courts with justices and judges who agree with the president on the proper role of government and its three branches. If a majority of senators are from the same political party as the president, these appointments easily receive Senate approval. If the president and a majority of the Senate are from different political parties, the appointments can result in political battles, especially for appointments to the Supreme Court. As of 2005, presidents have nominated 148 people to the Supreme Court. The Senate has rejected twelve. The most recent rejections were during the Reagan administration with Robert H. Bork (1927–) in 1987, and twice in the Nixon administration with Clement Haynsworth Jr. (1912–1989) in 1969 and G. Harrold Carswell (1919–1992) in 1970. The Senate also has taken no action on five, and postponed voting on three, leading to unofficial rejection of these nominees.

The final significant check on the power of the judiciary is the power to remove judges from office. All officers of the federal government, including the president, vice president, and judges of the Supreme Court and lower courts, can be impeached and removed if convicted of treason, bribery, or other high crimes and misdemeanors. The House of Representatives has the sole power to impeach, or accuse, a judge of such crimes, and the Senate has the sole power to try, convict, and remove the judge from office.

As of 2005, only seven judges in the nation's history have been removed from office as a result of impeachment. The very first was John Pickering (c. 1738–1805), a federal district court judge who was impeached, convicted, and removed from office in

March 1803 for drunkenness. The Pickering impeachment was a test run for Congress's real target, Supreme Court justice Samuel Chase (1741–1811), who was making speeches critical of the presidential administration of Thomas Jefferson. The House of Representatives impeached Chase in 1804. The Senate, however, voted not to convict, so Chase remained on the bench. As of 2005, he is the only Supreme Court justice to have been impeached.

For More Information

BOOKS

Beard, Charles A. *American Government and Politics*. 10th ed. New York: Macmillan Co., 1949.

Kelly, Alfred H., and Winfred A. Harbison. *The American Constitution: Its Origins and Development*. 5th ed. New York: W. W. Norton & Co., 1976.

McClenaghan, William A. *Magruder's American Government 2003*. Needham, MA: Prentice Hall School Group, 2002.

Roelofs, H. Mark. *The Poverty of American Politics*. 2nd ed. Philadelphia: Temple University Press, 1998.

Shelley, Mack C., II. *American Government and Politics Today*. 2004–2005 ed. Belmont, CA: Wadsworth Publishing, 2003.

Volkomer, Walter E. *American Government*. 8th ed. Upper Saddle River, NJ: Prentice Hall, 1998.

Woll, Peter. *American Government: Readings and Cases*. 15th ed. New York: Longman, 2003.

Zinn, Howard. *A People's History of the United States*. New York: HarperCollins, 2003.

Historic Roots of the Executive Branch

The president is the head of the executive branch of the federal government under the U.S. Constitution. The executive branch is responsible for enforcing America's laws, operating the military, and maintaining relations with foreign nations. Presidents are elected to serve a four-year term, and may not serve more than two terms since adoption of the Twenty-second Amendment in 1951.

According to Mark Roelofs in *The Poverty of American Politics,* William H. Seward (1801–1872) once said, "We elect a king for four years, and give him absolute power within certain limits, which after all he can interpret for himself." Seward was secretary of state under presidents Abraham Lincoln (1809–1865; served 1861–65) and Andrew Johnson (1808–1875; served 1865–69).

Seward's comparison of the U.S. presidency to a monarchy, a government headed by a king or queen, is interesting. When the Federal Convention met in Philadelphia, Pennsylvania, in 1787 to write the Constitution, monarchy was the world's primary kind of executive power. According to Michael Nelson in *The Evolving Presidency,* Virginia delegate James Madison (1751–1836) and most other delegates "feared both executive power and executive weakness, regarding the former as the seed of tyranny [extreme rule by one person] and the latter as the well-spring of anarchy [great chaos]."

In writing the Constitution, the convention delegates strove to create a presidency that would be powerful enough to lead the country but not powerful enough to dominate it. The presidency

Words to Know

checks and balances: The specific powers in one branch of government that allow it to limit the powers of the other branches.

executive branch: The branch of the federal government that enforces the nation's laws. The executive branch includes the president, the vice president, and many executive departments, agencies, and offices.

Founding Fathers: General term for the men who founded the United States of America and designed its government. The term includes the men who signed the Declaration of Independence in 1776 and the Constitution of the United States in 1787.

monarchy: A government under which power is held by a monarch, such as a king or queen, who inherits power by birth or takes it by force.

president: The highest officer in the executive branch of the federal government, with primary responsibility for enforcing the nation's laws.

republicanism: Theory of government under which power is held by the people, who elect public servants to represent them in the bodies of government.

separation of powers: Division of the powers of government into different branches to prevent one branch from having too much power.

they developed had roots in the histories of the Roman Republic, the British Empire, and the American colonies and states, in the writings of political philosophers, and in America's experience under the Articles of Confederation.

Roman Republic

The Roman Republic, which was centered around the city of Rome in what is now the country of Italy, lasted from around 509 BCE to 27 BCE. The governments that ruled during this period were republican to some extent. A republican government is one in which power rests with the people, who exercise that power through elected representatives. During the Roman Republic, all free adult men were generally allowed to vote to elect representatives. Women and slaves could not vote, so it was not a true republic.

The Roman Republic government that most influenced the men who wrote the U.S. Constitution was the one that operated until about 200 BCE. It contained two consuls, or diplomats, a Senate, and two assemblies of representatives. The consuls were military generals who served as executive heads of the republic, much like the president of the United States. The consuls were elected by the men who served in one of the two representative assemblies, called the centuriate assembly. The other representative assembly was called the tribal assembly. It made laws with unofficial approval by the Senate.

The Roman consuls had powers similar to their predecessors, the Roman kings, who served prior to 509 BCE. According to Forrest McDonald in *The American Presidency,* these included the power to assemble and command armies, spend public money on government projects, serve as religious leaders, call the Senate and assemblies into session, preside over the Senate, propose legislation, and judge serious crimes.

The powers of the U.S. presidency under the Constitution resemble the powers of the consuls in many respects. The president is commander in chief of the armed forces. The president has a constitutional duty to recommend legislation to Congress. The vice president, who serves under the president, is president of the Senate, with power to cast the deciding vote when the whole Senate is evenly split.

A consul's relationship with the Roman Senate and assemblies resembled the president's relationship with Congress under the Constitution. The consuls had to get approval from the Senate before going to war. In practice, laws proposed by the consuls had to pass both an assembly and the Senate to become law. The consuls were responsible for administering the Republic's finances.

Similarly under the Constitution, the president is supposed to lead troops into war only after Congress declares war. (In practice, though, most American military action happens without a congressional declaration of war. Presidents often think they have to protect America's interests in other regions of the world without the long, public process of congressional action. In addition, a declaration of war has consequences under international laws that America can avoid by going to war without declaring war.) Bills proposed by the president become law only after they pass both chambers of Congress, namely the Senate and the House of Representatives. Finally, the president administers the nation's finances through the Department of the Treasury.

The Guarantee Clause

Article IV, Section 4, of the Constitution begins, "The United States shall guarantee to every State in this Union a Republican Form of Government." A republican government is one in which power is held by the people, who elect public servants to represent them in the bodies of government.

Just as the Founding Fathers wrote the Constitution to prevent monarchy in the federal government, they wrote the Guarantee Clause to prevent monarchies in the state governments. According to the *Records of the Federal Convention* (as reprinted in *The Founders' Constitution*), Virginia delegate Edmund Randolph (1753–1813) said at the convention on June 11, 1787, "A republican government must be the basis of our national union; and no state in it ought to have it in their power to change its government to a monarchy."

British Empire

The government of the British Empire was a primary model for the U.S. Constitution. To be sure, America had separated from Great Britain in 1776 to escape the tyranny of King George III (1738–1820; reigned 1760–1820) and the British Parliament, or legislature. Many of the delegates at the Federal Convention, however, considered the eighteenth-century constitutional monarchy of Great Britain to be history's finest example of powerful government upon which to build.

The constitutional monarchy of Great Britain had three main bodies: the monarch, the House of Lords, and the House of Commons. The monarch, such as a king or queen, was the symbolic head of the empire. He or she had the power to make laws with Parliament, a legislative body composed of the House of Lords and the House of Commons. The monarch also had the power to execute the kingdom's laws.

The House of Lords was the chamber of Parliament that represented the noblemen and wealthy class of Britain. The other chamber, the House of Commons, represented the merchants and working people of Britain, also known as the common people.

America's Founding Fathers used Britain's separation of powers as a model for the U.S. Constitution. They strove, however, to make America's legislature, Congress, strong enough to prevent a president from becoming a monarchical tyrant. (A tyrant is a person who rules in an oppressive manner without regard to the people's rights.) In doing so, the Founding Fathers

Engraving of King John of England signing the Magna Carta in June 1215. © Bettmann/ Corbis.

were mindful of Great Britain's history of tyrants, such as King John (1167–1216; reigned 1199–1216) and King James II (1633–1701; reigned 1685–88).

Magna Carta In 1215, King John of England taxed his subjects and the Church of England heavily to cover the expenses of government. That year, church authorities and the king's barons (part of the English nobility) threatened a civil war if the king did not sign a document to proclaim and protect their freedoms. That document was called the Magna Carta, or Great Charter.

The Magna Carta protected the rights of free men only, and even free men would not truly be able to enforce their rights for many centuries. The principles of the Magna Carta, however, became mythic and influenced the design of the presidency in the U.S. Constitution.

One of the president's chief duties, for instance, is to enforce the nation's laws. The Constitution, as amended by the Bill of Rights in 1791, limits this enforcement power. (The Bill of Rights is the first ten amendments, or changes, to the Constitution.) Under the Bill of Rights, the president's enforcement agencies may not arrest a person except in accordance with the law. An accused criminal must be tried by a jury of citizens from the community. Punishment for criminals is not supposed to be cruel or unusual. Finally, the executive branch cannot take away a person's property without giving fair compensation for it. All of these restrictions have roots in the liberties proclaimed by the Magna Carta of 1215.

English Bill of Rights The Magna Carta did not end tyrannical government in Great Britain. From 1685 to 1688, King James II violated the religious freedoms and other liberties of his people. After James II was deposed, or removed as king, in what became known as the Glorious Revolution of 1688–89, King William III (1650–1702; reigned 1689–1702) and Queen Mary II (1662–1694; reigned 1689–94) shared the throne, but were restricted in their powers by a new English Bill of Rights. Adopted by the British Parliament in 1689, the English Bill of Rights strengthened Parliament's power in the constitutional monarchy.

The Bill of Rights influenced the design of the U.S. presidency mainly in terms of restricting the powers of the presidency. For example, the English Bill of Rights forbade the monarch from independently, without consultation, suspending British laws at his or her pleasure. Similarly, the U.S. Constitution says the president "shall take care that the laws be faithfully executed."

The English Bill of Rights made it illegal for the British monarch to spend money on projects not approved by Parliament. The U.S. Constitution gives Congress the power to appropriate, or assign, money to government projects.

The English Bill of Rights made it illegal for British monarchs to maintain standing armies during peacetime without

Parliament's approval. The Constitution gives Congress the sole power to create and make the rules for the army and navy, leaving to the president the job of commanding the armed forces under Congress's rules.

Monarchical power in the eighteenth century From 1765 to 1769, an English scholar named Sir William Blackstone (1723–1780) published a four-volume treatise, or essay, called *Commentaries on the Laws of England.* It contained a thorough description of English law at the time, including the powers of the British monarch. Most of the men who wrote the U.S. Constitution two decades later were familiar with Blackstone's work.

Despite restrictions rooted in the Magna Carta and the English Bill of Rights, British monarchs had great power. This included almost absolute power over foreign relations. British monarchs could send and receive ambassadors, or representatives, to and from foreign nations. They could also negotiate treaties, or formal agreements, with those nations. In addition, monarchs commanded England's military forces. The president of the United States has all these powers, too, except that the Senate must approve treaties by a two-thirds vote.

In domestic affairs, British monarchs had the power to appoint judges to the courts and to enforce the laws made by Parliament. They also could issue pardons. A pardon officially excuses someone from being punished for violating the law. Under the U.S. Constitution, the president has these powers, too, except that the Senate must approve the presidential appointment of judges by a simple majority vote.

Political philosophers

The men who wrote the Constitution in 1787 had read the works of well-known political philosophers. According to Forrest McDonald in *The American Presidency,* the Founding Fathers sometimes had little regard for political philosophy, preferring instead to rely on the actual experience of history. There is no doubt, however, that in designing the U.S. presidency, the convention delegates used ideas from political philosophers, including John Locke (1632–1704), Charles Montesquieu (1689–1755), and Jean Louis Delolme (1740–1806).

English scientist and philosopher John Locke, who helped launch the Age of Enlightenment in the late seventeenth century.

Locke and the separation of powers John Locke was an English scientist and philosopher who helped launch the Age of Enlightenment. The Age of Enlightenment was a period in the seventeenth and eighteenth centuries during which men used reason to change the study of philosophy and politics.

Locke's most famous political work was *Two Treatises of Government,* which he wrote from 1679 to 1681. The second treatise, published in 1689 at the height of England's Glorious Revolution, contained his theory of how government should be organized. As reprinted in *The Founders' Constitution,* Locke argued in the second treatise that the lawmaking branch of government must be separate from the executive branch:

> Because it may be too great a temptation to humane frailty apt to grasp at Power, for the same Persons who have the Power of making Laws, to have also in their hands the power to execute them, whereby they may exempt themselves from Obedience to the Laws they make, and suit the Law, both in its making and execution, to their own private advantage, and thereby come to have a distinct interest from the rest of the Community, contrary to the end of Society and Government....
>
> But because the Laws, that are at once, and in a short time made, have a constant and lasting force, and need a *perpetual* [ongoing] *Execution,* or an attendance thereunto: Therefore 'tis necessary there should be a *Power always in being,* which should see to the *Execution* of the laws that are made, and remain in force. And thus the *Legislative* and *Executive Power* come often to be separated....
>
> In all Cases, whilst the Government subsists [exists], the *Legislative is the Supream Power.* For what can give Laws to another, must needs be superiour to him.

The U.S. Constitution follows this advice by giving Congress the power to make the laws, and the president the power to execute them. Although the president can veto, or reject, laws passed by Congress, Congress can override a veto by a two-thirds vote in both chambers. Hence the president, at least in theory, has less lawmaking power than Congress, making Congress superior to the president in this regard.

French philosopher Charles Montesquieu wrote of the importance of a checks and balances system in the mid-1700s. Four decades later, the Founding Fathers who wrote the Constitution were influenced by his writings. Library of Congress.

Montesquieu and the separation of powers Charles Montesquieu was a French philosopher. His book *The Spirit of Laws,* which was published in 1748, influenced the men who wrote the Constitution four decades later. Like Locke, Montesquieu (as reprinted in *The Founders' Constitution*) wrote of the importance of separating the executive power of government from the legislative and judicial powers:

> When the legislative and executive powers are united in the same person, or in the same body of magistrates, there can be no liberty; because apprehensions [concerns] may rise, lest the same monarch or senate should enact tyrannical laws, to execute them in a tyrannical manner.
>
> Again, there is no liberty, if the judiciary power be not separated from the legislative and executive. Were it joined with the legislative, the life and liberty of the subject would be exposed to arbitrary control; for the judge would then be the legislator. Were it joined to the executive power, the judge might behave with violence and oppression.
>
> There would be an end of everything, were the same man or body, whether of the nobles or of the people, to exercise those three powers, that of enacting laws, that of executing the public resolutions [orders], and of trying the causes [court cases] of individuals.

Montesquieu's formula appears in the Constitution, which gives Congress the power to make the laws, the president the power to enforce the laws, and the Supreme Court the power to hear court cases under the laws.

Delolme and the power of the presidency Jean Louis Delolme, from the city of Geneva, wrote a book called *The Constitution of England; Or, An Account of the English Government.* The book was published in many editions during the 1780s, when America adopted the U.S. Constitution. According to McDonald, Delolme was popular with many Americans, including Founding Father Alexander Hamilton (1757–1804), because he was a strong supporter of both republicanism and the constitutional monarchy of Great Britain.

A number of Delolme's political philosophies ended up in the Constitution. Fearing tyranny, many Americans, including some delegates to the Constitution, believed the executive power should be split between two or more people, perhaps serving as a council. Delolme's writings recommended placing the executive power in one person. He felt the members of an executive council would end up in a struggle for supreme power. The delegates settled on placing the executive power in one person, the president of the United States.

Delolme also wrote about the role of the executive branch in crafting legislation. He supported the British system, under which the monarch could recommend legislation to Parliament but could not introduce legislation personally. Under the Constitution, the president has the authority to recommend legislation to Congress, but Congress has the power to write the laws. In practice in both England and America, however, the chief executives have close relationships with many members of the legislative branches, who introduce legislation written by the executives' advisors.

American colonies

When the delegates wrote the Constitution in 1787, they had 150 years of experience under colonial and state governments from which to learn. Generally speaking, when the colonies were part of Great Britain, each had a governor, a council, and an assembly. The governors were appointed by Great Britain and wielded the executive power of government. Governors appointed judges and often acted as a supreme court of appeals in court cases. The same person sometimes served as governor of two colonies.

The councils were legislative bodies that represented the interests of Great Britain. Councils had a role in the executive branch of government and often served as the supreme court of appeals. The assemblies were legislative bodies elected by the free men of the colonies.

A colonial governor had executive powers that resembled the powers of the British monarch. In the area of foreign affairs, he served as commander in chief of the colony's armed forces, often negotiating with or declaring war against Native American tribes. Similarly, the American president is commander in chief of the national armed forces and manages the country's relations with foreign nations. (Congress, however, is supposed to have the sole power to declare war.)

In the realm of domestic affairs, governors exerted legislative power with the ability to veto any law passed by the assembly and council. The assembly and council could not override a veto. According to the *Records of the Federal Convention* (as reprinted in *The Founders' Constitution*), delegate Benjamin Franklin (1706–1790) described the bribery that often resulted from the executive veto power in the colony of Pennsylvania:

> The negative [veto power] of the Governor was constantly made use of to extort [obtain by threat] money. No good law whatever could be passed without a private bargain with him. An increase of his salary, or some donation, was always made a condition; till at last it became regular practice, to have orders in his favor on the Treasury, presented along with the bills to be signed, so that he might actually receive the former before he should sign the latter. When the Indians were scalping the western people, and notice of it arrived, the concurrence [agreement] of the Governor in the means of self-defence could not be got, till it was agreed that his Estate [property] should be exempted [excused] from taxation, so that the people were to fight for the security of his property, whilst he was to bear no share of the [tax] burden.

During the 1700s, power struggles between governors and assemblies intensified in the colonies. By 1748, according to McDonald, assemblies had used their appropriations power (the allocation of money to government programs) to take control of the important administrative departments, including the military. The assemblies even used the appropriations power to restrict the salaries of governors to bend them to their will.

The men who wrote the Constitution sought to avoid these kinds of problems in the U.S. presidency. They gave the president the power to veto laws of Congress, but gave Congress the power to override presidential vetoes by a two-thirds vote in both chambers. They also wrote the Constitution to guarantee every president a salary that Congress could not raise or lower during the president's term in office.

King George III of Great Britain sent troops to America to fight against the colonists in the American Revolutionary War. National Archives and Records Administration.

American states

On July 4, 1776, the thirteen American colonies officially separated from Great Britain by signing the American Declaration of Independence (see box). Written primarily by Thomas Jefferson (1743–1826), the Declaration contained a list of the colonists' grievances against Great Britain and its monarch, King George III.

According to McDonald, King George III had been popular with the colonists until shortly before the American Revolutionary War (1775–83). Many Americans thought the British Parliament or the King's corrupt ministers were the main source of their problems with the mother country. Monarchical tradition held that the king was an agent of God who could do no wrong, and some people liked to cling to this myth.

By the time of the Declaration of Independence, King George III had sent troops to America to fight the colonists. This destroyed the love many Americans had for their king, and left them feeling betrayed. Viewing the monarch in this light, Americans could see how he was part of a government that was passing unfair laws for America and striking down laws that the colonists had passed for themselves. These were among the grievances listed in the Declaration of Independence.

As newly independent states, the thirteen American colonies had to set up state governments. The antimonarchical spirit that fueled the Revolution affected the process. Ten of the thirteen colonies adopted state constitutions around the time of independence. All ten made the legislature the most powerful branch of the government. South Carolina's constitution gave the chief executive the power to veto laws passed by the legislature, but the legislature took this power away in 1778. Pennsylvania's constitution did not even provide for a chief executive officer. Instead, it gave executive power to a council of twelve elected officials.

The state executive position that most resembled the eventual U.S. presidency was the governor of New York. This person served on a council that could veto laws passed by the legislature. The legislature, however, could override a veto by two-thirds majorities in both chambers. The governor was required to give the legislature reports on the condition of New York and to make recommendations for legislation. The governor could execute the laws, grant pardons and reprieves, conduct relations with other states, and command New York's armed forces. The president of the United States has similar powers under the Constitution of 1787.

Articles of Confederation

Revolutionary figure Thomas Paine (1737–1809) captured the antimonarchical spirit in his pamphlet *Common Sense*. Published in January 1776, the pamphlet criticized the British system of checks and balances as "farcical," or absurd. Paine said the only reason the House of Commons should need to check the king was if the king could not be trusted. If the king could not be trusted, then it was absurd to give the king power to veto the laws of Parliament.

Paine suggested that the American colonies set up their own constitutional government without a chief executive officer. This is exactly what they did when the Continental Congress wrote the Articles of Confederation in 1777. (The Continental Congress was the first American government, an organization of delegates representing the American colonies and states during most of the Revolutionary War.)

The Articles of Confederation gave all the powers of the federal government to Congress, a representative body of delegates from the thirteen states. The powers Congress received included some that the president would get under the Constitution of 1787. Congress, for example, could appoint ambassadors to, and make treaties with, foreign nations. Congress also had the power to direct the operations of America's military and naval forces.

The United States officially began to operate under the Articles of Confederation in 1781. Congress created four departments to oversee certain aspects of the government: foreign affairs, finance, war, and marine. Congress appointed men to be the heads, or secretaries, of each department. The departments were forerunners of the Departments of State, Treasury, and War that would operate under President George Washington (1732–1799; served 1789–1797) beginning in 1789. (The Department of the Navy was not set up until 1798.)

Congress had many problems during the 1780s. It lacked power to raise taxes, relying instead on borrowed money and taxes voluntarily raised by the states. This left the government always short of money. In June 1783, a group of four hundred to five hundred American soldiers surrounded Congress in Philadelphia, demanding pay for their service in the Revolutionary War. The delegates lacked a ready army to command for their defense, and eventually left Philadelphia unharmed but shaken.

The Declaration of Independence

On July 4, 1776, delegates from the thirteen British colonies in America signed the Declaration of Independence. Thomas Jefferson, thirty-three years old at the time, wrote the document to explain to the world why the colonies were taking this step. Most of the Declaration contains a list of grievances against the British monarch, King George III, and against his ministers and Parliament, the British legislature.

> The History of the present King of Great-Britain is a History of repeated Injuries and Usurpations [illegal actions], all having in direct Object the Establishment of an absolute Tyranny over these States. To prove this, let Facts be submitted to a candid World.

> He has refused his Assent [approval] to Laws, the most wholesome and necessary for the public Good.

> He has forbidden his Governors to pass Laws of immediate and pressing Importance, unless suspended in their Operation till his Assent should be obtained; and when so suspended, he has utterly neglected to attend to them.

> He has refused to pass other Laws for the Accommodation of large Districts of People, unless those People would

relinquish [give up] the Right of Representation in the Legislature, a Right inestimable [priceless] to them, and formidable [threatening] to Tyrants only.

> He has called together Legislative Bodies at Places unusual, uncomfortable, and distant from the Depository [place] of their public Records, for the sole Purpose of fatiguing [tiring] them into Compliance with his Measures.

> He has dissolved [broken up] Representative Houses repeatedly, for opposing with manly Firmness his Invasions on the Rights of the People.

> He has refused for a long Time, after such Dissolutions, to cause others to be elected; whereby the Legislative Powers, incapable of Annihilation [destruction], have returned to the People at large for their exercise; the State remaining for the mean time exposed to all the Dangers of Invasion from without, and Convulsions [disturbances] within.

> He has endeavoured to prevent the Population of these States; for that Purpose obstructing the Laws for Naturalization of Foreigners; refusing to pass others to encourage their Migration hither [here], and raising the Conditions of new Appropriations [grants] of Lands.

During the winter of 1786–87, a revolt against the state government in Massachusetts, called Shays's Rebellion, fueled Congress's fear even more. The rebellion was a protest named for a farmer and local officeholder named Daniel Shays (c. 1747–1825). A U.S. soldier in the American Revolutionary War (1775–83), he led one of the regiments in Shays's Rebellion. The rebels, about two or three thousand in number, were

He has obstructed the Administration of Justice, by refusing his Assent to Laws for establishing Judiciary Powers.

He has made Judges dependent on his Will alone, for the Tenure [holding] of their Offices, and the Amount and Payment of their Salaries.

He has erected a multitude of new Offices, and sent hither Swarms of Officers to harass our People, and eat out their Substance.

He has kept among us, in Times of Peace, Standing Armies, without the consent of our Legislatures.

He has affected to render the Military independent of and superior to the Civil Power.

He has combined with others [Parliament] to subject us to a Jurisdiction [governmental power] foreign to our Constitution, and unacknowledged by our Laws; giving his Assent to their Acts of pretended Legislation:

For quartering large Bodies of Armed Troops among us:

For protecting them, by a mock Trial, from Punishment for any Murders which they should commit on the Inhabitants of these States:

For cutting off our Trade with all Parts of the World:

For imposing Taxes on us without our Consent:

For depriving us, in many Cases, of the Benefits of Trial by Jury:

For transporting us beyond Seas to be tried for pretended Offences:

For abolishing the free System of English Laws in a neighboring Province, establishing therein an arbitrary Government, and enlarging its Boundaries, so as to render it at once an Example and fit Instrument for introducing the same absolute Rule into these Colonies:

For taking away our Charters [for colonial government], abolishing our most valuable Laws, and altering fundamentally the Forms of our Governments:

For suspending our own Legislatures, and declaring themselves invested with Power to legislate for us in all Cases whatsoever.

He has abdicated [eliminated] Government here, by declaring us out of his Protection and waging War against us. ⟶

protesting the government's treatment of debtors, people who owed other people money. Many of these debtors were farmers like Shays. Secretary of War Henry Knox (1750–1806), however, created a different story. According to McDonald, Knox told George Washington that the rebels were twelve thousand to fifteen thousand trained, armed "Robin Hoods" who planned

He has plundered our Seas, ravaged our Coasts, burnt our Towns, and destroyed the Lives of our People.

He is, at this Time, transporting large Armies of foreign Mercenaries [hired soldiers] to compleat the Works of Death, Desolation, and Tyranny already begun with circumstances of Cruelty and Perfidy [treachery], scarcely paralleled in the most barbarous Ages, and totally unworthy the Head of a civilized Nation.

He has constrained our fellow Citizens taken Captive on the high Seas to bear Arms against their Country, to become the Executioners of their Friends and Brethren, or to fall themselves by their Hands.

He has excited domestic Insurrections [rebellions] against us, and has endeavoured to bring on the Inhabitants of our Frontiers, the merciless Indian Savages, whose known Rule of Warfare, is an undistinguished Destruction, of all Ages, Sexes and Conditions.

In every stage of these Oppressions we have Petitioned for Redress [relief] in the most humble Terms: Our repeated Petitions have been answered only by repeated Injury. A Prince, whose

Character is thus marked by every act which may define a Tyrant, is unfit to be the Ruler of a free People.

A facsimile of the Declaration of Independence, surrounded by portraits of (from left) John Hancock, George Washington, and Thomas Jefferson, and the arms of the original thirteen states. Library of Congress.

to rob the Bank of Massachusetts and march southward, taking property from the rich and giving it to the poor.

Events such as these planted the seeds of desire for a stronger executive branch. In February 1787, with many states wishing to revise the Articles of Confederation, Congress passed a resolution for a federal convention to be held in Philadelphia in May. Delegates to the convention were supposed to revise the Articles of Confederation to make the federal government stronger. By September, the delegates had scrapped the Articles entirely, drafting a whole new Constitution for the United States of America. Article II of the Constitution created the U.S. presidency.

For More Information

BOOKS

Beard, Charles A. *American Government and Politics.* 10th ed. New York: Macmillan Co., 1949.

Kelly, Alfred H., and Winfred A. Harbison. *The American Constitution: Its Origins and Development.* 5th ed. New York: W. W. Norton & Co., 1976.

Kurland, Philip B., and Ralph Lerner. *The Founders' Constitution.* 5 vols. Indianapolis: Liberty Fund, 1987.

Lintcott, Andrew. *The Constitution of the Roman Republic.* Oxford: Clarendon Press, 1999.

McClenaghan, William A. *Magruder's American Government 2003.* Needham, MA: Prentice Hall School Group, 2002.

McDonald, Forrest. *The American Presidency.* Lawrence: University Press of Kansas, 1994.

Milkis, Sidney M., and Michael Nelson. *The American Presidency: Origins & Development.* 3rd ed. Washington, DC: Congressional Quarterly Inc., 1999.

Millar, Fergus. *The Roman Republic in Political Thought.* Hanover and London: Brandeis University Press and Historical Society of Israel, 2002.

Nelson, Michael, ed. *The Evolving Presidency.* Washington, DC: Congressional Quarterly Inc., 1999.

Roelofs, H. Mark. *The Poverty of American Politics.* 2nd ed. Philadelphia: Temple University Press, 1998.

Volkomer, Walter E. *American Government.* 8th ed. Upper Saddle River, NJ: Prentice Hall, 1998.

Zinn, Howard. *A People's History of the United States.* New York: HarperCollins, 2003.

Constitutional Role of the Executive Branch

The U.S. Constitution contains the blueprint for the federal government. Article II focuses on the executive branch. The main role of the executive branch is to enforce the nation's laws. It also leads the country's relations with foreign nations, commands the armed forces, and even participates in the law-making process.

The Constitution makes the president of the United States the head of the executive branch. It authorizes the president to seek advice from the heads of the executive departments. Executive departments are offices responsible for large areas of the federal government. The Constitution also provides for a vice president to serve the same four-year term as the president.

Articles of Confederation

America's Founding Fathers wrote the Constitution during a federal convention in 1787 and adopted it in 1788. Prior to then, beginning in 1781, the blueprint for American government was the Articles of Confederation.

The Articles established a Congress with both legislative and executive powers. This included the power to make and enforce the laws and operate the military. There was no executive branch separate from the Congress, and no judiciary as would exist under the Constitution.

Delegates serving in the Continental Congress wrote the Articles in 1777, one year after America declared independence from Great Britain. The Continental Congress was the governmental

Words to Know

Articles of Confederation: The document that established the federal government for the United States of America from 1781 to 1789.

checks and balances: The specific powers in one branch of government that allow it to limit the powers of the other branches.

Constitution of the United States of America: The document written in 1787 that established the federal government under which the United States of America has operated since 1789. Article II covers the executive branch.

Constitutional Convention of 1787: Convention held in Philadelphia, Pennsylvania, from May to September 1787, during which delegates from twelve of the thirteen American states wrote a new Constitution for the United States.

executive branch: The branch of the federal government that enforces the nation's laws. The executive branch includes the president, the vice president, and many executive departments, agencies, and offices.

Founding Fathers: General term for the men who founded the United States of America and designed its government. The term includes the men who signed the Declaration of Independence in 1776 and the Constitution of the United States in 1787.

monarchy: A government under which power is held by a monarch, such as a king or queen, who inherits power by birth or takes it by force.

president: The highest officer in the executive branch of the federal government, with primary responsibility for enforcing the nation's laws.

ratification: The process of formally approving something, such as a treaty, constitution, or constitutional amendment.

republic: A government under which power is held by the people, who elect public servants to represent them in the bodies of government.

separation of powers: Division of the powers of government into different branches to prevent one branch from having too much power.

vice president: The second highest officer in the executive branch of the federal government. The vice president replaces the president if the president dies or becomes unable to serve. The vice president also serves as president of the Senate, with power to break tie votes when the whole Senate is equally divided on an issue.

body that represented the states in their conflicts with Great Britain before and during the American Revolution (1775–83). At the time, Americans were generally fearful of executive power because of how King George III (1738–1820) of England treated the colonists leading up to the Revolutionary War (1775–83).

One of the problems the colonists had with Great Britain was its domination of commerce, or business and trade, in America. George III and the British Parliament, for example, passed laws giving the East India Company, a British company, control over the tea trade in America. Parliament also levied taxes on tea purchases in America. American merchants who wanted to participate in the tea trade and colonists who found the taxes unfair expressed their displeasure by dumping tea into the harbor during the famous Boston Tea Party of 1773.

When the delegates wrote the Articles of Confederation, they were determined to create a government that could not dominate them. According to Sidney M. Milkis and Michael Nelson in *The American Presidency,* the states told their delegates that government under the Articles could only be as powerful as necessary to conduct the Revolutionary War. In other words, they only wanted the government to be powerful enough to raise and equip an army and navy for winning the war. They did not want their state governments to be replaced with a powerful central government. This is one reason why the delegates did not create a separate executive branch of government or give the executive power to one person, such as a monarch. Instead, they gave all governmental power to Congress, which could have between two and seven delegates from each state. Each state's delegation could cast one vote for the state on matters before Congress.

When all of the delegates were not assembled for full sessions of Congress, the Articles allowed the government to be run by "A Committee of the States." The committee contained one delegate from each state, and those delegates appointed one person to be president of the committee. No person could be president for more than one year in every three-year term of Congress. The president had just one vote, like every other member of the committee. The president of the committee is the closest thing America had to an executive president until adoption of the U.S. Constitution. Ten men served as president under the Articles of Confederation, including Massachusetts politician John Hancock (1737–1793), the first person to sign the Declaration of Independence on July 4, 1776.

The military under the Articles of Confederation

Some Americans felt government did not work very well under the Articles of Confederation. Congress, for instance, did not have power to tax the people or businesses of America directly. To get money for operating the government, it had to borrow money or ask the states to collect taxes to send to

Congress. States were generally unwilling to do this unless they were near American Revolution battles or conflicts with Native Americans requiring assistance from the American army. Congress had no power to force uncooperative states to collect and contribute their share of taxes.

After the American Revolution ended in 1783, financial problems left America with a weak military and unpaid debts to suppliers. This became a problem as Great Britain and Spain encouraged Native Americans to raid American frontier settlements.

Lack of a well-paid army proved personally scary to members of Congress. In the summer of 1783, unpaid American soldiers marched to Philadelphia, Pennsylvania, surrounding Congress to demand payment for their war service. The members of Congress escaped unharmed.

Some men in Congress wished they had a ready army to crush Shays's Rebellion in Massachusetts in the fall and winter of 1786. The rebels, including former American Revolution soldier Daniel Shays (c. 1747–1825), were farmers protesting debtor laws in that state. Debtor laws allowed the government to seize land and property from people who could not pay their debts, or bills. The people asked Massachusetts to issue paper money to help them pay their bills, but the government refused. To protest the government's actions, a group of citizens organized rebellions to shut down court proceedings against debtors. Without assistance from the federal army, Massachusetts crushed the rebellion with its militia, or armed soldiers.

Commerce under the Articles of Confederation

American commerce was another problem under the Articles of Confederation. The Articles gave Congress the ability to make treaties, or official agreements, concerning commerce with foreign nations. These treaties, however, could not prevent the states from regulating commerce with foreign nations on their own. The result was a mixture of laws concerning commerce with foreign nations. England and France, meanwhile, were banning the importation of manufactured goods from America. Congress lacked an executive leader or the legislative and treaty power to fix this state of affairs.

Guardian of Liberty

The Founding Fathers proposed a new Constitution by arguing that American government was too weak under the Articles of Confederation. They also argued that American commerce, or business and trade, could be strengthened under the Constitution.

Not everyone agreed with this assessment. A man writing under the pen name Centinel, which means "guard," published a newspaper essay on December 22, 1787. As reprinted in *The Founders' Constitution,* Centinel said America's problems were caused by large debts from the American Revolution, and by the American habit of spending money to import "merchandise and luxuries" from other countries.

Centinel said that if American commerce needed to be unified through federal regulation, the Articles of Confederation could be changed accordingly. Creating a wholly new government with greatly expanded powers, however, would "render the citizens of America tenants at will of every species of property, of every enjoyment, and make them the mere drudges of government. The gilded [gold-covered] bait conceals corrosives that will eat up their whole substance." In other words, Centinel thought the Constitution would destroy the states and individual liberty.

In 1786, the legislature of Virginia called for a national meeting to be held in Annapolis, Maryland, in September. Only six of the thirteen states sent delegates to the meeting. Their goal was to explore how to improve American commerce. Instead of finding answers, the delegates decided to call for a federal convention to be held in Philadelphia in May 1787 to explore how to fix the Articles of Confederation.

At first, Congress resisted the idea of a federal convention. When states began to appoint delegates anyway, and after Shays's Rebellion, Congress officially called for the convention by resolution of February 1787. According to Milkis and Nelson in *The American Presidency,* the resolution advised "that on the second Monday in May next [the following May] a Convention of delegates who shall have been appointed by the several states be held in Philadelphia for the sole and express purpose of revising the Articles of Confederation."

Separation of powers

Fifty-five men attended the Constitutional Convention from May to September 1787. The men were delegates from twelve of the thirteen American states. (Rhode Island refused to send delegates because the men in power there favored strong state governments, not a strong national government. They feared that a strong national government would be impossible for the people to control.)

According to Congress's February resolution, the delegates were supposed to explore how to change the Articles of Confederation to strengthen the national government. After their first meeting on May 25, however, the delegates decided to scrap the Articles and write a whole new plan of government.

Constitutional Convention Illegal?

The delegates to the Constitutional Convention of 1787 were not there to write a new constitution. They were there to discuss how to revise American government under the Articles of Confederation to make it stronger. According to *The Founders' Constitution,* for example, the legislature of Virginia sent its delegates to the convention with authority "to join with [the other delegates] in devising and discussing all such Alterations and farther Provisions as may be necessary to render the Foederal Constitution adequate to the Exigencies [urgent matters] of the Union [of thirteen states]."

Revising the Articles of Confederation by Convention might have been illegal. Under the Articles, only Congress could make changes, and then only with agreement by the legislatures of all thirteen states. There was no provision in the Articles for a federal convention.

The Articles also had no provision for ratification, or approval, of changes by less than all thirteen state legislatures. Yet the delegates who wrote the Constitution proposed that it be approved by state conventions instead of state legislatures. They also

proposed that only nine of the thirteen state conventions needed to approve it for it to become law between the approving states. Nine was the number of states that had to agree to important decisions under the Articles. The delegates probably feared that requiring unanimous approval by the thirteen states would make it easy for one state to block adoption of the Constitution. On the other hand, if nine states approved, the other four would feel pressured to join rather than attempt to survive as independent states.

In a letter to Secretary of War Henry Knox (1750–1806) on February 3, 1787 (as reprinted in *The Founders' Constitution*), convention delegate George Washington dismissed concerns about the legality of the Convention. He said the federal government would collapse if the country did not strengthen it as soon as possible:

> The legality of this Convention I do not mean to discuss, nor how problematical the issue of it may be. That powers are wanting, none can deny. Though what medium they are to be derived, will, like other matters, engage public attention. That which takes the shortest course to obtain them, will, in my opinion, under present circumstances, be

Forty-two of the delegates were current or former members of Congress, so they knew from experience the problems America had under the Articles of Confederation. An important reason for getting rid of the Articles was that it did not provide an energetic executive leader for the country.

The delegates, however, did not want an executive leader who was too powerful. Most of them agreed that the best government would be one that separated the legislative, executive, and judicial powers into different branches. Writing in *The Federalist,*

found best. Otherwise, like a house on fire, whilst the most regular mode of extinguishing it is contended for, the building is reduced to ashes.

George Washington presides over the signing of the Constitution of the United States on September 17, 1787, in Philadelphia, Pennsylvania. Painting by Howard Chandler Christy. Library of Congress.

Thomas Jefferson thought separation of the executive and legislative powers was essential to an effective government. National Portrait Gallery.

No. 47, delegate and future president James Madison (1751–1836) said, "The accumulation of all powers, legislative, executive, and judiciary, in the same hands, whether of one, a few, or many, and whether hereditary, self-appointed, or elective, may justly be pronounced the very definition of tyranny [dictatorship]."

Thomas Jefferson (1743–1826), who would be the third president of the United States, agreed. He thought separation of the executive and legislative powers was essential if government was to operate effectively. Writing a letter to Virginia delegate Edward Carrington (1748–1810) from Paris, where he was the

American ambassador to France in August 1787, Jefferson said (as reprinted in *The Founder's Constitution*):

> I think it very material to separate in the hands of Congress the Executive and Legislative powers, as the Judiciary already are in some degree. This I hope will be done. The want of it has been the source of more evil than we have ever experienced from any other cause. Nothing is so embarrassing nor so mischievous in a great assembly as the details of execution. The smallest trifle of that kind occupies as long as the most important act of legislation, and takes place of every thing else. Let any man recollect, or look over the files of Congress, he will observe the most important propositions hanging over from week to week and month to month, till the occasions have past them, and the thing never done. I have ever viewed the executive details as the greatest cause of evil to us, because they in fact place us as if we had no federal head, by diverting the attention of the head [Congress] from great to small objects.

To separate the powers of government, the delegates wrote the constitution to give the legislative power to Congress, the executive power to the president, and the judicial power to the Supreme Court and the lower courts beneath it.

Checks and balances

The broad separation of powers in the Constitution is a little misleading. In reality, the three branches share the powers of government through a system of checks and balances. Many political scientists say this system creates a government of shared powers instead of a government of separated powers.

Many delegates to the Constitutional Convention were interested in checks and balances to prevent the president from being too strong. They knew the history of monarchical (rule by one) power in the world and of the colonists' experiences under King George III. They knew the history of the abuse of executive power by colonial governors appointed by Great Britain.

Some convention delegates, however, wanted the president to be as powerful as the kings and queens of England. According to Forrest McDonald in *The American Presidency,* Maryland delegate John Francis Mercer (1759–1821) said more than twenty of the fifty-five delegates were monarchists. Speaking at the convention on June 2, 1787, Delaware delegate John Dickinson (1732–1808) said a limited form of monarchy, such as existed in Great Britain, was one of the best kinds of government in the world, but that the people of America would not accept it for themselves.

For the executive branch of the federal government, the system of checks and balances was a compromise between the monarchists and those who feared monarchy. Under the Constitution, Congress and the president actually share the power to make laws. The president and the Senate share the power to make treaties with foreign nations and to appoint people to important government offices. The president enforces the nation's laws, but the judicial branch decides the cases brought by the president's enforcement agencies. (For more information on checks and balances, see chapters 7 and 8.)

Election of the president and vice president

One of the most difficult decisions at the Convention was how the president should be elected. The delegates considered many proposals. New York delegate Gouverneur Morris (1752–1816) and Pennsylvania delegate James Wilson (1742–1798) suggested that the people, meaning free men, elect the president by popular vote. The delegates strongly rejected this proposal. For various reasons, they did not believe democracy was wise on a national scale. Some feared giving the people too much power in government. Others thought the people were not intelligent or well enough informed to select a good president. Still others thought democracy worked only for local decisions.

New York delegate Alexander Hamilton (1757–1804) was at the other end of the political spectrum from Morris and Wilson. According to Milkis and Nelson in *The American Presidency,* Hamilton wrote, "The English model is the only good one on this subject." Hamilton wanted special electors from the states to select a president to serve for life, just like a king or queen. Virginia delegate James McClurg (1746–1823) and Delaware delegate Jacob Broom (1752–1810) agreed with the life-term idea but suggested that Congress select the president. The delegates rejected these proposals, too. Despite the existence

Virginia delegate and future U.S. president James Madison wrote the Virginia Plan, which proposed that the executive branch of government be selected by the legislature. National Archives and Records Administration.

of monarchists among them, most of the delegates feared giving one person the power of the presidency for life.

The very first constitutional plan the delegates considered was the Virginia Plan, written by Virginia delegate James Madison and presented by Virginia delegate Edmund Randolph (1753–1813). The Virginia Plan proposed that the executive branch of government be selected by the legislature. The delegates approved a form of this proposal in late August, less than a month before the Convention ended.

A problem with legislative selection of the president was that many delegates wanted the president to be eligible for reelection. They knew, however, that allowing Congress to reelect a president many times could lead to unfair deals between Congress and a president.

In the end, the delegates adopted a plan that had some of what most of the delegates wanted. The plan, called the electoral system, appears in Article II, Section 1, of the Constitution. It provides for selection of a president and vice president for a term of four years, with reelection allowed. To be president, a person must be at least thirty-five years old, a citizen of the United States, and a resident of the United States for at least fourteen years.

The electoral system gives each state a number of electors equal to the total number of representatives and senators they have in Congress. Each state gets to decide how to choose its electors. Once chosen, the electors meet in their state capitals on a day chosen by Congress.

What's in a Name?

During most of the Constitutional Convention, the delegates referred to the head of the executive branch of government simply as "the Executive." When it came time to finish a draft of the Constitution, they had to choose an official name for the chief executive officer. "President" and "governor" were two possibilities. One draft even proposed that the president be referred to as "His Excellency."

In the end, the delegates chose "president" and dropped "His Excellency." Article I, Section 9, even specifies that the United States cannot use titles of nobility. Given their experiences under King George III, most Americans did not want the president to seem like a king or queen.

Under the Constitution originally, each elector was to vote for two people, one of whom had to be from outside the elector's state. The votes would then be tallied and sent to the president of the Senate, who would open them in front of the whole Congress. If one person received a simple majority of votes, that person would become the next president, and the person with the second most votes would become the vice president. The House of Representatives got to select the president and the Senate got to select the vice president in cases of tie votes or failure of one person to receive a simple majority.

This system was used for the nation's first four presidential elections. In the election of 1800 (the nation's fourth), Vice President Thomas Jefferson and New York politician Aaron Burr (1756–1836) received the same number of electoral votes. Even though the electors clearly intended Jefferson to be president and Burr to be vice president, the Constitution required the House of Representatives to resolve the tie vote. A power struggle ensued between the Republican Party, to which Jefferson and Burr belonged, and the Federalist Party. The Federalists, the party of incumbent president John Adams (1735–1826; served 1797–1801), did not want Jefferson to be president. The Federalists in the House tried to give the election to Burr, but on the thirty-sixth ballot, Jefferson won. To prevent such a situation from happening again, Congress proposed and America adopted the Twelfth Amendment in 1804. Under the Twelfth Amendment, electors cast separate ballots for president and vice president. (See chapter 4, "Changes in the Executive Branch.")

Executive powers

Under the Articles of Confederation, Congress had sole authority to enforce the nation's laws. Its enforcement powers, however, were not very strong. The men who wrote the Constitution created the executive branch so the federal government would have stronger enforcement powers. These powers come mainly from the general vesting clause, the enforcement clause, the executive departments clause, and the pardons clause.

General vesting clause Article II, Section 1, of the Constitution begins, "The executive power shall be vested in a president of the United States of America." The Constitution does not define the term "executive power," so scholars have argued that the term means different things. Some scholars think executive power is limited to the specific presidential powers contained in the Constitution.

Others think the vesting clause gives presidents general power not mentioned in the Constitution. Delegate Alexander Hamilton, who was the first secretary of the treasury under President George Washington (1732–1799; served 1789–97), favored such an interpretation. Hamilton believed that limiting a government to specific powers would prevent the government from handling unforeseen circumstances.

John Locke (1632–1704) was a philosopher whose writings influenced the men who wrote the Constitution. He also thought executive rulers should have undefined powers. In *Second Treatise on Government* (as quoted by Milkis and Nelson in *The American Presidency*), Locke wrote that rulers should have power "to do several things of their own free choice, where the law was silent, or sometimes, too, against the direct letter of the law, for the public good."

Whatever they think "executive power" means, most scholars agree that it includes the power to enforce the nation's laws. When referring to the separation of powers, the founders talked about the need to separate the power to *make* the laws from the power to *enforce* them. Under the Constitution, Congress has the primary lawmaking power, and the executive branch, headed by the president, is the primary law enforcer.

Enforcement clause The power to enforce the laws also appears in Article II, Section 3. It says the president "shall take care that the laws be faithfully executed." This means that the president not only has the power to enforce the laws, but has a duty to do so. English monarchs throughout history often chose not to enforce the laws against favored people. Requiring a president to execute the laws "faithfully" is supposed to prevent the president from giving people special treatment under the laws.

In reality, though, presidents and their enforcement agencies get to use their judgment to decide when to enforce a law and when not to. Time and financial limitations prevent the executive branch from prosecuting all violations of the law. Political considerations, such as the power or popularity of an accused criminal, also affect the process. The combination of executive judgment, practical limitations, and political considerations makes it impossible to prevent the executive branch from giving special treatment to particular people.

Executive departments Article II, Section 2, says the president "may require the opinion, in writing, of the principal officer in each of the executive departments, upon any subject relating to the duties of their respective offices." This clause gives the president power to use executive departments to run the government and enforce the nation's laws.

Executive departments are government offices that focus on a large area of the government's duties. Congress has sole power to create executive departments, and the president has primary power to run them. Each department has a leader who is usually called the secretary. When the federal government began to operate under the Constitution in 1789, there were only three departments: State, Treasury, and War. During the administration of Harry S. Truman (1884–1972; served 1945–53), the Department of War became the National Military Establishment, and then was renamed the Department of Defense. In 1789, there also was an Office of the Attorney General, who is the head lawyer for the government. This office later became known as the Department of Justice.

The Department of Justice is the president's main law enforcement agency. The head of the department is called the attorney general. The Department of Justice investigates federal crimes through the Federal Bureau of Investigation (FBI). Attorneys who work for the Department of Justice, called U.S. attorneys, prosecute cases against accused criminals to enforce the nation's laws.

Pardons Article II, Section 2, of the Constitution gives the president "power to grant reprieves and pardons for offences against the United States, except in cases of impeachment." A reprieve is temporary relief from punishment for a crime. Reprieves give convicted criminals time to ask a court to change their punishment. A pardon is complete forgiveness for a crime. A pardon eliminates all punishment that a person might suffer if convicted of a crime.

The delegates to the Constitutional Convention had different feelings about the pardon power. Some feared presidents would use the power to pardon their friends, or even to pardon people who helped them commit a crime. Others, including Alexander Hamilton, argued that presidents needed the pardon power to help end rebellions against the government.

The delegates compromised by giving the president power to grant pardons except in cases of impeachment. Under the Constitution, the president and all other federal officers can be impeached and removed from office for committing treason, bribery, or other high crimes and misdemeanors. The Constitution defines treason as levying war against the United States or giving aid and comfort to its enemies. Bribery means giving something of value to influence official government action. The phrase "high crimes and misdemeanors" is completely undefined. The president cannot pardon himself or anyone else to avoid an impeachment.

Legislative powers

Congress has the primary lawmaking power under the Constitution. The system of checks and balances, however, gives the president lawmaking power too. The state of the union clause, recommendations clause, and veto power are the main sources of the president's lawmaking power.

State of the union message and recommendations Article II, Section 3, of the Constitution begins, "He shall from time to time give to the Congress information of the state of the union, and recommend to their consideration such measures as he shall judge necessary and expedient."

This clause did not cause much controversy when America was considering whether to adopt the Constitution. It requires the president to give Congress reports on how the country is doing, and to recommend laws that Congress should pass, change, or eliminate. In practice, these powers are more important than they seem. They allow presidents, especially popular ones, to set the tone for a session of Congress, influencing Congress's legislative agenda, or plan. For example, in his State of the Union address just after the start of his second term on February 2, 2005, President George W. Bush (1946–; served 2001–) asked Congress to pass laws to reduce lawsuits in America and to make Social Security investments private instead of public. (Social Security is a retirement and disability plan operated by the federal government, as of 2005.) Bush signed new legislation to reduce lawsuits by the end of that month.

Veto power The veto power is the power to reject laws passed by Congress. It appears in Article I, Section 7, of

Pardoning the Politicians and the People

The Constitution gives the president power to grant pardons and reprieves for offenses against the United States. A pardon is forgiveness for a crime, preventing the criminal from being punished. A reprieve is temporary suspension of a sentence. A reprieve gives a convict time to ask the court to change his or her sentence.

Presidents sometimes grant pardons to high-ranking government officials. The most famous example is President Gerald Ford's (1913–; served 1974–77) pardon of former president Richard Nixon (1913–1994; served 1969–74) on September 8, 1974. President Nixon had resigned from office one month earlier as the House of Representatives was about to impeach him for his involvement in covering up the Watergate scandal. (Impeachment is an official accusation of wrongdoing by the House of Representatives that can lead to conviction and removal from office by the Senate.) The Watergate scandal involved burglary of the offices of the Democratic National Committee. Ford said he pardoned Nixon to prevent the country from suffering through divisive criminal proceedings. The pardon was unpopular with many Americans, leading to Ford's defeat by former Georgia governor Jimmy Carter (1924–; served 1977–81) in the election of 1976, according to some scholars.

Another famous pardon happened in December 1992, when President George Bush (1924–; served 1989–93) pardoned six members of the administration of President Ronald Reagan (1911–2004; served 1981–89). The six men had been accused of criminal conduct in connection with the Iran-Contra scandal. The scandal involved the Reagan administration's sale of weapons to Iran for money illegally used to support rebels (called Contras) who were fighting the government in Nicaragua. The Reagan administration disapproved of the Nicaraguan government, which was based on socialism. Socialism involves government ownership of the means of production in an economy. Reagan's announcement of the Iran-Contra scandal, which he denied knowledge of, only slightly tarnished his overall popular approval in America.

History also has examples of presidents pardoning people who were not in positions of power. In 1792, President George Washington (1732–1799; served 1789–97) helped end the Whiskey Rebellion by granting a full pardon to the rebels. The Whiskey Rebellion was a protest by grain farmers against a tax on whiskey, which is made from grain.

When a pardon covers a group of people instead of specific persons, it can be called an amnesty. Presidents Abraham Lincoln (1809–1865; served 1861–65) and Andrew Johnson (1808–1875; served 1865–69), for example, granted amnesty to the Constitution. Under this section, Congress must present every bill it passes to the president. The president then has ten days (excluding Sundays) to consider and either approve or reject the bill. If the president signs the bill within ten days, or does nothing with the bill within ten days, the bill becomes law.

There are two ways a president can veto a bill. The first method, called a return veto, is when the president returns a

Confederate soldiers and leaders who had rebelled against the United States in the American Civil War (1861–65). Over a century later, presidents Gerald Ford and Jimmy Carter (1924–; served 1977–81) signed amnesties for people who had evaded the military draft during the Vietnam War (1954–75).

President Gerald Ford tells the nation that he is pardoning former president Richard Nixon for all Watergate-related offenses. AP/Wide World Photos.

bill to Congress with a veto message within ten days of getting it. A veto message explains why the president is vetoing a bill.

The second method is called a pocket veto. It happens when a president does nothing with a bill, but Congress adjourns, or takes an official recess break, before the president has the bill for ten days. In such cases, the bill is rejected even though the president did not use a return veto.

If the president vetoes a bill, it does not become law unless Congress overrides the veto by a two-thirds vote in both chambers, the Senate and the House of Representatives. History shows that overriding a presidential veto is very hard. According to a study by the Congressional Research Service in April 2004, presidents used the return veto 1,484 times and the pocket veto 1,065 times to that point in history. Congress voted to override only 106, or 7.1 percent, of the 1,484 return vetoes. (It is impossible to override a pocket veto, because a pocket veto occurs when Congress has adjourned.)

Military powers

Article II, Section 1, makes the president "commander in chief of the army and navy of the United States." Article I, Section 8, gives Congress the power "to make rules for the government and regulation of the land and naval forces" and "to declare war." This means that, in theory, Congress and the president share power over the armed forces.

In August 1787, a month before the end of the Constitutional Convention, a draft of the Constitution gave Congress the general power "to make war." On August 17, delegates James Madison and Elbridge Gerry (1744–1814) suggested changing "make war" to "declare war." The president, they said, should have the power to defend America from attack without a declaration of war. The delegates approved this change. Presidents have since used their power as commander in chief to conduct military operations, even offensive ones, without a declaration of war. As of 2005, Congress has declared war eleven times for five wars, including the War of 1812 (1812–15; one declaration against the United Kingdom), the Mexican-American War (1846–48; one declaration against Mexico), the Spanish-American War (1898; one declaration against Spain), World War I (1914–18;

Constitutional delegate and future U.S. vice president Elbridge Gerry suggested changing the language in the Constitution so that Congress could "declare war," rather than "make war." National Portrait Gallery.

declarations against Germany and Austria-Hungary), and World War II (1939–45; declarations against Japan, Germany, Italy, Bulgaria, Hungary, and Romania). Every other war, including the Korean War (1950–53), Vietnam War (1954–75), and the Persian Gulf Wars, has been undeclared, though often supported by a congressional resolution.

Foreign affairs

The executive branch of government has the primary authority to conduct relations with foreign nations. This power comes from the clauses on ambassadors and treaties.

An ambassador is a person who represents a nation in relations with another nation. Article II, Section 2, gives the president power to appoint ambassadors with the advice and consent of the Senate. This means the Senate must approve presidential appointments to ambassador posts by a simple majority.

Article II, Section 3, gives the president the power to receive ambassadors and other public ministers from foreign nations. The power to appoint American ambassadors and receive foreign ambassadors makes the executive branch the focal point for America's relations with foreign nations. The president conducts these relations through the Department of State, which is run by the secretary of state.

Article II, Section 2, gives the president the power to make treaties with other nations. A treaty is an official

President Gerald Ford stands with the U.S. ambassador to Ghana, Shirley Temple Black, in 1976. Presidents have the power to appoint American ambassadors, with Senate approval. AP/Wide World Photos.

agreement that governs the relations between nations. It creates an international law that the countries agree to obey and enforce. Under the Constitution, the president cannot make a treaty unless two-thirds of the Senate concurs, or agrees. This encourages presidents to work with senators while they negotiate treaties with other nations. On May 24, 2002, for example, President George W. Bush and President Vladimir Putin (1952–) of Russia signed the Moscow Treaty on Strategic Offensive Reductions. The Moscow Treaty was an agreement to reduce the number of strategic nuclear warhead arsenals in America and Russia to between 1,700 and 2,200 each by December 2012. The U.S. Senate ratified the treaty unanimously in March 2003.

Since the Senate must approve treaties, scholars debate whether the Senate must approve when a president cancels a treaty. Some scholars think presidents may cancel treaties on their own as part of their power over foreign affairs. Others think treaties are laws under the Constitution, and that letting presidents cancel them unconstitutionally gives one person the power to repeal a law. In December 2001, for example, President Bush notified Russia and the world that America was withdrawing from the Antiballistic Missile Treaty, which it had made with the Soviet Union in 1972. Bush withdrew from the treaty so America could work on an antimissile defense system, which the treaty would have prohibited. Bush said such a system was necessary to fight terrorism, and he did not seek Senate approval for his action.

Appointments

Under Article II, Section 2, the president has the power to appoint not only ambassadors, but also "other public ministers and consuls, judges of the Supreme Court, and all other officers of the United States, whose appointments are not herein otherwise provided for, and which shall be established by law." Just as with ambassadors, the Senate must approve such appointments by a simple majority.

Vice president

When they wrote the Constitution, the delegates struggled with what would happen if a president died or left office before the end of his term. Their solution was to create the position of vice president.

The vice president is chosen at the same time as the president for the same four-year term. Article II, Section 1, of the Constitution says, "In case of the removal of the president from office, or of his death, resignation, or inability to discharge the powers and duties of the said office, the same shall devolve on [be passed to] the vice president and the Congress may by law provide for the case of removal, death, resignation or inability, both of the president and vice president." The vice president has taken over as president nine times in history, eight times following the death of the president and once after the president resigned.

The only other job the vice president has in the Constitution is to serve as president of the Senate. In that role, the vice president has the power to break tie votes when the whole Senate is evenly split on a decision. The vice president does not get to vote in the Senate at any other time. The delegates to the Constitutional Convention, however, imagined that the vice president would attend Senate sessions fairly regularly. The vice president's role as president of the Senate is another way the executive branch participates in the law-making process.

Removal

The delegates to the Constitutional Convention decided to allow presidents to be reelected an unlimited number of times. In practice, only Franklin D. Roosevelt (1882–1945; served 1933–45) chose to run for more than two terms. (This was changed in 1951 by the Twenty-second Amendment, which allows a president to serve a maximum of two terms, or two terms and two years if the president was finishing no more than half of his predecessor's term.) The delegates wanted, however, a way to remove presidents who committed serious violations of law. The procedure for doing this is called the impeachment process. Under Article II, Section 4, presidents and other civil officers can be impeached and removed from office for "treason, bribery, or other high crimes and misdemeanors."

Congress alone has the impeachment power, which is divided between the House of Representatives and the Senate. The House has sole power to impeach a president or other federal officer. Impeachment is an official accusation that a president or other officer has committed treason, bribery, or other high crimes and misdemeanors.

If the House impeaches a president (or other federal officer), the Senate conducts an impeachment trial. The purpose of the trial is to determine whether the president should be removed from office for committing the crimes charged by the House. The Senate can convict and remove an impeached president (or other officer) only by a two-thirds majority.

As of 2005, only two presidents have been impeached by the House: Andrew Johnson (1808–1875; served 1865–69) in 1868 and Bill Clinton (1946–; served 1993–2001) in 1998. Neither was convicted or removed from office by the Senate.

A videotape still shows President Bill Clinton testifying before a grand jury in November 1998. He was impeached a month later.
© Wally McNamee/Corbis.

For More Information

BOOKS

Beard, Charles A. *American Government and Politics.* 10th ed. New York: Macmillan Co., 1949.

Beard, Charles A. *An Economic Interpretation of the Constitution of the United States.* New York: Macmillan, 1935.

Charleton, James H., Robert G. Ferris, and Mary C. Ryan, eds. *Framers of the Constitution.* Washington, DC: National Archives and Records Administration, 1976.

Cronin, Thomas E. *Inventing the American Presidency.* Lawrence: University Press of Kansas, 1989.

Kelly, Alfred H., and Winfred A. Harbison. *The American Constitution: Its Origins and Development.* 5th ed. New York: W. W. Norton & Co., 1976.

Kurland, Philip B., and Ralph Lerner. *The Founders' Constitution.* 5 vols. Indianapolis: Liberty Fund, 1987.

Levy, Leonard W. *Original Intent and the Framers' Constitution.* New York: Macmillan, 1988.

McClenaghan, William A. *Magruder's American Government 2003.* Needham, MA: Prentice Hall School Group, 2002.

McDonald, Forrest. *The American Presidency.* Lawrence: University Press of Kansas, 1994.

Milkis, Sidney M., and Michael Nelson. *The American Presidency: Origins & Development.* 3rd ed. Washington, DC: Congressional Quarterly Inc., 1999.

Nelson, Michael, ed. *The Evolving Presidency.* Washington, DC: Congressional Quarterly Inc., 1999.

Volkomer, Walter E. *American Government.* 8th ed. Upper Saddle River, NJ: Prentice Hall, 1998.

Zinn, Howard. *A People's History of the United States.* New York: HarperCollins, 2003.

WEB SITES

Sollenberger, Mitchel A. "Congressional Overrides of Presidential Vetoes." CRS Report for Congress, April 7, 2004. *United States House of Representatives.* http://www.senate.gov/reference/resources/pdf/98-157.pdf (accessed on February 14, 2005).

Sollenberger, Mitchel A. "The Presidential Veto and Congressional Procedure." CRS Report for Congress, February 27, 2004. *United States House of Representatives.* http://www.senate.gov/reference/resources/pdf/RS21750.pdf (accessed on February 14, 2005).

Changes in the Executive Branch

The Constitution of the United States was written at the Federal Convention in 1787 and adopted in 1788. It divides the federal government into three main branches. The legislative branch, Congress, is the main lawmaker. The executive branch is the primary law enforcer. The judicial branch, made up of the Supreme Court and lower federal courts, hears and decides cases under federal law.

The Constitution makes the president the head of the executive branch. Under the Constitution, the president has power to enforce the nation's laws, command the army and navy, veto laws passed by Congress, and oversee relations with foreign nations.

The Constitution also provides for a vice president to be elected with the president. The vice president replaces the president if he or she dies or leaves office before the end of the presidential term. The vice president has taken over as president nine times in history, eight times following the death of the president and once after the president resigned. The vice president also serves as president of the Senate, with the power to break tie votes when the whole Senate is evenly divided on an issue. As of 2005, vice presidents have cast tie-breaking votes about 233 times. More than half of these happened before 1850, when fewer states meant a smaller Senate with more chances of an even split. Most vice presidents since the 1870s have cast fewer than ten tie-breaking votes.

The executive branch has changed greatly since adoption of the Constitution. Many changes have been the result of

Words to Know

Constitution of the United States of America: The document written in 1787 that established the federal government under which the United States of America has operated since 1789. Article II covers the executive branch.

executive branch: The branch of the federal government that enforces the nation's laws. The executive branch includes the president, the vice president, and many executive departments, agencies, and offices.

executive privilege: A privilege that allows the president to keep information secret, even if Congress, federal investigators, the Supreme Court, or the people want the president to release the information. The privilege is designed to protect information related to national security, or public safety.

president: The highest officer in the executive branch of the federal government, with primary responsibility for enforcing the nation's laws.

ratification: The process of formally approving something, such as a treaty, constitution, or constitutional amendment.

separation of powers: Division of the powers of government into different branches to prevent one branch from having too much power.

vice president: The second highest officer in the executive branch of the federal government. The vice president replaces the president if the president dies or becomes unable to serve. The vice president also serves as president of the Senate, with power to break tie votes when the whole Senate is equally divided on an issue.

constitutional amendments. An amendment is a change to the Constitution agreed to by at least three-fourths of the states. Many constitutional amendments have affected the powers of the executive branch or the way the president and vice president are elected.

The Constitution, however, does not contain a thorough description of the powers of the executive branch. Instead, the powers have grown and changed over the years through presidential interpretation and congressional legislation. Congress can affect presidential power because while the executive branch enforces the laws, Congress makes the laws in the first place.

Housing soldiers in private homes: the Third Amendment

Nine of the thirteen American states had to ratify, or approve, the Constitution for it to become law between the ratifying states. Some of the states were wary of giving so much power to the federal government without including a bill of rights in the Constitution. A bill of rights is a law that protects the rights and freedoms of the people from unfair government action.

Ratification of the Constitution was done by state conventions, which contained delegates elected by the free men of the states. Some of the delegates refused to ratify the Constitution unless Congress promised to add a bill of rights to it soon after ratification. The delegates who supported the Constitution made this promise, and by summer 1788, ten states had ratified the Constitution.

Virginia delegate James Madison (1751–1836), who would be the fourth president of the United States, took it upon himself to draft the bill of rights. The bill that he and Congress proposed contained twelve amendments. By 1791, the states had ratified ten of them. Those ten amendments have come to be called the Bill of Rights.

The Third Amendment says, "No soldier shall, in time of peace be quartered [housed] in any house, without the consent of the Owner, nor in time of war, but in a manner to be prescribed by law." This amendment was important to Americans then because years earlier, British monarchs had housed soldiers in private homes against the will of the owners.

The Third Amendment prevents the president of the United States from housing soldiers in private homes as the British monarchs had done. It reflects the fact that many Americans felt the federal government should be required to respect the privacy of home life in America.

Searches and seizures: the Fourth Amendment

The Fourth Amendment says: "The right of the people to be secure in their persons, houses, papers, and effects, against unreasonable searches and seizures, shall not be violated, and no Warrants shall issue, but upon probable cause, supported by Oath or affirmation, and particularly describing the place to be searched, and the persons or things to be seized."

The purpose of the Fourth Amendment is to protect people from unreasonable searches and seizures. A search is when the government looks through a person's house, car, or other property for evidence of a crime. A seizure is when the government arrests a person suspected of committing a crime, or takes a person's property to hold as evidence of a crime.

Under the Fourth Amendment, searches and seizures must be reasonable. In general, a search or seizure is unreasonable unless the government has probable cause to believe a crime has been committed. Probable cause means a reasonable belief that a crime probably has been committed. If the government has probable cause to believe a crime has been committed, it can arrest the suspected criminal and seize evidence of the suspected crime.

Before it conducts a search or seizure, however, the government usually needs to obtain a warrant. A warrant is a document from a court saying that the government has probable cause to conduct the search or seizure. Courts issue warrants after the government shows them evidence that a crime probably has been committed. The evidence often includes a sworn statement by the victim or by a criminal investigator.

Because the executive branch has primary responsibility for law enforcement, the president's law enforcement agencies are the main departments that must obey the Fourth Amendment. For example, the Federal Bureau of Investigation (FBI) is the agency in the Department of Justice that investigates violations of federal law. When conducting investigations, the FBI often needs to arrest people suspected of committing crimes or seize evidence of suspected crimes.

In general, the FBI and other law enforcement agencies are not supposed to conduct searches or seizures without getting a warrant based on probable cause that a crime has been committed. Through interpretation of the Fourth Amendment, however, the Supreme Court has created many exceptions to this rule. For example, law enforcement personnel can arrest someone without a warrant when they catch him or her committing a crime.

Criminal prosecutions: the Fifth and Sixth Amendments

After a law enforcement agency conducts an investigation, it might decide to charge someone with committing a federal crime. If it has enough evidence for the charge, the agency can have the Department of Justice prosecute the suspected criminal. The Department of Justice is the agency in the executive branch that prosecutes criminal and civil cases for the federal government. Criminal cases involve violations of criminal laws, such as murder laws, which serve to protect society from harm. Civil cases involve private disputes that are not necessarily crimes, such as when one person breaks a contract, or agreement, with another person. Wrongful conduct, however, can violate both criminal and civil law, such as when one person hits another person, injuring her seriously. The government can file criminal charges against the attacker for criminal battery, and the injured person can file a civil case to recover money for her injuries.

The Fifth and Sixth Amendments give accused criminals specific rights in criminal prosecutions. The Fifth Amendment has four such rights. First, a person may not be prosecuted for a capital or infamous offense unless a grand jury decides that the government has enough evidence against the suspect. A capital offense is one punishable by death, such as first degree murder. An infamous offense involves treason, dishonesty, or a crime punishable by imprisonment for more than a year. Treason means levying war against the United States or giving aid and comfort to its enemies. A grand jury is a group of citizens that reviews the government's evidence to decide whether the evidence is enough to justify a criminal trial.

Second, the government cannot try a person twice for the same crime. Third, prosecutors cannot force a suspected criminal to testify at his or her trial. (When a prosecutor or investigator questions a suspect and he or she refuses to answer, it is called "taking the fifth." This means that instead of answering the question, the suspect is asserting his or her fifth amendment right not to incriminate himself or herself.) Fourth, the government cannot take away a person's life, liberty, or property without due process of law. Due process generally means that accused criminals cannot be punished without notice of the charges against them and a fair trial.

The Sixth Amendment gives an accused criminal five rights. First, an accused criminal must be tried in a speedy, public trial by a fair jury in the state or district where the crime was committed. A fair jury means a jury of people who have not made up their minds about the guilt or innocence of the accused before trial. Second, accused criminals must be informed of the charges against them. Third, an accused criminal has the right to cross-examine witnesses who testify against him or her. Fourth, an accused criminal has the right "to have compulsory process for obtaining witnesses in his favor." This means that if there is a witness who has testimony favorable to the defendant, the defendant can use the power of the court to force that witness to appear at his or her trial to testify. Fifth, an accused criminal has the right to have an attorney represent him or her.

Election of the president and vice president

The delegates to the Constitutional Convention struggled with the question of how the president of the United States should be elected. Some thought the people should elect the president directly in popular elections. Others thought Congress should select the president. The system the delegates settled on is called the electoral college, or electoral system.

Under this system, each state gets to choose a number of electors equal to the total number of senators and representatives it has in Congress. The electors meet in their state capitals on a day chosen by Congress to select the president and vice president for a four-year term. As the Constitution was written in 1787, electors each voted for two people. The person who received the most number of electoral votes became the next president, and the person who received the second most number of votes became the next vice president. Over the years, this system caused problems and situations that were eventually eliminated with the Twelfth, Twenty-second, and Twenty-third Amendments to the Constitution. Even so, discussion over the merits of the electoral college periodically surface, most recently after the 2000 presidential election, when Vice President Al Gore (1948–) received more popular votes than his challenger, Texas governor George W. Bush (1946–), but still lost the election because Bush received more electoral votes. This also happened in the presidential elections of 1824, 1876, and 1888.

The Twelfth Amendment: presidents and vice presidents The presidential election of 1800 was the fourth under the Constitution. Thomas Jefferson (1743–1826; served 1801–9) was the presidential candidate for the Democratic-Republican Party. Aaron Burr (1756–1836) was the Republican Party's candidate for vice president. After the electoral votes were tallied, Jefferson and Burr tied with seventy-three votes each.

The Constitution required the House of Representatives to break the tie. Each state had one vote in the House for this purpose. The Democratic-Republicans controlled eight states, the Federalist Party controlled six, and two states were evenly divided. Even though the Democratic-Republican electors intended for Jefferson to be president, it was possible for Burr to win the election in the House. When the House failed to come to a majority result for days, the Federalists considered passing a law making the president pro tem of the Senate the president of the United States until the election of 1804. (The president pro tem is a senator appointed by the Senate to preside over the Senate when the vice president of the United States, whose constitutional duty is to preside, cannot be there.) The president pro tem of the Senate at the time was a Federalist.

In the end, Jefferson won the election in the House. The situation, however, led Congress to propose the Twelfth Amendment in December 1803. Under the Twelfth Amendment, electors still vote for two people, but they cast one vote specifically for the presidency and the other for the vice presidency. The Twelfth Amendment became part of the Constitution in September 1804.

The Twenty-second Amendment: a presidential term limit

The delegates to the Constitutional Convention wanted presidents to be able to serve more than one four-year term. Scholars say the delegates expected George Washington (1732–1799; served 1789–97) to be the first president, and Washington was well liked among them. Sure enough, Washington was elected in 1788 and 1792, serving two four-year terms from 1789 to 1797.

Washington set an example by deciding not to seek a third term of office. Every president followed Washington's example until Franklin D. Roosevelt (1882–1945) served over three full terms from 1933 to 1945. Roosevelt, who was a member of the Democratic Party, died in 1945, three months into his fourth term.

In 1947, when Congress was controlled by the Republican Party, it proposed an amendment to limit presidents to two terms in office. Over three-fourths of the state legislatures approved the amendment by March 1951, making it the Twenty-second Amendment to the Constitution.

The Twenty-second Amendment is controversial. Some Americans think it is healthy to require the country to elect a new person at least every eight years. Others think restricting America's choice of the president is undemocratic. President Ronald Reagan (1911–2004), a popular president who served two terms from 1981 to 1989, called the Twenty-second Amendment the most undemocratic part of the Constitution.

Twenty-third Amendment The city of Washington in the District of Columbia is the seat of government for the United States. It was

House and Senate Roles in Presidential Elections

Every four years in November, Americans go to the polls to vote in a presidential election. Under the Constitution, however, the president and vice president are not elected by the voters. They are selected by people called electors. This system is called the electoral college.

The Constitution allows each state to appoint a certain number of electors. The number for each state is equal to the total number of representatives and senators the state has in Congress. In addition, the District of Columbia, which is not a state, gets at least three electors.

Under state law as of 2005, the electors are chosen by the voters in each state at the time of the November presidential election. After the election, the electors meet in their state capitals to cast votes for the president and the vice president. Electors usually cast their votes for the candidates who won the popular vote in their state in the November election (or in their district, in the case of Nebraska and Maine). The Constitution, however, does not require electors to vote like this.

After all the electors in all the states have voted, their votes are tallied in Congress. The people who get a majority of the votes for president and vice president win the election.

If nobody gets a majority of the votes for president, the Constitution requires the House of Representatives to choose the president. The House chooses between the people who got the first, second, and third most electoral votes. The members of the House do not vote individually, but instead vote in groups based on the states they represent. The person who receives votes from a majority of states becomes the president.

If nobody gets a majority of the votes for vice president, the Senate makes the choice. Senators vote individually, choosing from the people who got the first and second most electoral votes. A majority of senators must vote for a person for that person to become the vice president.

As of 2005, two presidential elections have been determined by the House. In 1800, Thomas Jefferson and vice presidential candidate Aaron Burr (1756–1836) received an equal number of electoral votes. The Constitution then did not distinguish between electoral votes for the president and those for the vice president. This sent the election to the House.

The House voted thirty-six times before electing Jefferson by a majority. Although voters clearly wanted Jefferson to be the president, members of the House from the Federalist Party were fearful of created in 1790 from land given to the federal government by Maryland. Until 1964, the residents of Washington, D.C., were not allowed to participate in presidential elections.

In 1961, America adopted the Twenty-third Amendment to the Constitution. The amendment allows Washington, D.C., to select a number of electors equal to the number of senators and representatives it would have if it were a state, but no more than the number of electors allowed for the least populous state (currently, Wyoming). Electors from Washington, D.C., get to vote for the president and vice president just like electors from the fifty states.

a Jefferson presidency. Jefferson was a strong supporter of state power and people's rights, whereas the Federalist Party wanted the nation's government to be stronger than the states. The Twelfth Amendment to the Constitution, adopted in 1804, changed the Constitution to prevent presidential candidates and their vice presidential running mates from getting equal numbers of electoral votes. Instead of simply casting two votes as they had under the original Constitution, electors under the Twelfth Amendment label their two votes, one for president and the other for vice president.

The election of 1824 produced another electoral conflict. U.S. senator Andrew Jackson (1767–1845) of Tennessee received 99 electoral votes, Secretary of State John Quincy Adams (1767–1848) received 84, Secretary of the Treasury William H. Crawford (1772–1834) got 41, and Speaker of the House Henry Clay (1777–1842) received 37. Because nobody got a majority, the House had to choose between the leading three vote-getters. Adams won on the first House ballot because the candidate who was no longer eligible, Clay, convinced the states that had voted for him to support Adams. This resulted in Adams receiving the necessary majority of state support to be elected. Adams, in return, appointed Clay as his secretary of state. Jackson's supporters called it a "corrupt bargain," accusing Adams of promising Clay the position in

exchange for getting support from the states that had voted for Clay during the election.

After none of the presidential candidates received a majority in the electoral voting, John Quincy Adams was chosen president in a House of Representatives vote. Library of Congress.

An editorial cartoon shows two-term president Franklin D. Roosevelt smoking a cigarette whose smoke curls up into a question mark, with the words "3rd Term Question" present. Roosevelt is the only president to be elected to more than two terms. He died three months into his fourth term. National Archives and Records Administration.

Voting rights: the Fifteenth, Nineteenth, Twenty-fourth, and Twenty-sixth Amendments

When the delegates wrote the Constitution in 1787, voting rights were a matter of state law. In general, the thirteen American states allowed only free men to vote, and only if they owned a certain amount of property or paid a poll tax. (A poll tax is a tax that a person must pay in order to be allowed to vote.) The delegates thought about including a property requirement in the Constitution for federal voting rights, but decided against it.

The gradual growth of democracy since 1787 is reflected in constitutional amendments that have expanded voting rights for Americans. The Fifteenth Amendment, adopted in 1870, made it illegal to deny a person the right to vote based on his or her race or color. The Nineteenth Amendment, ratified in 1920, gave women the right to vote. The Twenty-fourth Amendment, adopted in

Women suffragettes march in support of voting rights for women in 1912. The Nineteenth Amendment, ratified in 1920, gave women those rights. Library of Congress.

1964, made it illegal to charge a poll tax for presidential and congressional elections. Finally, the Twenty-sixth Amendment, ratified in 1971, extended voting rights to citizens at least eighteen years of age (most states had used twenty-one).

The veto power as a policy tool

Article I, Section 8, gives the president the power to veto, or reject, laws passed by Congress. Congress can override a veto only by a two-thirds vote in both the House of Representatives and the Senate.

Aware that his actions would set an example, President Washington used the veto power only twice, when he thought Congress had passed a law that violated the Constitution. Presidents through Abraham Lincoln (1809–1865), who served from 1861 to 1865, generally used the veto power sparsely, too.

Starting with Andrew Johnson (1808–1875), who served from 1865 to 1869, presidents began to use the veto power aggressively. They became more willing to veto laws of which they simply disapproved, whether or not the law might violate the Constitution. President Franklin Roosevelt, for example, used the veto power 635 times during his twelve years and three months in office.

Although the Constitution makes Congress the primary lawmaker, aggressive use of the veto power has led scholars to call the president the chief legislator. A veto threat gives the president great power to shape Congress's overall legislative agenda, or plan. It also gives the president great power to influence the content of the individual laws passed by Congress. This comes from the fact that it is very hard to override a presidential veto. According to a study by the Congressional Research Service in April 2004, Congress had overturned only 106, or 7.1 percent, of the 1,484 return vetoes to that point in history.

The budget process

The federal budget is the plan for how the government is going to spend money during the year. Under the Constitution, Congress is the branch that assigns federal money to the government's departments and agencies, including those in the executive and judicial branches. This makes Congress responsible for preparing the government's budget each year.

Until 1921, departments and agencies from all branches submitted budget requests directly to Congress. Congress used the requests to prepare a budget for the upcoming year. In making the budget, Congress was not bound by the budget requests. Instead, it could adjust the requests up or down to arrive at a final budget.

In 1921, Congress passed a law called the Budget and Accounting Act. The law gave the president responsibility to assemble budget requests and submit a proposed budget to Congress each year. It also created a new executive office, the Bureau of the Budget, to help the president with this task. In 1939, President Franklin Roosevelt moved the Bureau of the Budget from the Department of the Treasury into the Executive Office of the President, which is the office that helps the president run the executive branch. In 1970, President Richard Nixon (1913–1994; served 1969–74) renamed the bureau the Office of Management and Budget (OMB).

Every year in the spring, federal departments and agencies submit budget requests to the OMB. OMB officials spend the rest of the year helping the president transform these requests into a proposed budget. The president presents the proposed budget to Congress the following February. From there, Congress works the budget into revenue and spending laws for the fiscal year that runs from the upcoming October 1 through September 30.

In theory, Congress is not bound by the president's proposed budget. In practice, the president's proposal carries a lot of weight. This means that although Congress had the most budget power before 1921, the president has had greater power since passage of the Budget and Accounting Act that year.

Growth of the bureaucracy

A major change in the executive branch since 1789 has been the growth of the number and size of its departments, agencies, and other offices. In 1789, President George Washington's administration had only three departments: State, Treasury, and War. There were other offices, too, such as the Office of the Attorney General, who is the lead lawyer for the federal government. Washington's administration employed just a few hundred people at the time.

As of 2005, the executive branch contains fifteen departments, hundreds of agencies and offices, and many regulatory commissions, employing a total of about 2.7 million people altogether. Departments are offices with responsibility for large areas of the federal government. The fifteen departments are: Agriculture, Commerce, Defense, Education, Energy, Health & Human Services, Homeland Security, Housing & Urban Development, Interior, Justice, Labor, State, Transportation, Treasury, and Veterans Affairs.

Agencies are offices that handle specific areas of government, such as the American Battle Monuments Commission, the Environmental Protection Agency, and the Federal Aviation Administration. The Federal Aviation Administration, for example, regulates airlines and air traffic in the United States and investigates aircraft accidents. Regulatory commissions are offices that regulate a particular area of the economy. Examples include the Food and Drug Administration (FDA), which regulates food and drug safety, and the Occupational Safety and Health Administration (OSHA), which

WASHINGTON AND HIS CABINET.

President George Washington (left) and the nation's first cabinet: Secretary of War Henry Knox, Secretary of the Treasury Alexander Hamilton, Secretary of State Thomas Jefferson, and Attorney General Edmund Randolph. © Corbis.

regulates workplace safety. Regulatory commissions wield tremendous power in their areas of expertise. The FDA, for example, has the final say on what drugs are allowed to reach the shelves of America's pharmacies and drugstores.

Executive Office of the President

As the executive branch grew, it became difficult for presidents and their staffs to manage it. In 1939, President Franklin D. Roosevelt created the Executive Office of the President (EOP). The purpose of the EOP is to help the president manage the executive branch.

As of 2005, the EOP contains over a dozen separate councils, boards, and offices. Most presidents have either a White House Office or an Office of Chief of Staff that oversees the president's White House operations and close advisors. These advisors include people who schedule the president's appointments and write his speeches. The White House press secretary answers questions from, and feeds information to, the nation's newspaper, television, and other journalists. The press secretary often holds press conferences at the White House to make important announcements or answer questions about significant events.

The EOP contains many offices outside the White House Office. The OMB helps the president prepare a proposed federal budget each year The National Security Council (NSC) helps the president plan national security, or safety, and foreign policies. The National Economic Council and the Council of Economic Advisors inform the president about the nation's economy. The Office of National Drug Control Policy helps the president set the nation's drug control policies. The Office of Administration helps the entire EOP run by providing financial management and information technology support, human resources management, library and research assistance, facilities management, purchasing, printing and graphics support, security, and mail and messenger operations.

Executive orders

An executive order is an order signed by the president for exercising a power or duty of the executive branch. The Constitution does not mention executive orders. As of 2005, however, executive orders have been used by every president except William Henry Harrison (1773–1841), who died after just one month in office. According to the *Congressional Quarterly's Powers of the Presidency,* presidents mainly use executive orders to establish agencies, change bureaucratic rules and procedures, and carry out laws passed by Congress.

On January 29, 2001, for example, President George W. Bush signed an executive order to create the White House Office of Faith-Based and Community Initiatives. The office develops policies to allow religious and community groups in America to compete for federal funding for fighting social problems such as poverty, hunger, homelessness, and drug addiction. Supporters say the program will allow religious and community groups to help improve America. Opponents say the program will unconstitutionally give federal money to programs for spreading religion. The First Amendment says the federal government may not respect an establishment of religion, which means to favor one or more religions over others.

President Washington signed only eight executive orders (that historians know about) during his eight years in office. The second president, John Adams (1735–1826; served 1797–1801), signed just one, and the third president, Thomas Jefferson, signed just four. Use of executive orders became more frequent with the presidency of Abraham Lincoln and increased dramatically with the presidency of Theodore Roosevelt (1858–1919; served 1901–9) at the start of the twentieth century.

Many executive orders are routine, but they can also be controversial. If Congress passes a law that does not clearly define

President Bill Clinton signs an executive order at the Department of Agriculture on August 12, 1999, that will enable crop and timber waste to be turned into sources of energy. © Reuters Corbis.

how a president is supposed to enforce it, executive orders issued under the law can essentially create new law. Presidents sometimes use executive orders to avoid congressional involvement in important policy decisions. For example, some people think it should be up to Congress, not the president alone, to set national policies for including religious organizations in federal funding programs. Finally, many executive orders are written to keep government information secret. Some scholars believe these kinds of executive orders are undemocratic, giving the president power that nobody can challenge. Others think they are necessary executive functions.

Executive privilege

Executive privilege is presidential power to keep information secret from Congress, investigators, the courts, and the public. The Constitution does not mention an executive privilege. Instead, presidents have created it through practice.

The question of executive privilege first arose after November 1791, during President Washington's first term in office. That month, General Arthur St. Clair (1736–1818) led a failed military expedition against Native Americans in which hundreds of American lives were lost. In March 1792, the House of Representatives created a committee to investigate the expedition. The committee asked Washington's office to provide testimony and documents concerning the expedition.

Washington met with his cabinet to consider the request. (The cabinet is a group of the president's most important advisors, including the heads of the executive departments.) With his cabinet's advice, Washington decided that Congress could request information from a president, but that presidents could withhold information that might harm the public good. Although the failed expedition was embarrassing, Washington decided that disclosing information about it would not harm the public good, so he gave the House committee the information it wanted.

Following Washington's example, presidents generally have used the executive privilege to shield information relating to national security, diplomatic negotiations, and other governmental functions for which secrecy is arguably important. Some experts agree that secrecy is necessary for presidents to handle matters relating to national safety and the well-being of the public. Others believe secrecy is undemocratic because citizens cannot hold presidents accountable for their actions if the actions are secret.

During the presidencies of Richard Nixon and Bill Clinton (1946–; served 1993–2001), the issue of executive privilege became particularly controversial. Nixon tried to use the privilege in 1973 to hide information about the Watergate scandal from a Senate investigation. The Watergate scandal involved burglary of the offices of the Democratic National Committee in 1972 by men hired by the Republican Party. High-level officials in the Nixon administration may have had knowledge of the planned burglary,

The Pullman Strike of 1894

Just as the Roman consuls of the Roman Republic were in charge of the military and the monarchs of England controlled its soldiers, the president of the United States is commander in chief of American military forces. Military forces serve to protect a nation from foreign attack.

The U.S. Constitution also authorizes the federal government to use the military internally. The Militia Clause of Article I, Section 8, says Congress may "provide for calling forth the [State] militia to execute the laws of the union, suppress insurrections and repel invasions." The Protection Clause of Article IV, Section 4, says, "The United States ... shall protect each of [the States] against invasion; and on application of the legislature, or of the executive (when the legislature cannot be convened) against domestic violence."

The Founding Fathers wrote the Protection Clause to allow the federal government to use the military to suppress rebellions against state governments. The federal government, however, has also used the military to suppress strikes by workers against businesses.

The Pullman Strike of 1894 is one of the most famous examples of this tactic. As told by Howard

Zinn in A People's History of the United States, the Pullman Palace Car Company manufactured railway cars in the town of Pullman near Chicago, Illinois. Company workers lived in Pullman, paying the company for rent and utilities. As of June 1894, in the midst of a nationwide economic recession, the company had lowered worker pay five times without dropping rent charges. For these and other reasons, the workers went on strike. (A strike is a work stoppage to protest working conditions.)

According to Zinn:

> The American Railway Union [an organization for railroad workers] ... asked its members all over the country not to handle Pullman cars. Since virtually all passenger trains had Pullman cars, this amounted to a boycott of all trains—a nationwide strike. Soon all traffic on the twenty-four railroad lines leading out of Chicago had come to a halt. Workers derailed freight cars, blocked tracks, pulled engineers off trains if they refused to cooperate.... On July 6, hundreds of cars were burned by strikers.

President Grover Cleveland (1837–1908; served 1885–89, 1893–97) decided to send the federal military to help the local police and state militia end the strike. Cleveland reasoned that the strike and Nixon himself may have participated in efforts to cover up the burglary. Clinton tried to use the privilege to hide information from a federal prosecutor relating to whether he lied under oath when he denied having a sexual relationship with Monica Lewinsky (1973–), a twenty-one-year-old White House intern.

In both cases, federal courts forced Nixon and Clinton to disclose the requested information. The general public sentiment held that Nixon and Clinton abused the privilege by using it to try to hide personal information that did not relate to matters of national security or other important governmental functions.

was interfering with commerce between the states, which Congress has the power to regulate. On July 7, fourteen thousand troops, militia, and police clashed with the strikers. Fourteen people died, fifty-three were seriously wounded, and seven hundred were arrested, ending the strike.

Workers pull spikes from switches in the Western Indiana Railroad yards during the Pullman Strike of 1894. Getty Images.

War powers

The Constitution makes the president the commander in chief of the army and navy. Congress, however, has the power to create the army and navy, assign government money to them, make rules for their operation, and declare war.

Historians generally agree that the delegates to the Constitutional Convention carefully divided the military powers in the Constitution. They feared giving the president absolute control over the armed forces. They even rejected a proposal that the president have the power to declare war.

By giving Congress the power to declare war, the delegates intended to prevent offensive military operations without congressional authorization. In other words, the power to declare war is not supposed to be a mere formality. Presidents are supposed to have the power to use military forces without a declaration of war only when necessary to defend against a sudden attack.

In practice, American military activity has not been constrained to declarations of war and defensive operations. As of 2005, Congress has declared war for only five wars, including the War of 1812 (1812–15), the Mexican-American War (1846–48), the Spanish-American War (1898), World War I (1914–18), and World War II (1939–45). American forces, however, have engaged in hundreds of offensive military conflicts. Congress often approves military action after it happens, but it also criticizes presidents for engaging in military activity without congressional authorization.

Some scholars think presidents must have the power to engage in military activity whenever they think it is necessary, even without congressional approval. Others think such activity violates the Constitution and gives dangerous power to the president.

In 1973, Congress passed the War Powers Resolution to try to strengthen the constitutional separation of military powers. President Nixon vetoed the bill, but both chambers of Congress voted to override the veto.

The War Powers Resolution says presidents should send troops into hostile situations only with a congressional declaration of war or other congressional authorization, or to defend against an attack. It also says presidents must consult with Congress whenever possible before committing troops to hostile situations. Finally, it requires presidents to remove troops from hostile situations within

Panamanian military leader Manuel Noriega, following his capture in 1989. President George Bush had sent fourteen thousand troops to Panama without congressional approval to capture Noriega, who was eventually accused of election fraud and drug violations. A P / W i d e W o r l d P h o t o s .

sixty days unless there is a congressional declaration of war or other congressional authorization.

Every president since the passage of the resolution has called it unconstitutional, or violated its terms, or both. Presidents generally say their duty as commander in chief gives them power to use military forces without congressional approval. Occasionally some members of Congress protest when a president violates the resolution, but Congress usually does nothing to enforce it. On December 20, 1989, for example, President George Bush (1924–; served 1989–93) sent fourteen thousand military forces to Panama to join thirteen thousand American forces already there to capture General Manuel Noriega (1938–), then a military leader of Panama. Noriega was accused of election fraud and drug violations. Bush never asked for congressional approval for the invasion. Because the invasion was popular with Americans, Congress did not complain.

The president as chief economist

The economy is a term that means the business and employment activity in a nation. When business activity is strong and employment rates are high, meaning most working people have a job, the economy is in an inflationary state. When business activity sags and unemployment rates rise, the economy is in a recession.

The Constitution does not mention the national economy. Congress, however, has the power to regulate things that affect the economy, such as taxes, commerce, and money. When the Constitution was written in 1787, people generally did not think the government was responsible for the health of the economy.

That thinking changed with the presidency of Franklin Roosevelt. Roosevelt became president in 1933 when the American economy was in the middle of the Great Depression (1929–41). At the worst point of the Depression, one out of every three to four working Americans did not have a job. In those desperate times, people began to look more to the federal government for help with the economy. Roosevelt responded with his famous New Deal, a set of government programs designed to pump federal money into the economy to spur job growth.

As of 2005, the president is often considered the chief economist for the nation. Presidential candidates often include their own economic plans. When the economy is doing well, people generally credit the president, and when the economy is doing poorly, people generally blame the president.

The expectation that presidents can control the economy is unrealistic. Presidents have the power to affect the economy to some extent through the policy decisions they and their advisors make. The overall health of the economy, however, is determined by many complicated factors, all of which are beyond the power

President Franklin D. Roosevelt talks to a young boy and a farmer who is receiving a drought relief grant during the Great Depression in 1936. Library of Congress.

of the government to control completely. Even professional economists cannot always predict what will happen to the economy from one year to the next. Still, Americans have come to expect presidents to have a plan for improving a bad economy or making a good one even better.

The future

America is often called the land of opportunity. Americans are generally free to choose the kinds of jobs they want, although people with more money have more choices than people with less money. One of the key reasons immigrants from around the world move to America is to improve their job or career opportunities. Many American children grow up with dreams of becoming the president of the United States.

In spite of the opportunities in America, the office of the presidency is out of reach for most people. As of 2005, every American president has been a white, Christian man of European ancestry. Presidents are typically much wealthier than most Americans before ever setting foot in the White House. And despite the existence of many political parties, every president has been a member of either the Republican or Democratic Party since 1853, when Democrat Franklin Pierce (1804–1869; served 1853–57) took office.

Gender and religious diversity According to the U.S. Census Bureau, 78 percent of Americans age eighteen and older considered themselves to be Protestant or Catholic Christians in 2002. It is not surprising, then, that all of the presidents have been Christian, since people tend to elect representatives and leaders they perceive to be most like themselves.

Women, however, make up about 51 percent of the population, but a woman has never occupied the office of the presidency. America is behind other nations in this regard. Prime Minister Indira Gandhi (1917–1984; served 1966–77, 1980–84) of India; Prime Minister Golda Meir (1898–1978; served 1969–74) of Israel; Presidents Mary Robinson (1944–; served 1990–97) and Mary McAleese (1951–; served 1997–) of Ireland; Prime Minister Margaret Thatcher (1925–; served 1979–90) of Great Britain; and President Tarja Halonen (1943–; served 2000–) of Finland are notable female leaders from around the world.

Most Americans say they would vote for a female president. Presidents, however, tend to be former vice presidents, governors, members of Congress, and high-ranking military officers. Women are underrepresented in these positions, but that is changing with growing political and social equality for women.

In 1984, for example, U.S. congresswoman Geraldine Ferraro (1935–) of New York became the first female vice presidential candidate on a major party ticket, running with the Democratic presidential contender, former vice president Walter Mondale (1928–). (They lost to President Ronald Reagan and Vice President George Bush). In 1981, Sandra Day O'Connor (1930–) became the first female Supreme Court justice; Ruth Bader Ginsburg (1933–) was the second, in 1993. In

1997, Madeleine Albright (1937–) became the first woman secretary of state; Condoleezza Rice (1954–) held the same position following her appointment in 2005. As of 2005, many people speculate that former first lady and U.S. senator Hillary Clinton (1947–) of New York will run for president in 2008.

Financial diversity Presidential campaigns cost hundreds of millions of dollars, much of which goes to advertising, hiring advisors, election experts, and other staff members, and conducting research into people and issues to determine the best way to win an election. It is not surprising, therefore, that presidents tend to be wealthy. Wealthy people can use as much of their own money as they want to in their presidential campaigns. Wealthy people also have more money to donate to presidential campaigns, giving them greater financial influence in the electoral process.

Some Americans think contributing money to presidential campaigns is a right protected by the First Amendment. (The First Amendment protects the right to speak, assemble in groups, and petition the government for laws and programs.) These Americans do not want to limit the ability to contribute to such campaigns.

Other Americans think the high cost of becoming president makes the position undemocratic because it favors the wealthy. They favor laws that would change the way campaigns are financed so that people who are not wealthy have a better chance to become president.

Political diversity As of the 2004 elections, five parties besides the Republicans and Democrats regularly run candidates for presidential and congressional elections, including the Constitution, Green, Libertarian, Natural Law, and Reform parties. There are also at least five more parties working to gain nationwide support, including the Communist, Labor, New, Socialist, and Workers World parties. There are millions of Americans who do not belong to a specific political party, and millions of Americans do not vote in presidential elections. So while the Democratic and Republican parties dominate American politics, they do not represent all Americans.

The Democratic and Republican parties, however, are the largest political parties in America as of 2005. This means that most elected government officials, including those in Congress

Green Party presidential candidate Ralph Nader speaks at a news conference in 2000. The environmentalist Green Party is just one of many parties that serve as alternatives to the traditional Democratic and Republican parties. AP/Wide World Photos.

and the state legislatures, come from these parties. Legislatures have passed election and ballot access laws that make it harder for candidates from the so-called third parties to get elected. (For example, Democrats and Republicans generally need to collect far fewer signatures from party members to get onto primary ballots than third-party members need to collect to get on general election ballots.) Democrats and Republicans regularly exclude third parties from candidate debates, making it harder for third-party candidates to get their messages to the voters and to receive serious consideration on election day. One notable recent exception was Texas businessman H. Ross Perot, who was included in the 1992 presidential debates with his opponents, Arkansas governor Bill Clinton and President George Bush; Perot fared better than any other third-party candidate in history, receiving 18.9 percent of the popular vote.

Direct popular elections and instant runoff voting The electoral system makes it possible for a presidential candidate to lose the popular vote but win the presidency. This has happened four times in history. John Quincy Adams (1767–1848; served 1825–29), Rutherford B. Hayes (1822–1893; served 1877–81), Benjamin Harrison (1833–1901; served 1889–93), and George W. Bush (1946–; served 2001–) won their presidential elections even though they received fewer popular votes than their nearest competitors. (For Bush, this was the case in the 2000 election, but not in 2004.)

President Bush's victory in the election of 2000 revived national interest in direct popular election of the president. Under a system of direct popular election, the person who receives the most votes wins the election. Russia, for instance, elects its president through direct popular elections. People in favor of direct popular elections say it is a purer test of who the country wants at the helm. Some people against direct popular election say it would harm small states, which have a stronger say in the election under the current electoral system.

Other people against direct popular elections know it could eventually hurt the two major parties because it could lead to Instant Runoff Voting (IRV). Under IRV systems, voters rank all of the candidates in order of preference. The ballots are then counted using a system that ensures that the person who wins the election ultimately receives a simple majority of votes. IRV voting would give voters more choices in elections, making it possible for a third-party candidate to win an election. IRV voting also would prevent candidates who lose the popular vote from becoming president of the United States.

For More Information

BOOKS

Beard, Charles A. *American Government and Politics.* 10th ed. New York: Macmillan Co., 1949.

Congressional Quarterly Inc. *Powers of the Presidency.* 2nd ed. Washington, DC: Congressional Quarterly Inc., 1997.

Cronin, Thomas E. *Inventing the American Presidency.* Lawrence: University Press of Kansas, 1989.

Hart, John. *The Presidential Branch.* 2nd ed. Chatham, NJ: Chatham House Publishers, 1995.

Kelly, Alfred H., and Winfred A. Harbison. *The American Constitution: Its Origins and Development.* 5th ed. New York: W. W. Norton & Co., 1976.

Kurland, Philip B., and Ralph Lerner. *The Founders' Constitution.* 5 vols. Indianapolis: Liberty Fund, 1987.

Levy, Leonard W. *Original Intent and the Framers' Constitution.* New York: Macmillan, 1988.

McClenaghan, William A. *Magruder's American Government 2003.* Needham, MA: Prentice Hall School Group, 2002.

McDonald, Forrest. *The American Presidency.* Lawrence: University Press of Kansas, 1994.

Milkis, Sidney M., and Michael Nelson. *The American Presidency: Origins & Development.* 3rd ed. Washington, DC: Congressional Quarterly Inc., 1999.

Nelson, Michael, ed. *The Evolving Presidency.* Washington, DC: Congressional Quarterly Inc., 1999.

Rozell, Mark J. *Executive Privilege.* Lawrence: University Press of Kansas, 2002.

Rozell, Mark J., William D. Pederson, and Frank J. Williams. *George Washington and the Origins of the American Presidency.* Westport, CT: Praeger, 2000.

Volkomer, Walter E. *American Government.* 8th ed. Upper Saddle River, NJ: Prentice Hall, 1998.

WEB SITES

Sollenberger, Mitchel A. "Congressional Overrides of Presidential Vetoes." CRS Report for Congress, April 7, 2004. *United States House of Representatives.* http://www.senate.gov/reference/resources/pdf/98-157.pdf (accessed on February 14, 2005).

Sollenberger, Mitchel A. "The Presidential Veto and Congressional Procedure." CRS Report for Congress, February 27, 2004. *United States House of Representatives.* http://www.senate.gov/reference/resources/pdf/RS21750.pdf (accessed on February 14, 2005).

U.S. Census Bureau. http://www.census.gov (accessed on February 16, 2005).

White House. http://www.whitehouse.gov (accessed on February 16, 2005).

Key Positions in the Executive Branch

The federal government has three main branches. Congress is the legislative branch, the one that makes the laws. The president is the head of the executive branch, which enforces the laws. The Supreme Court is the head of the judicial branch, which decides cases brought under the laws.

After the president, the key positions in the executive branch are the vice president, the cabinet, key officers in the Executive Office of the President, the heads of the executive agencies, and commissioners of the regulatory commissions.

President

The Constitution is the blueprint for American government. In Article II, Section 1, it says, "The executive power shall be vested in a president of the United States of America." This makes the president the head of the executive branch of the federal government. To become president, a person must be at least thirty-five years old, a natural born American citizen, and a resident of the United States for at least fourteen years.

Presidential powers The Constitution gives the president the power to enforce the nation's laws, command the army and navy, and send and receive foreign ambassadors. The president also has the power to recommend laws to Congress and to veto, or reject, laws passed by Congress. Congress, however, can override a veto with a two-thirds vote in both chambers, the Senate and the House of Representatives.

Words to Know

cabinet: A group of executive officials who advise the president on important policy matters and decisions. By law, the cabinet includes the heads of the executive departments. Presidents can also include other important executive officials in their cabinets, such as the vice president.

Constitution of the United States of America: The document written in 1787 that established the federal government under which the United States of America has operated since 1789. Article II covers the executive branch.

executive branch: The branch of the federal government that enforces the nation's laws. The executive branch includes the president, the vice president, and many executive departments, agencies, and offices.

executive departments: Departments in the executive branch responsible for large areas of the federal government. As of 2005, there are fifteen departments: Agriculture, Commerce, Defense, Education, Energy, Health & Human Services, Homeland Security, Housing & Urban Development, Interior, Justice, Labor, State, Transportation, Treasury, and Veterans Affairs. The heads of the departments, called secretaries, make up the president's cabinet.

president: The highest officer in the executive branch of the federal government, with primary responsibility for enforcing the nation's laws.

separation of powers: Division of the powers of government into different branches to prevent one branch from having too much power.

vice president: The second highest officer in the executive branch of the federal government. The vice president replaces the president if the president dies or becomes unable to serve. The vice president also serves as president of the Senate, with power to break tie votes when the whole Senate is equally divided on an issue.

The president shares two constitutional powers with the Senate. First, the president can make treaties, or agreements, with foreign nations if two-thirds of the Senate approves. Second, the president appoints people to serve as judges or high-level officers in the federal government. The Senate, however, must approve the appointments by a simple majority.

Unofficial duties Presidents have other roles that do not come specifically from the Constitution. A president serves as chief-of-state, the symbolic leader of the country, even though he is head of just one of three branches.

The power to recommend and veto legislation has led some scholars to call the president the chief legislator. This is because the president's legislative powers can allow him to set the tone for Congress's legislative agenda, or plan.

Finally, Americans today expect the president to have plans for the national economy. They want plentiful, well-paying jobs and strong businesses. This leads some scholars to consider the president the chief economist, even though most presidents are not trained economists.

Election and removal Presidents are elected to a four-year term of office. The nation's first president, George Washington (1732–1799; served 1789–97), set a two-term example by refusing to run for a third term of office. Future presidents followed Washington's example until Franklin D. Roosevelt (1882–1945; served 1933–45) ran for and won a record four terms (though he died at the beginning of the fourth). Roosevelt's accomplishment led the nation to adopt the Twenty-second Amendment in 1951. Under the Twenty-second Amendment, a person may not be elected to the presidency for more than two terms.

The only way to remove a president from office before the expiration of his term is by impeachment in the House and conviction in the Senate. Presidents (and other government officials) can be impeached only for committing treason, bribery, or other high crimes and misdemeanors. The Constitution defines treason as levying war against the United States or giving aid to its enemies. Bribery involves influencing official government action with money or some other benefit.

The Constitution does not define "high crimes and misdemeanors," so scholars disagree over what it means. Some think it means only serious crimes. Others think it means any conduct that is inappropriate for a president. Because the House of Representatives has sole power to impeach and the Senate has sole power to convict, they get to determine what "high crimes and misdemeanors" means in specific cases. Two presidents have been impeached by the House: Andrew Johnson (1808–1875; served 1865–69) in 1868 for violating a congressional law, and Bill Clinton (1946–; served 1993–2001) in 1998 for lying under oath. In both cases, the Senate failed to convict the president, so they remained in office. In August 1974, President Richard M. Nixon (1913–1994; served 1969–74) resigned from office because the House was almost certainly about to impeach him for his role in covering up a 1972 burglary of the offices of the Democratic National Committee by members of the Republican Party, a scandal that became known as Watergate.

John Tyler became the first vice president to become president upon the death of his predecessor. When William Henry Harrison died in 1841, Tyler insisted that the Constitution allowed him to fill out the remainder of Harrison's term. © Bettmann/Corbis.

Vice president

The Constitution requires the United States to elect a vice president to serve the same four-year term as the president. Under the Twelfth Amendment, adopted in 1804, a person cannot be vice president unless he or she satisfies the same qualifications required for the presidency. This means vice presidents must be natural born American citizens who are at least thirty-five years old and who have been U.S. residents for at least fourteen years.

Constitutional roles The Constitution gives the vice president just two jobs. First, the vice president serves as president of the Senate. In this role, the vice president has the power to cast tie-breaking votes when the whole Senate is equally divided on an issue. The vice president does not get to speak during Senate debates, however, and does not get to vote in any other situation. The position, however, makes the vice president part of the legislative branch in addition to being a high-ranking officer in the executive branch.

The vice president's other job under the Constitution is to replace a president who dies, resigns, or becomes unable to do the job. This power initially came from Article II, Section 1. The Constitution, however, left it unclear whether vice presidents would replace presidents for the remainder of their terms, or only until a special election could be held to select a new president. According to Sidney M. Milkis and Michael Nelson in *The American Presidency,* historical evidence suggests that the men who wrote the Constitution in 1787 wanted special elections.

History, however, led to a different result. In April 1841, President William Henry Harrison (1773–1841; served 1841) died after only a month in office. His vice president, John Tyler (1790–1862; served 1841–45), insisted that the Constitution allowed him to fill the office of the presidency for the remainder of Harrison's term, until 1845. At the time, historians did not have access to the evidence that the men who wrote the Constitution preferred a special election. So Tyler served the remainder of Harrison's term, establishing a tradition that future vice presidents followed when taking over for presidents who had died or otherwise left office before the end of a term.

Despite the fact that seven presidents died in office over the course of 126 years, the tradition of a vice president being sworn in as president did not become official until 1967 when the Twenty-fifth Amendment was adopted. Section 1 says, "In case of the removal of the president from office or his death or resignation, the vice president shall become president."

History of the vice presidency The vice presidency was not a very powerful position for well over a century from its beginning. The first vice president, John Adams (1735–1826), got to cast the tie-breaking vote twenty-nine times during his eight years as president of the Senate. Still, as quoted in *The American Presidency,* Adams once wrote to his wife, Abigail Adams (1744–1818), "My country has in its wisdom contrived for me the most insignificant office that ever the invention of man contrived or his imagination conceived."

As the country grew and the number of senators grew with it, tie-breaking votes in the Senate became less common. This reduced the power of the vice presidency even further. Vice President John Nance Garner (1868–1967), who served from 1933 to 1941 under president Franklin D. Roosevelt (1882–1945; served 1933–45), said (as quoted in *The American Presidency*), "The vice presidency isn't worth a pitcher of warm spit."

Growth of vice presidential power Prior to 1940, political parties picked the vice presidential candidates at election time. This often forced presidents to serve with vice presidents whom they did not like or trust. In fact, during the nation's first four elections, the vice president was simply the person who came in second in the presidential race. The result of the nation's third election in 1796 was that Federalist president John Adams (1735–1826) served with a Democratic-Republican vice president, Thomas Jefferson (1743–1826), from 1797 to 1801.

In 1940, towards the end of his second term in office, President Franklin Roosevelt told the Democratic Party he would not run again unless they selected Secretary of Agriculture Henry A. Wallace (1888–1965) as his vice presidential running mate. The party granted Roosevelt's wish. Since then, presidential candidates have picked their running mates on their own, usually with advice from a team of close advisors. This has strengthened relationships in the White House, making presidents more willing to give important duties to vice presidents.

Franklin D. Roosevelt (left) with Henry Wallace on April 15, 1935. At this time, Wallace was secretary of agriculture, but five years later, near the end of Roosevelt's second term, the president said he would not run for a third term unless party officials selected Wallace as his running mate. That marked the first time that presidential candidates selected their vice presidential running mates. © Bettmann / Corbis.

As of 2005, vice presidents tend to have three important duties outside those assigned by the Constitution. First, they frequently represent the president in visits to foreign countries for meetings, funerals, and other ceremonies.

Second, they typically serve in the president's cabinet, which consists of the heads of the executive departments and other important executive officials. Presidents meet with their cabinets for advice on important decisions and crises.

Third, a congressional law makes the vice president part of the National Security Council, which meets with and advises the president on issues relating to national safety.

According to a popular saying, the vice president is only a heartbeat away from the presidency. Because vice presidents must be able to replace the president at a moment's notice, modern presidents tend to keep vice presidents well informed about the workings of the executive branch. They let vice presidents attend important meetings and read secret reports. Starting with President Gerald Ford (1913–; served 1974–77) and Vice President Nelson Rockefeller (1908–1979), presidents have met privately with their vice presidents once a week, often over lunch. Beginning with Walter Mondale (1928–) in 1977, vice presidents have had an office in the West Wing of the White House.

Cabinet and department heads

The president's cabinet consists of the heads of the executive departments plus a few other high-ranking executive officers. Departments are responsible for large areas of government in the executive branch. As of 2005, there are fifteen departments: Agriculture, Commerce, Defense, Education, Energy, Health & Human Services, Homeland Security, Housing & Urban Development, Interior, Justice, Labor, State, Transportation, Treasury, and Veterans Affairs.

Presidents consult their cabinets for information and advice on important policy matters and decisions. Usually, however, presidents do not meet with the entire cabinet at the same time. Instead, they consult with cabinet members individually or hold meetings with the members who can help with a particular issue.

The head of a department is usually called the secretary, except the head of the Department of Justice, who is the attorney general. Secretaries are normally assisted by various deputy, under-, and assistant secretaries (or attorneys general). Presidents have the power to select these officials, but the Senate must approve the selections by a simple majority. Presidents can fire these officials at will, without Senate approval.

Secretary of agriculture The secretary of agriculture is head of the U.S. Department of Agriculture (USDA). President Abraham Lincoln (1809–1865; served 1861–65) created the USDA in 1862, when 58 percent of working Americans were farmers.

An Appointed President: Gerald Ford

Gerald Ford became president on August 9, 1974. As of 2005, he is the only person to serve as both president and vice president without being elected to either office.

On October 10, 1973, Ford was serving as a member of the House of Representatives from the fifth congressional district of Michigan. That day, Vice President Spiro T. Agnew (1918–1996) resigned from office. Agnew had failed to report almost $30,000 on his federal income tax return in 1967 while he was governor of Maryland. He also was accused of taking bribes while serving as a county official in Maryland.

Under the Twenty-fifth Amendment of the Constitution, President Richard M. Nixon (1913–1994; served 1969–74) had to nominate someone to replace Agnew. Nixon nominated Ford, who was the Republican Party leader in the House at the time. Under the Twenty-fifth Amendment, both chambers of Congress had to vote on whether to approve Nixon's nomination. Both chambers approved the nomination, and Ford took office as vice president on December 6, 1973.

Less than a year later, Nixon resigned from the presidency. Nixon was being investigated for possible crimes connected with the cover-up of the Watergate scandal. The scandal began in 1972 when members of the Republican Party burglarized the offices of the Democratic National Committee. Nixon resigned on August 9, 1974, after the Judiciary Committee of the House of Representatives recommended that Congress impeach Nixon and remove him from office.

Ford took the presidential oath of office the day Nixon resigned. He spent the next month trying to restore American confidence in the office of the presidency. On September 8, 1974, President Ford granted Nixon a full pardon for all crimes Nixon may have committed. (A pardon is official forgiveness for a crime, preventing the criminal from being prosecuted and punished.) Ford said he pardoned Nixon to allow the nation to heal instead of suffering through a long and disruptive criminal proceeding against a former president. Ford's approval rating, which had been high up to that point, dropped significantly because many Americans believed Nixon should face criminal charges. Ford never fully recovered, and he ultimately lost the 1976 election to former Georgia governor Jimmy Carter (1924–; served 1977–81).

Gerald Ford, the first man in history to be appointed vice president under the auspices of the Twenty-fifth Amendment, and then the first vice president to become president following the resignation of his predecessor. Library of Congress.

The secretary of agriculture runs a $81.7 billion department that has seventeen agencies and twelve offices as of 2005. It employs nearly 110,000 people. Agencies run the department's government programs. Offices manage the department and its interactions with other government offices and the public.

According to the USDA's Web site in 2005, USDA agencies operate in seven mission areas. The Farm and Foreign Agricultural Services mission gives government money to agricultural businesses. Food, Nutrition, and Consumer Services provides science-based dietary guidance and administers dietary assistance programs. Food Safety regulates the country's meat, poultry, and egg supply. Marketing and Regulatory Programs creates markets for agricultural products and sets standards for animal health and care. Natural Resources and Environment runs programs to protect land and water. Research, Education, and Economics uses research and education to create a strong agricultural economy. Rural Development gives government money to businesses and housing and utility projects in rural America, where farmers work and live.

Secretary of commerce The U.S. Department of Commerce is the "voice of business in government," according to its Web site. The secretary of commerce is head of the department, which has around thirty-six thousand employees and an annual budget of $6.1 billion as of 2005. The department collects economic data, issues trademarks and patents, sets technical standards, forecasts the weather, conducts ocean and coastal zone research, manages marine fisheries and sanctuaries, enforces international trade laws, and develops national policy for telecommunications and technology.

Secretary of defense The secretary of defense is head of the U.S. Department of Defense (DOD), which was created in 1947 by combining the War Department, the Navy Department, and the Department of the Air Force. As of 2005, the DOD has three million military and civilian employees and an annual budget of nearly $429 billion.

The office of the secretary of defense plans and implements national security and defense policy for the DOD. It also oversees the department's budgets, managerial staffs, military force readiness, and purchasing.

President James Monroe, standing at the globe, speaks with members of his cabinet. Library of Congress.

Under the Office of the Secretary, the DOD is divided into three main areas. One area contains the military departments, including the U.S. Army, Navy, Marine Corps, Air Force, and National Guard and Reserve forces. The DOD also helps train and equip the U.S. Coast Guard, which is in the Department of Transportation.

The second main area under the secretary is the Office of the Chairman of the Joint Chiefs of Staff. The Joint Chiefs of Staff contains a chairman appointed by the president plus the heads of the U.S. Army, Navy, Marine Corps, and Air Force. They work together to coordinate the manpower, intelligence, operations, logistics, strategic plans, command and control operations, communications, operational plans, and resources of all the military departments.

The third main area under the secretary is the Unified Commands. As of 2005, this area has nine military commanders who have direct access to the president and the secretary of defense. Five of the commanders oversee military operations in five different sections of the world. Four of the commanders oversee worldwide operations, with specific concern for transportation of the military forces, special operations, strategic command issues, and joint forces command issues.

Secretary of education The secretary of education heads the U.S. Department of Education, which Congress created in 1980. As of 2005, the department has about forty-five hundred employees and an annual budget of $64.3 billion.

According to its Web site, the Department of Education has four primary missions. It establishes policies and administers programs for distributing federal financial aid to state programs, schools, and students. It conducts and publishes research on the condition and performance of America's schools. It runs programs to bring national attention to key educational issues. Finally, it promotes equal access to education for children and students regardless of race, color, and other potential features of discrimination.

Secretary of energy The secretary of energy is head of the U.S. Department of Energy. As of 2005, the department has around one hundred thousand employees and an annual budget of about $24 billion.

The Energy Department has four main areas of responsibility. It develops nuclear and other scientific technology for defense projects. It develops national policies for the development and use of energy sources, such as coal and petroleum. It conducts scientific energy research to support the nation's national security and economic goals. Finally, it works to dispose of the high-level radioactive waste left over from the government's Cold War nuclear weapons programs. (The Cold War was a period from the late 1940s to the early 1990s when the United States competed with the former Soviet Union to be the world's strongest superpower. Development of nuclear weapons was a major part of the Cold War.)

Secretary of health & human services The secretary of health & human services heads the U.S. Department of Health & Human

Services. As of 2005, the department has nearly sixty-eight thousand employees and an annual budget of about $575 billion.

The department has over three hundred programs run by eleven operational agencies. Eight of them are U.S. Public Health Services Agencies. The National Institutes of Health conducts medical research on the cause, prevention, treatment, and cure of common and rare diseases. The Food and Drug Administration (FDA) regulates the safety of food, cosmetics, drugs, biological products, and medical devices. The Centers for Disease Control and Protection works to prevent and control diseases. The Indian Health Service works to provide health services to Native Americans through hospitals, health centers, and other facilities. The Health Resources and Services Administration funds health centers to provide health care to people who are poor or who do not have health insurance or access to health care facilities. The Substance Abuse and Mental Health Services Administration funds programs to prevent drug and alcohol abuse and to provide mental health services. The Agency for Healthcare Research and Quality funds research on the quality and cost of health systems and access to them.

The three other operational agencies in the department are human services agencies. The Centers for Medicare and Medicaid Services provides health insurance to elderly, disabled, and low-income Americans. The Administration for Children and Families runs welfare and other aid programs for needy children, families, and communities. The Administration on Aging provides aid and services to elderly Americans.

Secretary of homeland security The secretary of homeland security is head of the U.S. Department of Homeland Security (DHS). The DHS began in October 2001 as the Office of Homeland Security, an office President George W. Bush (1946– ; served 2001–) created after the terrorist attacks of September 11, 2001. Congress made the office a full department in the executive branch in October 2002, filling it with twenty-two agencies from throughout the government.

As of 2005, the DHS employs over 180,000 people and has an annual budget of $31 billion. Its mission is to deter and prevent terrorist attacks in America. The department has five divisions, including Border & Transportation Security, Emergency Preparedness & Response, Science & Technology,

The nation's first secretary of homeland security, Tom Ridge, on March 12, 2002, unveiling the agency's five-level, color-coded terrorist warning system. AP/Wide World Photos.

Information Analysis & Infrastructure Protection, and Management.

Secretary of housing & urban development The secretary of housing & urban development heads the U.S. Department of Housing & Urban Development (HUD). HUD's mission is to increase homeownership in America, fund community development projects, and implement fair housing laws to prevent discrimination in housing. As of 2005, HUD has an annual budget of nearly $39 billion and employs over ten thousand people.

One of HUD's primary offices is the Federal Housing Administration (FHA), which administers mortgage and loan insurance to help people buy homes. Another main project is the Community Development Block Grants program. It gives money to communities to help them develop local economies, create jobs, and fix rundown housing.

Secretary of the interior The secretary of the interior is head of the U.S. Department of the Interior (DOI). Employing about seventy thousand people with a budget of nearly $9 billion as of 2005, the DOI's mission is to regulate land use and federally owned land in America, and manage the country's relationships with Native American tribes.

The DOI has eight agencies that operate in four primary areas. The National Parks Service and the U.S. Fish and Wildlife Service manage America's national parks and wildlife. The Bureau of Indian Affairs manages America's relationship with Native American tribes. The Bureau of Land Management, Office of Surface Mining Reclamation and Enforcement, and Minerals Management Service regulate the extraction of resources from American lands. The U.S. Geological Survey does earth and minerals science for the DOI. The Bureau of Reclamation distributes water and electricity for seventeen western states.

Attorney general: the Justice Department The attorney general is head of the U.S. Department of Justice (DOJ). The attorney general oversees the nation's primary law enforcement activities in the DOJ's offices, divisions, and bureaus. As of 2005, the department employs over 110,000 people and has a budget of $23.7 billion.

The Office of the Solicitor General handles the federal government's side of the case in appeals to the U.S. Supreme Court. The associate attorney general oversees legal offices that handle antitrust, civil rights, environment, tax, and other civil litigation. The deputy attorney general oversees offices concerned with criminal law enforcement, such as the Criminal Division of the DOJ, the Federal Bureau of Investigation (FBI), the Drug Enforcement Administration (DEA), the Bureau of Alcohol, Tobacco, Firearms, and Explosives, and the Bureau of Prisons.

Secretary of labor The secretary of labor heads the U.S. Department of Labor. As of 2005, the department employs over seventeen thousand people and has a budget of over $57 billion. The Labor Department administers programs and laws relating to labor and employment in America. Some of its major bureaus and agencies include the Bureau of Labor Statistics, which compiles employment data. The Employee Standards Administration implements federal laws concerning minimum wages, overtime pay, and other employment standards. The Occupational Safety and Health Administration (OSHA) regulates safety in American workplaces.

First Lady Hillary Rodham Clinton

The wife of the president of the United States is called the first lady. Hillary Rodham Clinton (1947–) was the first lady during the presidency of Bill Clinton (1946–), from 1993 to 2001.

First ladies usually do not play a large role in making public policy. Instead, they normally have ceremonial duties and devote time to public service projects. Laura Bush (1946–), for example, is a former schoolteacher and librarian who worked to bring attention to children's education and women's health issues during the first term of President George W. Bush from 2001 to 2005.

Hillary Clinton, a lawyer, departed from the normal role for first ladies. In 1993, she was the first presidential wife to set up her own office in the West Wing of the White House. That year, President Clinton appointed his wife to lead a task force on national health care. The task force investigated and reported to Congress on ways to improve health insurance coverage in America. Congress, however, declined to implement the task force's recommendations.

Hillary Clinton's work in the White House received both criticism and praise. Opponents criticized her for serving in policy roles without being an elected official or an appointed officer approved by the Senate. Supporters praised her for setting an example of strong leadership for future first ladies.

In 1999, Hillary Clinton became the first woman to run for elective office while serving as first lady. She sought to become a U.S. senator from New York,

and won the election of 2000 against her opponent, Rick Lazio (1958–). Vice president Al Gore (1948–) swore in Hillary Clinton as a senator in January 2001, just weeks before President Clinton left office to be replaced by George W. Bush.

Hillary Rodham Clinton became the first presidential wife to run for public office while still first lady. Victorious, she was sworn in as a U.S. senator from New York on January 3, 2001, just weeks before her husband, Bill Clinton, left office. Library of Congress.

Secretary of state The secretary of state is head of the U.S. Department of State. The State Department is one of only three departments created in 1789, at the start of the first administration of President George Washington (1732–1799; served 1789–97). (The other two are the Department of the Treasury and the Department of War, now called the Department of Defense.) As of 2005, the department employs over 30,000 people and has a budget of nearly $28 billion.

As head of the State Department, the secretary works directly with the president to develop America's foreign affairs policies. These are policies that guide the country's relationships

Who's in Charge?

The Constitution says that the vice president is in charge if the president dies, resigns, or is unable to discharge his duties. By congressional law, the next three people in the line of succession are the Speaker of the House of Representatives, the president pro tempore of the Senate, and the secretary of state.

The issue became important on March 30, 1981, when John Hinckley (1955–) shot President Ronald Reagan (1911–2004; served 1981–89) as Reagan left the Hilton Hotel in Washington, D.C. The Secret Service rushed Reagan to a hospital at George Washington University. Surgeons removed a bullet that bounced off Reagan's limousine, lodging one inch from his heart.

As Reagan underwent surgery, members of his administration met in the Situation Room at the White House to discuss the crisis. Among them was Secretary of State Alexander Haig (1924–). One thing they discussed was who was in charge while the president was in surgery. According to tapes of the meeting

released in 2001, Haig said, "So the helm is right here. And that means right in this chair for now, constitutionally, until the vice president gets here." Haig repeated the statement at a press conference soon afterwards, saying, "As of now, I am in control here in the White House pending return of the vice president."

Vice President George Bush (1924–) was returning to the White House from Texas at the time. Haig received a lot of criticism for saying he was in control, because under the Constitution, Bush was in control, wherever he was, if President Reagan was unable to do his job.

During a *Larry King Live* television program on the twentieth anniversary of the assassination attempt, former attorney general Edwin Meese III (1931–) said criticism of Haig had been unfair: "[Haig] had heard from the press room that the statement was made that they weren't sure who was in charge, and he went bounding up there. And I think that was really his motivation, to make it clear to foreign leaders that we were not adrift and there was no vacuum."

with foreign nations. The secretary also oversees the department's many operations.

The United States Agency for International Development is a State Department agency that spends government money to develop economies worldwide. The United States Permanent Representative to the United Nations is the office for American ambassadors to the United Nations (UN). The UN is a cooperative organization of governments from around the world. As of 2005, 191 countries belong to the UN. According to its charter, or document of organization, the UN's goals are to maintain international peace and security, develop friendly relations among

Secretary of State Alexander Haig speaks to the press following the assassination attempt on President Ronald Reagan, March 30, 1981. National security advisor Richard Allen looks on as a shaken Haig declares, "I am in control here pending return of the vice president" (George Bush, who was flying back to Washington from Texas at the time). © Bettmann/Corbis.

nations, solve international problems, promote human rights, and harmonize the conduct of member nations.

The secretary of state has many undersecretaries. The undersecretary for political affairs oversees the offices of American ambassadors, who represent America before governments and organizations around the world. The undersecretary for economic, business, and agricultural affairs advises the secretary on matters relating to international economies. The undersecretary for arms control and international proliferation works with the president to develop policies for controlling the kinds of weapons that other countries have. The undersecretary for public diplomacy and public affairs educates the public both abroad and in America about foreign affairs issues. The undersecretary for global affairs coordinates worldwide foreign affairs on specific subjects, including democracy, human rights, labor, the environment, and women's issues.

Secretary of transportation The secretary of transportation heads the U.S. Department of Transportation (DOT). Established in 1967, the DOT employs nearly sixty thousand people with an annual budget of nearly $59 billion as of 2005. According to its mission statement, the DOT works to ensure a fast, safe, efficient, accessible, and convenient transportation system in America.

The DOT has many agencies for carrying out its mission. The Federal Aviation Administration (FAA) regulates the safety of commercial aircraft and airlines. The Federal Highway Administration (FHA) funds programs for repairing and expanding the National Highway System, which is approximately 160,000 miles of U.S. roadways. The Federal Motor Carrier Safety Administration regulates commercial vehicles. The Federal Railroad Administration regulates the nation's railways. The Federal Transit Administration funds mass transit systems, such as subways and buses, in the urban areas. The National Highway Traffic Safety Administration regulates safety on the National Highway System.

Secretary of the treasury The secretary of the treasury is head of the U.S. Department of the Treasury, which began in 1789. As of 2005, the department employs nearly 116,000 people and has a budget of $52 billion. The Treasury Department has primary responsibility for America's financial affairs. Bureaus and offices in the Treasury Department, including the Internal Revenue Service (IRS), collect taxes and enforce tax laws. The department also pays America's bills, manages the national debt, produces postage and currency, and regulates national banks. The secretary of the treasury works directly with the president to develop financial, monetary, economic, trade, and tax policies, both national and international.

Secretary of veterans affairs The secretary of veterans affairs heads the U.S. Department of Veterans Affairs. Veterans Affairs is the second largest employer (nearly 220,000 people) in the executive branch, after the Department of Defense. The department has a budget of $67 billion. The secretary oversees the department's various offices, which administer programs for veterans and their families. The main programs include health care through veterans hospitals and clinics, pension, disability, and death benefits, GI bill benefits for education and training, counseling services, homeless benefits, home loan assistance, life insurance, and national cemeteries.

Other cabinet officers In addition to the heads of the fifteen executive departments, other executive officers can serve in the cabinet if the president wishes. As of 2005, for example, the cabinet of President George W. Bush included the vice president of the United States, the president's chief of staff, the administrator of the Environmental Protection Agency, the director of the Office of Management and Budget, the U.S. trade representative, and the director of the Office of National Drug Control Policy.

Executive Office of the President

The executive branch is enormous, employing millions of Americans. To help him run it, President Franklin D. Roosevelt created the Executive Office of the President (EOP) in 1939. As of 2005, the EOP contains over a dozen offices. Four of the most important positions in the EOP are the chief of staff, director of the Office of Management and Budget, director of the National Economic Council, and national security advisor.

Chief of staff The White House chief of staff is the highest-ranking official in the EOP. Generally, the chief of staff supervises the White House staff and manages the president's schedule. By managing the president's schedule, the chief of staff decides who has access to the president. The chief of staff can also serve as a trusted advisor to the president on policy issues and important decisions.

Director of the Office of Management and Budget The Office of Management and Budget (OMB) helps the president prepare a budget proposal each year. A budget proposal is a plan for how much government money Congress should give the federal branches, departments, and agencies for their operations. Congress uses the OMB's proposal to prepare tax and spending laws for the year. Congress does not have to follow the OMB's proposal, but the proposal greatly affects what Congress does.

The head of the OMB is called the director. The director of the OMB has one of the most powerful positions in the EOP. This is because the OMB's annual budget proposal influences how much money the executive departments, agencies, and other offices get from Congress.

Director of the National Economic Council The National Economic Council (NEC) was created in 1993. Its role is to help the president develop and implement economic policies, both domestic and international. The head of the NEC is called the director.

National security advisor The national security advisor is officially called the assistant to the president for national security affairs. The national security advisor is a lead member of the National Security Council (NSC). The NSC was created in 1947, after the end of World War II (1939–45), which America was drawn into after Japan attacked a military base at Pearl Harbor, Hawaii, in 1941.

The NSC helps the president develop policies on national security, or safety, and coordinates those policies among the departments and agencies of the executive branch. The president serves as chairperson of the NSC. In addition to the national security advisor, other regular members of the NSC are the vice president and the secretaries of the Defense, State, and Treasury Departments. The chairperson of the Joint Chiefs of Staff is the military advisor to the NSC, and the director of the Central Intelligence Agency (CIA) is its intelligence advisor. Other senior executive officials attend NSC meetings that relate to their areas of concern.

Bureau and agency heads

Many executive departments are divided into bureaus. Bureau chiefs serve as heads of the various bureaus. Just as with department secretaries, presidents get to appoint bureau chiefs with the advice and consent of the Senate.

The executive branch also contains dozens of agencies. An agency is a government office that handles a very specific government function. Agencies are usually controlled by the president but are independent of any executive department. Examples include the Central Intelligence Agency (CIA), the Environmental Protection Agency (EPA), and the National Aeronautics and Space Administration (NASA).

The heads of executive agencies are often called directors or administrators. Like department secretaries and bureau chiefs, agency heads are appointed by the president with the advice and consent of the Senate.

Regulatory commissioners

A regulatory commission is a government body that regulates a specific area of the economy. Examples include the Federal Communications Commission (FCC), the Federal Trade Commission (FTC), the Federal Reserve Board, the Securities and Exchange Commission (SEC), and the National Labor Relations Board (NLRB).

The heads of the commissions are called commissioners. Each commission typically has a panel of five commissioners. Commissioners are appointed by the president with the advice and consent of the Senate. Unlike department secretaries, bureau chiefs, and agency heads, however, commissioners cannot be removed by the president at will. They can only be removed for reasons provided by congressional law, such as criminal conduct. This gives regulatory commissions a degree of independence from the executive branch.

For More Information

BOOKS

Congressional Quarterly Inc. *Powers of the Presidency.* 2nd ed. Washington, DC: Congressional Quarterly Inc., 1997.

Hart, John. *The Presidential Branch.* 2nd ed. Chatham, NJ: Chatham House Publishers, 1995.

Janda, Kenneth, Jeffrey M. Berry, and Jerry Goldman. *The Challenge of Democracy.* 5th ed. Boston: Houghton Mifflin Company, 1997.

McClenaghan, William A. *Magruder's American Government 2003.* Needham, MA: Prentice Hall School Group, 2002.

McDonald, Forrest. *The American Presidency.* Lawrence: University Press of Kansas, 1994.

Milkis, Sidney M., and Michael Nelson. *The American Presidency: Origins & Development.* 3rd ed. Washington, DC: Congressional Quarterly Inc., 1999.

Nelson, Michael, ed. *The Evolving Presidency.* Washington, DC: Congressional Quarterly Inc., 1999.

Volkomer, Walter E. *American Government.* 8th ed. Upper Saddle River, NJ: Prentice Hall, 1998.

WEB SITES

King, Larry. "Remembering the Assassination Attempt on Ronald Reagan." *CNN.com.* http://transcripts.cnn.com/TRANSCRIPTS/0103/30/lkl.00.html (accessed on February 16, 2005).

"The Reagan Tapes." *NPR.* http://www.npr.org/programs/morning/features/2001/mar/010320.reagan.html (accessed on February 16, 2005).

U.S. Department of Agriculture. http://www.usda.gov/wps/portal/usdahome (accessed on March 4, 2005).

U.S. Department of Commerce. http://www.commerce.gov/ (accessed on March 4, 2005).

U.S. Department of Defense. http://www.defenselink.mil/ (accessed on March 4, 2005).

U.S. Department of Education. http://www.ed.gov/index.jhtml (accessed on March 4, 2005).

U.S. Department of Energy. http://www.energy.gov/engine/content.do (accessed on March 4, 2005).

U.S. Department of Health & Human Services. http://www.os.dhhs.gov/ (accessed on March 4, 2005).

U.S. Department of Homeland Security. http://www.dhs.gov/dhspublic/ (accessed on March 4, 2005).

U.S. Department of Housing and Urban Development. http://www.hud.gov/ (accessed on March 4, 2005).

U.S. Department of the Interior. http://www.doi.gov/ (accessed on March 4, 2005).

U.S. Department of Justice. http://www.usdoj.gov/ (accessed on March 4, 2005).

U.S. Department of Labor. http://www.dol.gov/ (accessed on March 4, 2005).

U.S. Department of State. http://www.state.gov/ (accessed on February 24, 2005).

U.S. Department of the Treasury. http://www.ustreas.gov/ (accessed on March 4, 2005).

U.S. Department of Transportation. http://www.dot.gov/ (accessed on March 4, 2005).

U.S. Department of Veterans Affairs. http://www.va.gov/ (accessed on March 4, 2005).

White House. http://www.whitehouse.gov (accessed on February 16, 2005).

Daily Operations of the Executive Branch

The executive branch is the branch of government that administers and enforces the nation's laws and public programs. It is an enormous operation, employing around three million civilian and military people as of 2005. The daily operations of the branch include work by the president, vice president, fifteen executive departments, and hundreds of bureaus, agencies, and minor offices.

A day in the life of the president

The president of the United States is head of the executive branch. A typical day on the president's job involves meeting with advisors and foreign leaders, signing bills and executive orders, working on the federal budget, and making public appearances.

Many people think of the president as the nation's chief of state, the symbolic leader of the country. This role requires the president to make public appearances at special events, attend press conferences, and address the nation in times of crisis.

The constitutional power to send ambassadors to foreign countries and receive their ambassadors makes the president the chief diplomat. In this role, the president meets with high-ranking foreign officials to work on foreign relations.

The Constitution makes the president the commander in chief of the armed forces. When the country is at war or engaged in military hostilities, the president meets frequently with military advisors for status reports. Sometimes he has to make difficult decisions concerning military action.

Words to Know

cabinet: A group of executive officials who advise the president on important policy matters and decisions. By law, the cabinet includes the heads of the executive departments. Presidents can also include other important executive officials in their cabinets, such as the vice president.

Constitution of the United States of America: The document written in 1787 that established the federal government under which the United States of America has operated since 1789. Article II covers the executive branch.

executive branch: The branch of the federal government that enforces the nation's laws. The executive branch includes the president, the vice president, and many executive departments, agencies, and offices.

executive departments: Departments in the executive branch responsible for large areas of the federal government. As of 2005, there are fifteen departments: Agriculture, Commerce, Defense, Education, Energy, Health & Human Services, Homeland Security, Housing & Urban Development, Interior, Justice, Labor, State, Transportation, Treasury, and Veterans Affairs. The heads of the departments, called secretaries, make up the president's cabinet.

president: The highest officer in the executive branch of the federal government, with primary responsibility for enforcing the nation's laws.

separation of powers: Division of the powers of government into different branches to prevent one branch from having too much power.

vice president: The second highest officer in the executive branch of the federal government. The vice president replaces the president if the president dies or becomes unable to serve. The vice president also serves as president of the Senate, with power to break tie votes when the whole Senate is equally divided on an issue.

The constitutional power to propose legislation to Congress and to veto, or reject, bills passed by Congress makes the president the chief legislator, according to many scholars. A day in the president's life can involve speaking publicly about important legislation, signing a bill of which he approves, or vetoing a bill he dislikes.

As head of the executive branch, the president oversees a vast organization containing fifteen departments and hundreds of bureaus, agencies, and minor offices. A day in the president's life can involve signing executive orders that affect the way these offices operate. The president also meets with advisors from the Office of Management and Budget (OMB) to discuss budget proposals for the federal government. (A budget is a plan for how much money the government intends to spend each year.)

The role of the vice president

The vice president is the second-highest ranking official in the executive branch. In reality, though, the vice president is only as powerful as the president allows him to be. The vice president's only constitutional powers are to serve as president of the Senate, and to replace the president if he dies, resigns, or is unable to do his job.

When the Senate is in session, the vice president usually attends to start the official proceedings each day. If there is a tie vote on a bill or other issue, the vice president gets to break the tie. Otherwise, he does not get to vote, and he never gets to participate in Senate debate, or discussions, about bills and decisions, because the Constitution does not give him such power.

Besides breaking tie votes, the vice president's only other job as president of the Senate is to preside over its daily business, interpreting and enforcing the Senate's rules for conducting its proceedings. Normally after opening a session, the vice president leaves the Senate to do other work. When this happens, the president pro tempore of the Senate or another senator presides over the session. (*Pro tempore* means "for the time being.") The president pro tempore is usually the senator from the majority party who has served longest in the Senate. The majority party is the political party who has the most members in the Senate.

Back at the White House, the vice president attends many meetings. Because of his relationship with the senators, the vice president often meets with the president and other advisors on legislative strategy. Presidents usually invite their vice presidents to attend cabinet meetings, where the president meets with senior officials from the executive departments. Finally, vice presidents attend meetings of the National Security Council (NSC), because a congressional law passed in 1949 made the vice president an official member of the NSC. (The NSC is a special group of presidential advisors on matters relating to national security, or safety, such as military action, terrorism, and spying.) Including the vice president in important meetings prepares him to take over in case the president dies in office. According to one famous story, when Vice President Harry S. Truman (1884–1972) became president after Franklin D. Roosevelt's (1882–1945) death in 1945, he did not know the United States was developing

A Day in the Life of President Gerald Ford (1913–)

Gerald Ford was president from 1974 to 1977. The Web site of the Gerald Ford Library and Museum contains an online exhibit called "A Day in the Life of the President." The exhibit includes a diary of President Ford's day on April 28, 1975. Each day in a president's life is different, but the diary gives a snapshot of what one day might be like.

On April 28, 1975, President Ford had breakfast at 6:50 AM and arrived at the Oval Office at 7:34. For the next two-and-a-half hours, Ford met with various advisors. This included a meeting with David A. Peterson, chief of the Office of Current Intelligence in the Central Intelligence Agency, and Lt. Gen. Brent Scowcroft, deputy assistant for national security affairs. The president also met separately with his legal counselor and assistant during the morning session in the Oval Office.

At 10:13 AM, President Ford left the Oval Office to speak to three thousand attendees at the sixty-third annual meeting of the U.S. Chamber of Commerce. Ford returned to the Oval Office at 10:57 and spent the rest of the morning and the whole afternoon in meetings with various people. One meeting was with Herman H. Zerfas, a school superintendent from Michigan, and Ival E. Zylstra, administrator at the National Union of Christian Schools. They were in Washington to talk to Ford about federal funding for private religious schools. Another meeting was a photo opportunity for Lisa Lyons, who had become Miss National Teenager 1974–75. The president also had meetings with members of his cabinet, including Secretary of State Henry A. Kissinger (1923–), Secretary of Health, Education and Welfare Caspar W. Weinberger (1917–), and Secretary of Transportation William T. Coleman Jr. (1920–).

At 5:47 PM, President Ford met with advisors to discuss White House negotiations with Congress on an energy plan to help the national economy. The meeting lasted 90 minutes.

At 7:12 PM, Ford met in the Oval Office with Vice President Nelson A. Rockefeller (1908–1979) and Kissinger. At 7:23, the three men went to the Roosevelt Room in the White House to meet with the National Security Council (NSC). The NSC is a council of senior executive officials who advise the president on matters relating to national safety. At the time, the United States was evacuating Americans from the South Vietnamese capital of Saigon at the end of the Vietnam War (1954–75). Ford described the situation in his autobiography, *A Time to Heal*:

> The final siege of Saigon began on April 25. Kissinger was on the telephone to U.S. Ambassador [to Vietnam] Graham Martin several times a day, and his reports convinced me that the country was going to collapse momentarily. In the late afternoon of April 28, I was chairing a meeting of my economic and energy advisers in the Cabinet Room when Brent Scowcroft entered and handed me a note. A message had just come in to the Situation Room downstairs. Our Air Force, it said, had been forced to halt evacuation flights from Saigon because Communist rockets and artillery shells were blasting the runways at Tan Son Nhut. A C-130 transport plane had been destroyed and several U.S. Marines killed. Nearly a thousand Americans still remained in Saigon, and we had to carry out our plans to evacuate them.

At 8:08, Ford returned to the Oval Office and, ten minutes later, went to the second floor of his residence in the White House. Over the next few hours, he met or spoke on the telephone about the crisis with senior advisors, including Secretary of Defense James R. Schlesinger (1929–). At 9:15 PM, Ford had dinner with first lady Betty Ford (1918–).

At 11:28 PM, Ford returned to the Oval Office, and three minutes later went to the Situation Room, where White House officials meet during crisis situations. In his autobiography, Ford described the evening leading up to the meeting in the Situation Room:

> I decided to wait an hour or so to see if the shelling stopped. If it did, we could resume the evacuation flights. The firing did cease, but we had a new problem to solve. Refugees were streaming out onto the airport's runways, and our planes couldn't land. The situation there was clearly out of control. The only option left was to remove the remaining Americans, and as many South Vietnamese as possible, by helicopter from the roof of the U.S. embassy in Saigon. Choppers were standing by on the decks of U.S. Navy ships steaming off the coast, and just before midnight I ordered the final evacuation. Over the next sixteen hours we managed to rescue 6,500 U.S. and South Vietnamese personnel without sustaining significant casualties.

Five minutes after midnight, President Ford returned to his residence in the White House, making one last phone call before turning in for the night.

President Gerald Ford in a relaxed mood in the Oval Office in 1974. Getty Images.

an atomic bomb for possible use in World War II until he was told by U.S. secretary of war Henry L. Stimson (1867–1950).

Vice presidents also have ceremonial duties. They often greet visiting foreign officials or meet with them in place of the president. They also represent the government by traveling to foreign countries for important weddings, funerals, and other events the president cannot attend. George Bush (1924–), who served as vice president under President Ronald Reagan (1911–2004) from 1981 to 1989, once joked (according to *The Powers of the Presidency*), "I'm George Bush. You die, I fly." Vice presidents also attend ceremonies in America, either with or in place of the president.

President Harry S. Truman (left) is briefed by Secretary of War Henry L. Stimson on August 8, 1945, two days after the United States dropped an atomic bomb on Hiroshima, Japan. As vice president, Truman was unaware of U.S. plans for the atomic bomb; he was updated by Stimson shortly after Franklin D. Roosevelt's sudden death put Truman in the White House. © Bettmann/Corbis.

One of the primary duties of an American vice president is to represent the president at funerals. Here, Vice President George Bush (far left) attends the funeral of World War II general Omar Bradley on April 14, 1981. Bush is joined by (left to right) Barbara Bush, first lady Nancy Reagan, Secretary of State Alexander Haig, Patricia Haig, and Secretary of Defense Caspar Weinberger.
© Bettmann/Corbis.

Law enforcement: the Justice Department

The executive branch is divided into fifteen departments as of 2005, each of which handles a large area of government in the executive branch: Agriculture, Commerce, Defense, Education, Energy, Health & Human Services, Homeland Security, Housing & Urban Development, Interior, Justice, Labor, State, Transportation, Treasury, and Veterans Affairs.

One of the executive branch's main jobs is to enforce the nation's laws. This job is spread among various bureaus, agencies, and other offices, most of which have law enforcement duties relating to their area of specialty. In the Department of the Treasury, for example, the Internal Revenue Service (IRS) collects taxes and enforces the federal tax laws. The Department of Labor enforces laws relating to labor unions, wages, and job safety.

The department with primary law enforcement responsibility is the Department of Justice (DOJ). The head of the DOJ is called the attorney general and serves as the lead lawyer for the

United States in both criminal and civil cases. (A civil case involves illegal conduct that is not criminal.)

The attorney general is assisted by a deputy attorney general, solicitor general, associate attorney general, and hundreds of U.S. attorneys and assistant U.S. attorneys. The assistants are the ones who actually handle legal cases for the government on a daily basis because there is too much work for the attorney general to handle all of it personally.

A typical day in the Justice Department involves investigation, prosecution of civil and criminal cases, and other enforcement activities.

Investigation: the Federal Bureau of Investigation Investigating crimes is a large part of the job of law enforcement. Many agencies in the executive branch have responsibility for investigating specific kinds of crimes. The Federal Bureau of Investigation (FBI) in the DOJ is the agency that investigates all federal crimes not specifically assigned to another agency. As of 2005, the FBI is responsible for investigating over two hundred kinds of federal crimes, including civil rights crime, counterterrorism, foreign counterintelligence, organized crime, drug crime, violent crime, and financial crime.

A day of investigation in the FBI involves many activities. Special agents conduct surveillance, following and photographing suspects to try to catch them in criminal acts. Surveillance also involves getting court orders to place wiretaps on telephone lines, allowing agents to listen to private conversations. Courts are supposed to allow a wiretap only when there is probable cause to believe a crime is being committed. According to the federal courts, probable cause means reasonable belief based on actual evidence.

Other agents visit crime scenes to gather evidence for prosecutors. Agents investigating financial crime might ask a court to order the suspect to produce documents for inspection. Agents can get warrants from federal courts to search a home or other private area or arrest a criminal suspect. The FBI photographs and fingerprints suspects and tries to talk to them to get voluntary statements about their crimes. The FBI Laboratory analyzes evidence to determine whether a crime has been committed and who the criminal is.

The face of the FBI for 48 years was J. Edgar Hoover, standing here in July 1935 in front of a map that shows the locations of FBI agents. © Bettmann/Corbis.

Prosecution: U.S. attorneys U.S. attorneys are responsible for prosecuting civil and criminal cases for the federal government. As of 2005, there were ninety-three U.S. attorneys in districts throughout America, each of whom is assisted by many assistant U.S. attorneys.

During the course of an investigation, law enforcement agencies such as the FBI share the evidence they gather with U.S. attorneys. The U.S. attorneys decide whether or not to file a civil or criminal case against a suspect. In the most important cases, the attorney general, deputy attorney general, or associate attorney general might participate in the decision-making process.

Criminal cases are cases filed by the government against people or organizations suspected of violating a federal criminal law. Criminal laws are written to outlaw conduct that is particularly harmful to society, such as murder, rape, and kidnapping. Civil cases involve violations of law that are not criminal. Civil laws generally concern relationships between private persons or between a private person and the government. Examples include tax laws or laws governing contracts, or agreements, between people and businesses. The U.S. government files civil cases as a plaintiff against defendants who have violated a civil law. The U.S. government also defends civil cases when people or organizations sue the government for violating a law. U.S. attorneys represent the federal government in all such cases, whether the government is prosecutor in a criminal case, or plaintiff or defendant in a civil case. (For more information about the conduct of civil and criminal cases, see volume 3, chapter 6, "Daily Operations of the Judicial Branch.")

Antiwar Protest and the First Amendment

As the symbolic leader of the country, the president often makes public appearances around the nation. Protesters sometimes attend these events to voice opposition to the federal government or its policies and actions.

On October 24, 2002, President George W. Bush (1946–) was scheduled to arrive at Columbia Metropolitan Airport in Columbia, South Carolina. At the time, the president was threatening to send military troops into Iraq to overthrow President Saddam Hussein (1937–). Thousands of supporters were at the airport to greet President Bush on his arrival.

Brett A. Bursey was at the airport, too. He carried a sign that said, "No War For Oil." Bursey wished to protest the looming war with Iraq.

Before Bush arrived, police and Secret Service agents told Bursey he would have to take his protest to a "free speech zone" that was far away. Bursey replied that he was in a free speech zone, the United States of America. An airport police officer eventually told Bursey to put down his sign or leave. When Bursey asked if the content of his sign was the problem, the officer answered (according to the *New York Times*), "Yes, sir, it's the content of your sign."

Bursey refused to drop the sign or leave, so the police arrested him for trespassing. President Bush arrived while Bursey sat in the back seat of a patrol car. Local authorities eventually dropped the trespassing charges. Years earlier, the Supreme Court of South Carolina had ruled that protesters on public property cannot be charged with trespassing.

Enforcement: Drug Enforcement Administration Law enforcement agencies conduct many enforcement activities other than investigation and prosecution. Examples include the work of the U.S. Drug Enforcement Administration (DEA), which is part of the Justice Department. Under its Asset Forfeiture program, the DEA seizes profits and property from drug law violations. The profits and property go into a fund to help victims of drug crime and to pay for future law enforcement activities.

The DEA's Demand Reduction program educates the public about the dangers and harms of drug use to individuals, families, and communities. The Diversion Control program works to prevent legal prescription drugs, or medicine, from being sold illegally for recreational drug use.

The High Intensity Drug Trafficking Areas program works with state and local law enforcement officials to block the movement and sale of drugs in areas of the country where such activity is high. The Money Laundering program works to find and seize money from illegal drug activity that criminals are trying to

In March 2003, however, a U.S. attorney for the federal government filed charges against Bursey. He was accused of violating a federal law that allows the Secret Service to control areas the president visits. Eleven members of the U.S. House of Representatives wrote a letter to Attorney General John Ashcroft (1942–), urging him to drop the charges against Bursey. Echoing Bursey's feelings, U.S. congressman Barney Frank (1940–) of Massachusetts said (according to *Warblogging.com*), "As we read the First Amendment to the Constitution, the United States is a 'free speech zone.'" (The First Amendment is supposed to protect free speech in America.)

At Bursey's trial, the U.S. attorney said federal law allows the Secret Service to require protesters to go to free speech zones. Bursey's lawyer, Lewis Pitts, argued that the federal government was using free speech zones to hide government protest. He said there were Bush supporters near Bursey at the airport who were not asked to go to the free speech zone, and other supporters allowed to attend a rally area separate from the free speech zone. The prosecution argued that all unauthorized personnel, including Bush supporters, were required to leave the area Bursey was in when President Bush arrived. Bursey, the prosecution said, was the only person who refused to leave.

Later that year, a federal judge found Bursey guilty of the charges against him. In January 2004, the judge sentenced Bursey to a fine of $500. Bursey and his lawyer appealed the verdict to the U.S. Court of Appeals for the Fourth Circuit, which could either affirm, or agree with, the verdict or reverse it, clearing Bursey of the charge against him. As of early 2005, the Fourth Circuit Court of Appeals was getting ready to hear oral argument in the case, after which it would make a decision.

convert into assets that look like they come from legal sources. Under Operation Pipeline, DEA trains state and local law enforcement officials to recognize suspects who might be transporting illegal drugs in private motor vehicles on the nation's highways.

Executive agencies

The executive branch has dozens of agencies that operate independently. This means they report to the president without being part of one of the fifteen executive departments. Agencies typically handle very specific areas of the government's job. Examples of executive agencies include the Central Intelligence Agency (CIA), the Environmental Protection Agency (EPA), and the National Aeronautics and Space Administration (NASA).

Spying: the Central Intelligence Agency The Central Intelligence Agency (CIA) is America's spy headquarters. Its job is to collect intelligence and share it with government officials. Intelligence is information about military, government, or terrorist activity that could be harmful to the United States.

The CIA is led by the director of central intelligence, who is supported by a deputy director. The president of the United States appoints people to these positions with the advice and consent of the Senate. The director also serves as a member of the National Security Council, the president's closest group of advisors on national security issues.

Daily operations in the CIA involve three main offices. The Directorate of Science and Technology develops technology to use for gathering intelligence. The Directorate of Operations does the actual spying, employing agents who secretly collect foreign intelligence from around the world. Finally, the Directorate of Intelligence analyzes collected intelligence and shares it with the appropriate governmental officials.

Administrative law: the Environmental Protection Agency The Environmental Protection Agency (EPA) regulates the amount of pollution of air, land, and water in America. The head of the EPA is called the administrator. The president appoints the administrator with the advice and consent of the Senate.

The EPA is an example of an agency that enforces laws passed by Congress. Congress, for example, passed the Clean Water Act to regulate the amount of pollution of water by people, businesses, and government bodies. To enforce the Clean Water Act (and other environmental laws), different EPA offices serve as lawmaker, investigator, prosecutor, and judge.

Acting as lawmaker, the EPA Office of Water adopts regulations concerning water pollution. Regulations are like laws, but they usually are much more detailed. To enforce the regulations, the EPA Office of Compliance and Enforcement investigates suspected violations. If the EPA finds a serious violation and the person or business refuses to correct the situation, an enforcement office can file a civil or criminal action against the offender. Criminal actions are usually limited to cases in which a person or business violates an environmental law on purpose.

EPA administrative law judges (ALJs) hear most cases and decide them just like trial judges in court. ALJs can fine violators, make them clean up pollution, or find that the government has not proven a violation of the law. If a person or business disagrees with the result reached by an ALJ, an appeal can be made to the Environmental Hearings Board (EHB).

Space exploration: the National Aeronautics and Space Administration

The National Aeronautics and Space Administration (NASA) is the nation's space agency. The head of NASA is the administrator, who is assisted by a deputy administrator. The president appoints people to both positions with the advice and consent of the Senate.

NASA headquarters in Washington, D.C., is divided into offices. The Office of Exploration Systems oversees the development of space exploration projects. The Office of Aeronautics oversees research into aviation and aeronautics technology. This research helps both NASA and defense projects, such as military aircraft and missiles. Other offices at headquarters have specific responsibilities for engineering, health and medical systems, information technology, and management.

Outside headquarters, NASA has many centers and field facilities across the country. The Kennedy Space Center near Titusville, Florida, is where most space launches occur. The

Mission Control Center at the Johnson Space Center in Houston, Texas, manages manned flights, including space shuttle missions and the International Space Station. The Jet Propulsion Laboratory in Pasadena, California, manages unmanned space missions, such as exploratory satellites and rovers sent to other plants.

Many NASA centers conduct scientific and technological research, testing, and training. These include the Ames Research Center in Moffett Field, California; the Dryden Flight Research Center in Edwards, California; the Glenn Research Center in Cleveland, Ohio; the Goddard Institute for Space Studies in New York City; the Goddard Space Flight Center in Greenbelt, Maryland; the Independent Verification & Validation Facility in Fairmont, West Virginia; the Langley Research Center in

The National Aeronautics and Space Administration (NASA) oversees the U.S. space program. Here, the space shuttle Discovery *prepares for liftoff at the Kennedy Space Center in Florida.* National Aeronautics and Space Administration (NASA).

Hampton, Virginia; Wallops Flight Facility in Wallops, Virginia; the Marshall Space Flight Center in Huntsville, Alabama; the Stennis Space Center in southwest Mississippi; and the White Sands Test Facility in White Sands, New Mexico.

Regulating the economy: the Federal Trade Commission

Regulatory commissions regulate specific areas of the national economy. Examples include the Federal Communications Commission (FCC), the Federal Trade Commission (FTC), the Federal Reserve Board, the Securities and Exchange Commission (SEC), and the National Labor Relations Board (NLRB).

A board of commissioners leads each of the regulatory commissions. Boards contain an odd number of commissioners, often five. The president appoints people to be commissioners with the advice and consent of the Senate.

Commissioners serve fixed terms of office. They cannot be fired by the president except for misconduct specified in the congressional law that controls the commission. Commissions report to Congress on their actions. In theory, this set-up makes regulatory commissions independent from the executive branch. Independence is supposed to allow commissions to enforce laws without concern for loyalty to a particular presidential administration or political party. In reality, individual commissioners have political beliefs, so the work of regulatory commissions becomes political to some extent.

The work of the Federal Trade Commission (FTC) illustrates the work of regulatory commissions. The FTC has five commissioners. Their job is to enforce laws to protect consumers from two kinds of business conduct. The first is unfair, deceptive, or fraudulent business activity. The second is business mergers, or combinations, that hurt competition in an industry.

To enforce these laws, the FTC has offices that write rules and regulations. The Bureau of Consumer Protection writes rules related to unfair business activity. The Bureau of Competition writes rules related to mergers. Offices in these bureaus investigate suspected violations of congressional law and FTC rules.

If the FTC finds reason to believe a law or rule has been violated, it can file an enforcement action against the offending company. There are three main courses enforcement can take.

First, the accused company can reach an agreement with the FTC, promising to stop the challenged conduct.

Second, the company can dispute the charges in a hearing before an FTC administrative law judge (ALJ). ALJ hearings are much like court cases. If the company does not like the result, it can appeal the ALJ's decision to all five FTC commissioners.

The third thing the FTC can do is file a case in court or ask the appropriate office of the Department of Justice to file a lawsuit. These lawsuits can be for civil or criminal violations of federal trade laws.

The FTC has offices that do other kinds of work. The Bureau of Economics conducts economic research to support the rulemaking and enforcement activity of the rest of the FTC. The Office of Public Affairs informs the public about FTC matters. The Office of Congressional Relations is the FTC's link to Congress, which writes the laws that the FTC enforces and the rules it must obey in its enforcement activities.

For More Information

BOOKS

Congressional Quarterly Inc. *Powers of the Presidency*. 2nd ed. Washington, DC: Congressional Quarterly Inc., 1997.

DiClerico, Robert E. *The American President*. 5th ed. Upper Saddle River, NJ: Prentice Hall, 2000.

Ford, Gerald R. *A Time to Heal: The Autobiography of Gerald Ford*. New York: Harper & Row, 1979.

Hart, John. *The Presidential Branch*. 2nd ed. Chatham, NJ: Chatham House Publishers, 1995.

Janda, Kenneth, Jeffrey M. Berry, and Jerry Goldman. *The Challenge of Democracy*. 5th ed. Boston: Houghton Mifflin Company, 1997.

McClenaghan, William A. *Magruder's American Government 2003*. Needham, MA: Prentice Hall School Group, 2002.

McDonald, Forrest. *The American Presidency*. Lawrence: University Press of Kansas, 1994.

Milkis, Sidney M., and Michael Nelson. *The American Presidency: Origins & Development*. 3rd ed. Washington, DC: Congressional Quarterly Inc., 1999.

Nelson, Michael, ed. *The Evolving Presidency*. Washington, DC: Congressional Quarterly Inc., 1999.

Nelson, Michael, ed. *The Presidency and the Political System.* 7th ed. Washington, DC: CQ Press, 2003.

Rozell, Mark J. *Executive Privilege* Lawrence: University Press of Kansas, 2002.

Volkomer, Walter E. *American Government.* 8th ed. Upper Saddle River, NJ: Prentice Hall, 1998.

PERIODICALS

Eaton, Leslie. "Questions of Security and Free Speech: A Flashback to the 60's for an Antiwar Protester." *The New York Times* (April 27, 2003): p. 15.

Thurmond, J. Strom, Jr. "As Court Ruled, Bursey's Free Speech Not Trampled." *The State* (January 13, 2004).

WEB SITES

Central Intelligence Agency. http://www.cia.gov/ (accessed on February 17, 2005).

"Daily Diary of President Gerald Ford, April 28, 1975." *Gerald Ford Library & Museum.* http://www.ford.utexas.edu/library/exhibits/daylife/dailydia.htm (accessed on February 17, 2005).

"The Democracy Project: President for a Day." *PBSKids.org.* http://pbskids.org/democracy/presforaday/index.html (accessed on February 17, 2005).

Federal Bureau of Investigation. http://www.fbi.gov (accessed on February 17, 2005).

Federal Trade Commission. http://www.ftc.gov/ (accessed on February 17, 2005).

"Free Speech Zones and John Ashcroft." *Warblogging.com.* http://www.warblogging.com/archives/000655.php (accessed on February 17, 2005).

National Aeronautics and Space Administration. http://www.nasa.gov/externalflash/Vision/index.html (accessed on February 17, 2005).

U.S. Department of Justice. http://www.usdoj.gov/ (accessed on February 17, 2005).

U.S. Drug Enforcement Administration. http://www.dea.gov/ (accessed on February 17, 2005).

U.S. Environmental Protection Agency. http://www.epa.gov/ (accessed on February 17, 2005).

White House. http://www.whitehouse.gov (accessed on February 17, 2005).

Executive-Legislative Checks and Balances

The U.S. Constitution divides the powers of government into three branches: legislative, executive, and judicial. Generally speaking, the legislative branch, Congress, makes the nation's laws. The executive branch enforces the laws through the president and various executive offices. The judicial branch, made up of the Supreme Court and lower federal courts, decides cases that arise under the laws.

This division of government is called the separation of powers. The purpose of the separation of powers is to prevent tyranny, which is arbitrary (random) or unfair government action that can result when one person has all the power to make, enforce, and interpret the laws.

In addition to the broad separation of powers into three branches, the Constitution keeps the executive and legislative branches separate with various specific provisions. Article I, Section 6, prevents members of Congress from serving as officers of the government in the executive branch. Article I, Section 5, says each chamber of Congress, namely the House of Representatives and the Senate, is the sole judge of who wins congressional elections and who is qualified to serve there. The same part of the Constitution gives the House and Senate sole authority to make their rules of operation.

Article I, Section 6, is known as the Speech and Debate Clause and says representatives and senators cannot be punished for speeches made in Congress. Neither can they be arrested while in office, except for treason, felony, and

Words to Know

appropriations bill: A bill, or law, that assigns money to a government department or agency.

bicameralism: The practice of dividing the legislative, or lawmaking, power of government into two chambers.

checks and balances: The specific powers in one branch of government that allow it to limit the powers of the other branches.

Congress: The legislative, or lawmaking, branch of the federal government. Congress has two chambers, the Senate and the House of Representatives.

Constitution of the United States of America: The document written in 1787 that established the federal government under which the United States of America has operated since 1789. Article I covers the legislative branch and Article II covers the executive branch.

impoundment: The presidential practice of refusing to spend money that Congress appropriates for an executive department, agency, or program.

personnel floor: A congressional minimum on the number of employees a governmental department, agency, or program must employ.

president: The highest officer in the executive branch of the federal government, with primary responsibility for enforcing the nation's laws.

quorum: The number of members of Congress who must be present for Congress to conduct business, such as voting on bills. The U.S. Constitution says a chamber has a quorum when a simple majority of its members are present.

reprogramming: The practice of using money that Congress appropriates to one governmental program for a different program.

separation of powers: Division of the powers of government into different branches to prevent one branch from having too much power.

veto: Rejection of a bill, or proposed law, by the president of the United States. If the president vetoes a bill, it does not become law unless two-thirds of both chambers of Congress vote to override the veto.

breach of the peace. (Treason is defined as levying war against America or giving aid and comfort to its enemies. A felony is the most serious kind of crime, usually punishable by imprisonment for more than a year. Breach of the peace refers to disorderly conduct.)

Article II, Section 1, says the president must get a salary, which Congress sets, but that Congress may not raise or lower the salary while the president is in office. The same provision prevents the president from getting any compensation other than the salary set before the president entered office.

Checks and balances

The men who wrote the Constitution in 1787 wanted each branch's power to be separate, but not absolute. They considered absolute power, even over just a portion of the government, to be dangerous. They were especially fearful of giving too much power to the president, who might come to resemble an uncontrollable king. They were also fearful of giving too much power to the House of Representatives, which they saw as the chamber of Congress that would represent the popular will of America. The men who wrote the Constitution wanted to protect the wealthy class of society from the passions of popular democracy.

To prevent the power of any one branch from being absolute, the Founding Fathers wrote the Constitution to contain a system of checks and balances. These are powers that each branch has for limiting the power of the other branches. Some scholars say the system of checks and balances actually creates a government of shared powers instead of one with separated powers.

The checks and balances between the president and Congress are many. The most important are the president's power to veto, or reject, laws that Congress passes, and Congress's power to override a presidential veto. Other legislative-executive checks and balances are the executive recommendation power, the legislative appropriations power, senatorial advice and consent, the division of powers concerning war, congressional oversight work, and removal of the president and other executive officers by impeachment.

Veto power and override

The U.S. Constitution gives the president the power to veto laws passed by Congress. It also gives Congress the power to override a presidential veto. This gives both the executive and legislative branches a role in making America's laws.

Presidential veto To pass Congress, a bill must receive a simple majority of votes in both chambers. This means at least 218 of the 435 representatives in the House must vote in favor of a bill for it to pass. In the Senate, either 51 of the 100 senators or else 50 senators plus the vice president of the United States must vote in favor of a bill to pass it. When the Senate is split 50-50, the vice president gets to cast the tie-breaking vote as president of the Senate under Article I, Section 2, of the Constitution.

Article I, Section 7, of the Constitution says:

> Every bill which shall have passed the house of representatives and the senate, shall, before it become a law, be presented to the president of the United States; if he approve he shall sign it, but if not he shall return it, with his objections to that house in which it shall have originated.... If any bill shall not be returned by the president within ten days (Sundays excepted) after it shall have been presented to him, the same shall be a law, in like manner as if he had signed it, unless the Congress by their adjournment prevent its return, in which case it shall not be a law.

Under this procedure, there are four things that can happen to a bill when Congress passes it and presents it to the president for consideration. Two are ways the bill can become a law. If the president signs the bill within ten days, not counting Sunday, it becomes a law. The president can also choose to do nothing with the bill. If ten days pass, not counting Sunday, and Congress is still in session when the president has not acted on it, the bill becomes a law as if the president had signed it.

After Congress passes a bill, the president has the power to veto it. The usual way to do this is to send the bill back to Congress with a veto message within ten days of receiving it. The veto message explains to Congress and the nation why the president is rejecting a bill. This is called a return veto.

The other way to veto a bill happens when Congress adjourns, or takes an official break, before the president has had the bill for ten days. Because such an adjournment prevents the president from having a full ten days for a return veto, the Constitution provides that bills do not become laws in such situations. This kind of veto is called a pocket veto, for it is as if the president simply puts the bill in his pocket, waiting for Congress to adjourn.

Generally speaking, members of Congress believe that pocket vetoes can happen only at the end of each official two-year term of Congress. (Congress's two-year terms begin the January after every November election for the House of

President Calvin Coolidge signs the Mellon Bill on February 26, 1926. Library of Congress.

Representatives.) Presidents, however, use the pocket veto when Congress breaks between the first and second one-year sessions of its terms, and even during congressional recesses, or breaks, in the middle of a session. The Supreme Court has declined to decide the issue of when the president may use a pocket veto. The Supreme Court prefers to stay out of disputes between the executive and legislative branches of government.

The presidential veto is powerful. Obviously, it allows presidents to reject bills of which they disapprove. The mere threat of a veto can discourage Congress from considering or passing a bill in the first place. A veto threat also gives the president the power to encourage Congress to change a bill to the president's liking before passing it.

According to a study by the Congressional Research Service in April 2004, presidents used the return veto 1,484 times and the pocket veto 1,065 times up to that point in history. The number of pocket vetoes is high because Congress often passes many bills in a flurry of activity less then ten days before it adjourns. Many of these die from pocket vetoes.

As of 2005, Franklin D. Roosevelt (1882–1945; served 1933–45) holds the record for the president with the most vetoes—635. As of 2005, eight presidents never used the veto power. George W. Bush (1946–; served 2001–) did not use his veto power during his first term in office. Prior to Bush, the last president not to use the veto power was James A. Garfield (1831–1881), who served for only a short time in 1881 before dying after being shot by an assassin.

Congressional override When the president vetoes a bill by returning it to Congress while Congress is still in session, the Constitution allows Congress to try to override the veto. It says that if the president vetoes a bill:

> he shall return it, with his objections to that house in which it shall have originated, who shall enter the objections at large on their journal, and proceed to reconsider it. If after such reconsideration two-thirds of that house shall agree to pass the bill, it shall be sent, together with the objections, to the other house, by which it shall likewise be reconsidered, and if approved by two-thirds of that house, it shall become a law.

Under this provision, Congress can override a return veto when two-thirds of both chambers vote in favor of a bill after the veto.

The language of the Constitution makes it sound like Congress must vote on whether to override every return veto. In practice, however, the chamber that first gets the bill back from the president holds an override vote only if there is a chance that two-thirds of its members will vote in favor of the bill (as opposed to the simple majority required to pass the bill in the first place). Through practice, Congress also has established that only two-thirds of the members present for an override vote, not two-thirds of the entire membership, must vote for a bill to

Sumners Veto Proposal

The Constitution gives the president power to veto, or reject, laws passed by Congress. Congress can override a presidential veto only by a two-thirds vote in both chambers.

Early presidents rarely used the veto power. They generally vetoed a bill only if they thought it was unconstitutional. If they thought a bill was bad policy but also constitutional, they generally signed it, believing it was Congress's job to make policy through legislation.

This approach changed drastically through the years. During his eight years in office from 1829 to 1837, Andrew Jackson (1767–1845) vetoed twelve bills, more than the first six presidents before him combined. President John Tyler (1790–1862) vetoed ten bills from 1841 to 1845, and President Franklin Pierce (1804–1869) vetoed nine bills from 1853 to 1857. From there, the veto power grew into a strong policy tool for the president. By vetoing bills and threatening to veto others, presidents learned they could influence Congress's legislative agenda, or plan.

Use of the veto power reached a peak during the presidency of Franklin D. Roosevelt (1882–1945), a Democrat who was in office from 1933 to 1945. Roosevelt vetoed a total of 635 bills, an average of about fifty each year. Congress overrode only nine of them.

In 1943, after Roosevelt had used the veto power 592 times, Democratic congressman Hatton W. Sumners of Texas proposed that Congress amend the president's veto power. Sumners thought Roosevelt was abusing the

power, taking away Congress's control over legislative policy. Sumners wanted Congress to be able to override presidential vetoes by simple majorities rather than two-thirds majorities. Such a change required a constitutional amendment, and the proposal failed to attract enough support in Congress.

As of 2005, no president since Franklin Roosevelt has used the veto power as frequently as he did. The power, however, remains potent. It allows presidents to influence congressional agendas so greatly that many scholars call the president the nation's chief legislator.

U.S. representative Hatton W. Sumners of Texas, chairman of the U.S. House Judiciary Committee, in his office. Sumners proposed that Congress be allowed to override presidential vetoes by simple majorities rather than two-thirds majorities. Time Life Pictures/Getty Images.

override the veto. To hold an override vote or conduct any other business, however, a chamber must have a quorum of members in attendance. A quorum exists when a majority of the chamber's members are present.

If the president pocket vetoes a bill, Congress does not get a chance to override the veto. This is because a pocket veto happens when Congress adjourns before the president has the bill for ten days. Adjournment prevents Congress from reconsidering the bill and holding an override vote.

It is very hard, politically, to override a return veto. Normally, neither of the two major parties, the Republicans and Democrats, has two-thirds of the seats in the House or Senate. Members of the president's political party rarely vote to override a veto. According to a Congressional Research Service study in April 2004, Congress had overturned only 106, or 7.1 percent, of the 1,464 return vetoes to that point in history. As of 2005, the president whose vetoes were overruled the most times was Andrew Johnson (1808–1875). Congress voted to override fifteen of Johnson's twenty-nine return vetoes. This was the period of Reconstruction, in which Congress was trying to help bring the South back into the Union after the American Civil War (1861–65). Johnson disagreed with Congress's Reconstruction policies. The disagreement fueled the House's 1868 impeachment of Johnson for violation of a federal law. The Senate came one vote short of convicting Johnson and removing him from office.

Legislative veto The Constitution contains a veto power only for the president. Congress, however, created a veto power for itself. In 1932, for example, it passed a law giving the president the power to reorganize the offices of the executive branch without first getting congressional approval. Either chamber of Congress, however, could reject a reorganization by passing a simple resolution against it within sixty days of the president's action. (A resolution is a statement of congressional will or opinion.) This process gave each chamber of Congress the power to veto presidential action on reorganization.

Legislative vetoes have many forms. They can be simple resolutions by one chamber of Congress, concurrent resolutions by both chambers, and even resolutions by a single committee of Congress.

Congress has used its veto power to strengthen its control of the departments and agencies of the executive branch. Many laws, for example, have given Congress the power to disapprove a department or agency's spending decisions. Other laws have given Congress the power to disapprove department or agency action.

The legislative veto power has been challenged in court many times. In 1983, in *INS v. Chadha,* the U.S. Supreme Court decided that the legislative veto violates the Constitution. The Constitution says the only way Congress can pass a bill or resolution is when both chambers approve it and present it to the president for executive veto consideration. Legislative vetoes violate this by giving either one or both chambers of Congress the power to take official action that the president cannot veto.

Despite the Supreme Court's ruling, Congress continues to include the legislative veto power in the nation's laws. According to Louis Fisher in *The Politics of Shared Power,* Congress enacted four hundred legislative vetoes between the time of the decision in *INS v. Chadha* and the end of 1987. Congress also gets around the Supreme Court's decision by using informal arrangements with agencies. Through such arrangements, agencies agree to give Congress unofficial legislative veto power over agency spending or action. Agency officials make such arrangements to appease Congress in order to get the funding and programs they want.

Executive recommendation power

Article II, Section 3, of the Constitution says the president "shall from time to time give the Congress information of the state of the union, and recommend to their consideration such measures as he shall judge necessary and expedient [proper]." Every year in January, the president carries out this duty by giving a State of the Union address to Congress and the nation. The address outlines what the president would like to see Congress do in the upcoming year. The president conveys such information to Congress in reports during the year, too.

The power to recommend action to Congress serves as a check on Congress's power to pass laws. Congress is not required to do what the president asks. There can be political pressure, however, to do much of what a popular president recommends. For example, after Republican president Ronald

A good example of the popularity of a sitting president occasionally extending to the opposing party is President Ronald Reagan (left) and his friendship with Speaker of the House Tip O'Neill, shown here in February 1981. © Bettmann/ Corbis.

Reagan (1911–2004; served 1981–89) won a landslide reelection to a second term in 1984, he was able to get large tax cut bills through Congress even though the Democrats controlled the House of Representatives.

Legislative appropriations power

The Constitution gives the House of Representatives the power to write, and both chambers of Congress the power to pass, bills for raising revenue through taxes and other methods. By tradition, the House also writes appropriations bills. An appropriations bill, also called a spending bill, is one that gives money to a government department or agency. Under Article I, Section 9, of the Constitution, "No money shall be drawn from the Treasury, but in consequence of appropriations made by law."

The appropriations power is supposed to serve as a check on the president. It restricts the president and the various executive departments and agencies to spending only the money Congress appropriates. The power, however, has led to conflict between the legislative and executive branches. Three of those conflicts involve impoundment, reprogramming, and personnel ceilings and floors.

Impoundment Impoundment happens when the president refuses to spend money Congress has appropriated to a specific department, agency, or program. Presidents and executive agencies use impoundment to control government spending. They also use it to prevent the government from spending tax dollars on projects of which the president's administration does not approve.

The administration of President Richard Nixon (1913–1994; served 1969–74) used the impoundment power a lot from 1969 to 1974. Many in Congress felt this violated the Constitution, an opinion shared by prior members of Congress when presidents used impoundment. When Congress passes an appropriations bill, the only way for the president to strike it is by using the veto power under the Constitution. By signing appropriations bills but impounding money for specific programs, the president was creating a sort of line item veto, the power to strike only portions of a spending bill. In other words, impoundment was giving the president greater control over spending and violating the will of Congress concerning government funding.

To fix the situation, Congress passed the Budget and Impoundment Control Act of 1974. In addition to changing the whole federal budget process, the act changed the impoundment power. It requires the president to submit reports to Congress when the president impounds funds. If an impoundment is temporary, either chamber of Congress can disapprove it. If an impoundment is permanent, both chambers have to approve it before it takes effect.

Congressional power to disapprove impoundments is a form of legislative veto. As noted earlier, the Supreme Court declared legislative vetoes illegal under the Constitution in the 1983 case of *INS v. Chadha*. However, the executive and legislative branches continue to use the impoundment procedures in the Act of 1974 to guide the exercise of the impoundment power.

Reprogramming Each year the federal government sets a budget for spending for the period October 1 through September 30. The overall budget is based on detailed budget requests that the various departments and agencies submit to the president and Congress. Budget requests specifically identify the programs the departments and agencies want to fund.

Congress gets to set the final annual budget in its appropriations bills. These bills, however, do not contain specifics concerning the programs being funded. Instead, the bills appropriate lump sums of money to the various departments and agencies, such as the Central Intelligence Agency (CIA) or the U.S. Army. The details on the amount being appropriated for specific government programs appear in the reports of the congressional committees that write the appropriations bills.

Reprogramming happens when a department or agency takes money appropriated for one program and spends it on a different program. Reprogramming, like impoundment, can frustrate Congress. This is particularly true when an agency uses reprogramming to fund a project that Congress specifically decided not to fund in its appropriations bills. For example, in July 2002, President George W. Bush had $700 million transferred from unidentified programs into programs for planning an invasion of Iraq. Bush made the transfer without notifying Congress, as he was required by law to do. According to the Center for American Progress, White House allies in Congress told *USA Today* that Bush's move was acceptable because the amount was small compared to overall spending bills.

During the latter half of the twentieth century, Congress tried to gain control over reprogramming. It began by requiring some departments or agencies to advise Congress when reprogramming occurred. Next, some congressional committees required departments and agencies to ask permission for certain reprogramming. In 1974, the appropriations bill for the Department of Defense specifically made it illegal for the Pentagon to use reprogramming to fund projects rejected by Congress. Future defense appropriations bills have repeated this restriction.

Many scholars and government officials believe that requiring committee approval of reprogramming is a legislative veto that is illegal after *INS v. Chadha.* Departments and agencies, however, live with such procedures to appease the committees that are responsible for funding their projects. In addition, the federal government is so large that it is impossible for Congress to catch and correct every instance of reprogramming.

Personnel ceilings and floors Another way presidents have tried to control spending is through personnel ceilings. A personnel ceiling is a limit on the total number of employees a department or agency may hire.

Presidents, through the Office of Management and Budget (OMB), use personnel ceilings to prevent agencies from spending all the money appropriated by Congress for specific projects. In other words, if an agency cannot hire the people it needs for a particular project, the project goes nowhere and the money appropriated for it is saved or spent elsewhere.

Just as Congress tries to control impoundment and reprogramming, it also tries to control personnel ceilings. Its tactic for doing so is called personnel floors. A personnel floor is a minimum number of employees that a department or agency must hire. Congressional committees often write personnel floors into the reports supporting appropriations bills. Congress occasionally includes a personnel floor in an actual bill, making the floor a mandatory part of the law. Floors in committee reports are not absolute, but departments and agencies might follow them to appease their funding committees.

Senatorial advice and consent

There are two powers in the Constitution that the president shares with the Senate alone. One is the appointment of executive officers, judges, and other important positions in the federal government. The other is the making of treaties, or formal agreements, with other nations.

Executive appointments and removals Article II, Section 2, of the Constitution says the president "shall nominate, and by and with the advice and consent of the senate, shall appoint ambassadors, other public ministers and consuls, judges of the supreme court, and all other officers of the United States, whose appointments are not herein otherwise provided for, and which shall be established by law."

Under this provision, when Congress creates important positions in the federal government, the president gets to nominate, or recommend, people for those positions. The Senate then gets to consider and either approve or disapprove the nominations.

There are thousands of positions that the president gets to appoint under the nomination power. With support from trusted advisors, the president personally works on the most important nominations. These include the heads of the executive departments, called secretaries (except for the head of the Department of Justice, who is called the attorney general). The president also works personally to nominate the heads of important agencies (such as the Central Intelligence Agency), Supreme Court justices, and commissioners on the independent regulatory commissions (IRCs). IRCs are governmental bodies, such as the Federal Communications Commission (FCC), that regulate specific areas of the national economy.

Before making an important nomination, the president often checks with key members of the Senate to see if the Senate will approve the nomination. This helps the president eliminate people who have no chance of being appointed. Sometimes a person who is nominated, called a nominee, withdraws his or her name from consideration if it looks like the nomination will fail. For example, in December 2004, President George W. Bush nominated former New York City police commissioner Bernard Kerik (1955–) to be secretary of the Department of Homeland Security (DHS). The DHS is a department that Congress created after the terrorist attacks of September 11, 2001, to coordinate protection of the American homeland. One of the DHS's duties is to enforce immigration laws concerning illegal aliens. Illegal aliens are people from other countries who live and work in America without complying with immigration laws. One week after being nominated to lead the DHS, Kerik withdrew his name because he once employed a housekeeper and nanny who was an illegal alien, and he had failed to pay taxes on some of her wages. This information probably would have led the Senate to vote against Kerik for the DHS post.

When the president makes a nomination, the appropriate Senate committee holds hearings to consider the matter. For example, the Senate Judiciary Committee holds hearings to consider nominations to the U.S. Supreme Court and lower

President George W. Bush (right) and homeland security secretary nominee Bernard Kerik, on December 3, 2004. Kerik, the former New York City police commissioner, who was at the helm during the September 11, 2001, terrorist attacks, withdrew his name from consideration after it was revealed that he once employed an illegal alien and failed to pay taxes on some of her wages. © Kevin Lamarque/Reuters/Corbis.

federal courts. Upon recommendation from its committees, the Senate usually approves the president's nominations, but occasionally rejects them, requiring the president to make another nomination. If enough senators oppose a nominee, they can prevent the nomination from coming to a vote by using a procedure called a filibuster. A filibuster is a way to use up all of the time assigned to a particular issue without allowing the issue to come to a vote in the Senate. During the first term of Republican president George W. Bush, a minority of Democratic senators used the filibuster to block the Senate from voting on some of Bush's nominations of federal judges. The conflict led some senators to call for revising their filibuster rules to make it harder for a minority of senators to block Senate votes.

There are thousands of positions to fill that the president does not have time to handle personally. The president's cabinet and staff handle the details of these nominations. For less important positions located in a particular state, the president's staff usually checks with senators from that state who are also in the president's political party. If the president fails to extend this courtesy to senators for such appointments, the Senate might reject a nomination. The effect of this practice, called "senatorial courtesy," is to encourage presidents to check with senators before nominating people to positions located in a particular state.

The Constitution refers only to the power to make and approve appointments to federal offices. It does not address who has the power to remove people from important executive positions. Through case law, the Supreme Court has established that except in cases of impeachment, the president has the sole authority to remove people from purely executive positions, such as the heads of the executive departments. The president can remove such people at any time for any reason, because these positions must be held by people in which the president has complete confidence.

To remove commissioners from IRCs, the president must follow the guidelines set by Congress in the laws governing the commissions. Commissioners are supposed to be independent of the executive branch, so the president does not have the right to remove them at will.

Under the Constitution, justices of the Supreme Court and judges of the lower federal courts cannot be removed "during good behavior." Instead, they can only be removed by impeachment and conviction for "treason, bribery, or other high crimes and misdemeanors." Congress has the sole authority to remove judges through the impeachment process. As of 2005, Congress has removed just seven judges from office through impeachment.

Treaties A treaty is a formal agreement with another nation. The Constitution gives the president the power to make treaties "provided two-thirds of the senators present concur [agree]." When the president signs a treaty, the Senate Foreign Relations Committee studies it before submitting it to the entire Senate for a vote. Presidents starting with George Washington (1732–1799; served 1789–97) have involved the Senate in the process of negotiating treaties. This way a treaty has a greater likelihood of being approved by the Senate.

The Senate usually approves treaties signed by the president. One of the most famous exceptions was the Treaty of Versailles, which ended World War I (1914–18). The Treaty of Versailles created the League of Nations, an international organization that was the forerunner of the United Nations. President Woodrow Wilson (1856–1924; served 1913–21) negotiated this important treaty without Senate involvement, and the Senate refused to approve it.

The House plays no role in the process of negotiating and approving treaties. If a treaty program requires federal money, however, the House can determine whether the program gets money through its role in passing appropriations bills.

The Constitution does not say who has the power to cancel treaties. According to Louis Fisher in *The Politics of Shared Power,* treaties have been cancelled by congressional laws, Senate resolutions, new treaties, and presidential action. The Supreme Court has not resolved the issue. Generally speaking, the Supreme Court prefers to have Congress and the president work together to determine who has the power to cancel treaties.

In addition to treaties, presidents often sign executive agreements with the heads of other nations. Executive agreements are not officially treaties, so they do not require the consent of the Senate. The U.S. Supreme Court, however, has ruled that executive agreements are part of the supreme law of the land, just like treaties.

Presidents typically use treaties for the most important issues and executive agreements for less important issues. Sometimes, however, presidents use an executive agreement for an important issue. Presidents Franklin D. Roosevelt and Harry S. Truman (1884–1972; served 1945–53), for example, used executive agreements at meetings in Yalta and Potsdam to end World War II (1939–45). Using an executive agreement instead of a treaty is significant, because the Senate can require a president to change a treaty before the Senate will approve it.

War powers

The Constitution divides the nation's war powers between Congress and the president. Congress has the power to create an army and navy, and to make rules and appropriate money for their operation. Congress also has the sole power to declare war.

President Harry S. Truman meets with Soviet president Joseph Stalin and British Prime Minister Clement Attlee at the Potsdam Conference in July 1945. Getty Images.

The president is "commander in chief of the army and navy." This means the president ultimately controls the operations of the military forces.

This separation of war powers was important to the men who wrote the Constitution in 1787. According to Louis Fisher in *The Politics of Shared Power,* convention delegate James Madison (1751–1836) wrote:

> Those who are to conduct a war cannot in the nature of things, be proper or safe judges, whether a war ought to be commenced [begun], continued, or concluded. They are barred from the latter functions by a great principle in free government, analogous

[comparable] to that which separated the sword from the purse, or the power of executing from the power of enacting laws. Hence, the men who wrote the Constitution generally felt that the president would be able to use military forces without congressional approval only to defend against an attack. To wage an offensive attack would require a declaration of war by Congress.

Presidents have generally ignored this constitutional separation of powers. America has fought in several hundred military actions since the adoption of the Constitution in 1788. As of 2005, Congress has declared war only eleven times for five wars: the War of 1812 (1812–14), the Mexican-American War (1846–48), the Spanish-American War (1898), World War I (1914–18), and World War II.

During the Vietnam War (1954–75), Presidents Lyndon B. Johnson (1908–1973; served 1963–69) and Richard Nixon sent more than five hundred thousand American soldiers to fight without a congressional declaration of war. Over fifty–eight thousand of them died. When the war became politically unpopular, Congress passed the War Powers Resolution of 1973.

The War Powers Resolution requires the president to report to Congress "in every possible instance" within forty-eight hours after sending troops into hostile situations. The president is then supposed to withdraw the troops unless Congress declares war or otherwise authorizes the military action within sixty days. Presidents, however, have routinely ignored the requirements of the War Powers Resolution, taking for themselves absolute authority over America's military decisions, offensive and otherwise. Some members of Congress occasionally object when the president violates the War Powers Resolution. For example, in October 1983, President Ronald Reagan sent nineteen hundred troops to the Caribbean island of Grenada to take control away from communist Bernard Coard (1944–), who had taken control of Grenada in a military coup. Eleven members of Congress filed a lawsuit, saying Reagan's invasion violated the U.S. Constitution, which gives Congress sole power to declare war. A federal court of appeals dismissed the case because the invasion was over.

President Lyndon B. Johnson greets U.S. troops in Vietnam in 1966. National Archives and Records Administration.

Legislative oversight

To make sure the government is operating as Congress wants it to operate, Congress engages in legislative oversight. This is the process of reviewing the work of government departments and agencies and investigating specific problems. Congress has the power to engage in oversight by virtue of its power to make the laws and appropriate money for governmental operations.

Committees of Congress handle oversight of the departments and agencies for which they write laws and appropriate money. Oversight can take many forms. Much is informal, as when members of a congressional committee meet with federal bureaucrats to see how a program is working. Congress often takes the more formal step of asking an agency to submit an official report of its operations or a specific problem. If a problem is serious, a committee can hold hearings to investigate the situation. Oversight work can lead to informal correction of a problem by a department or agency or to official correction through new laws or different appropriations.

Congressional oversight often leads to conflict with the executive branch. Sometimes the president or executive agencies withhold information from Congress to protect national security, or safety. Other times they withhold information that has nothing to do with national safety, but that they do not want to share with Congress or the nation for some other reason. In the case of *United States v. Nixon* in 1974, the Supreme Court ruled that the executive branch can withhold information relating to "confidential executive deliberations," or discussions, unless there is a compelling, or strong, governmental interest for forcing the executive branch to release the information. Struggles between Congress and the president over withholding information often end up being resolved in federal court.

Impeachment

The Constitution says, "The president, vice-president and all civil officers of the United States, shall be removed from office on impeachment for, and conviction of, treason, bribery, or other high crimes and misdemeanors." This is called the impeachment process. It is the only way to remove the president, vice president, and federal judges from office.

Congress alone has the power to impeach and remove federal officers. The process has two parts. Under the first part, the House of Representatives holds hearings and votes on whether to impeach an officer. Impeachment is a formal charge that an officer has committed treason, bribery, or other high crimes or misdemeanors. To impeach someone, the House must vote for impeachment by a simple majority.

If an officer is impeached in the House, the second part of the process is an impeachment trial in the Senate. The Senate conducts the trial much like a courtroom trial, but there is no judge or jury apart from the Senate. (An exception to this is impeachment trials of presidents, over which the U.S. Constitution requires the chief justice of the Supreme Court to preside. Even then, however, the chief justice simply enforces the Senate's rules for the trial. He does not question witnesses or vote on whether to convict the president, as the senators do, because the Constitution limits his role to presiding over the trial.) At the end of the trial, the Senate votes on whether to convict the officer of the charges made by the House. Two-thirds of the senators present must vote in favor of conviction to convict an officer. If the Senate convicts an officer, the officer is removed from office. The Senate can also prevent a convicted officer from serving in another federal office in the future.

The Constitution says that when the House impeaches the president of the United States, the chief justice of the United States presides over the impeachment trial in the Senate. The chief justice is the head of the U.S. Supreme Court. Normally the vice president of the United States has the right to preside over Senate activities, but that would be

Iran-Contra Scandal

The Iran-Contra scandal illustrates the system of checks and balances in American government. The scandal involved congressional lawmaking power, executive foreign policy power, and the presidential power to pardon criminals.

In 1979, a group called the Sandinista National Liberation Front won a revolution in Nicaragua, a country in Central America. The Sandinistas installed a Marxist government. In theory, Marxists support government ownership of the means of production in a national economy. In practice, Marxist governments can be as unfair as governments that operate under capitalism, which means private ownership of the means of production.

In 1981, Ronald Reagan (1911–2004; served 1981–89) became president of the United States. One of Reagan's primary goals was to combat communism around the world. An outgrowth of Marxism, communism is a form of government in which the people share ownership of the means of production.

The Reagan administration wished to destroy the Sandinista government in Nicaragua. To accomplish this, the Central Intelligence Agency (CIA) trained a group of rebels, called Contras, to fight the Sandinistas. The CIA helped put mines in Nicaraguan harbors to destroy weapon shipments from the Soviet Union, a communist nation. According to Howard Zinn in *A People's History of the United States*, a Contra named Edgar Chamorro later testified before the World Court about the Contras' activities:

> We were told that the only way to defeat the Sandinistas was to use the tactics the agency [CIA] attributed to communist insurgencies elsewhere: kill, kidnap, rob, and torture.... Many civilians were killed in cold blood. Many others were tortured, mutilated, raped, robbed, or otherwise abused.... When I agreed to join ... I had hoped that it would be an organization of Nicaraguans.... [It] turned out to be an instrument of the U.S. government.

According to surveys, most Americans did not want the country involved in the conflict in Nicaragua. In inappropriate in a presidential impeachment trial because the vice president stands to get the president's job if the president is removed from office.

When presiding over a presidential impeachment trial, the chief justice gets to rule on what evidence may and may not be presented to the Senate for consideration. Under its own rules, however, the Senate may overrule any ruling that the chief justice makes. The chief justice, moreover, does not get to vote on whether to convict the accused president. The chief justice's main role is to see that the process runs smoothly.

As noted, impeachment can happen when a federal officer commits treason, bribery, or other high crimes and misdemeanors. The Constitution defines treason as levying war against America or giving aid and comfort to its enemies. Bribery is

1984, Congress passed a law called the Boland Amendment making it illegal for the United States to directly or indirectly support military operations in Nicaragua.

The president and the executive branch are supposed to enforce the nation's laws. President Reagan's administration wanted to continue helping the Contras, so they secretly decided to violate the Boland Amendment. Led by National Security Advisor Robert McFarlane (1937–), the administration devised and carried out a plan to sell antitank and antiaircraft missiles to Iran and use money from the sale for the Contras. In addition, they hoped the deal would buy the release of American hostages being held by a terrorist group in Lebanon, a country in the Middle East.

In 1986, a magazine article in Beirut, the capital of Lebanon, revealed the arms-for-hostages deal to the world. Many Americans were outraged. Iran was considered a country that supported terrorism. America had official policies that it would not support terrorist nations or bargain with terrorists for the release of hostages. The Reagan administration's arms deal violated both policies. The diversion of money to the Contras violated the Boland Amendment.

President Reagan accepted responsibility for the arms-for-hostages deal, but he and Vice President George Bush (1924–) denied knowledge of the diversion of funds to the Contras. Still, U.S. congressman Henry Gonzalez (1916–2000) of Texas introduced a resolution in the House of Representatives to impeach Reagan. Congress did not pursue it.

Many Reagan administration officials faced criminal charges as a result of the scandal. Bush pardoned six of them after he became president in 1989, including McFarlane, Elliott Abrams, Duane R. Clarridge, Alan Fiers, Clair George, and Caspar Weinberger. Bush and others in the Reagan administration considered the event, which they called the "Iran-Contra affair," to be the work of patriots trying to free hostages and protect America from communism, even though they were in violation of the law.

U.S. senator J. Strom Thurmond of South Carolina (far left) swears in Supreme Court chief justice William Rehnquist before the start of the Senate impeachment trial of President Bill Clinton on January 1, 1999. AP/Wide World Photos.

when someone gives a government officer money or something else of value to influence the officer's official conduct.

The Constitution does not define "high crimes and misdemeanors." Some scholars think it means a serious violation of a criminal law. Others think it means what Alexander Hamilton (1757–1804) called it in *The Federalist,* No. 65, "a violation of public trust." In practice, the House and Senate get to define the term themselves in the impeachment process. For example, in 1998, the House impeached President Bill Clinton (1946–; served 1993–2001) for lying under oath regarding whether he had an affair with White House intern Monica Lewinsky (1973–). The case generated much debate over whether lying under oath is a "high crime or misdemeanor" under the Constitutional requirements for impeachment.

Although the Supreme Court has not addressed the issue as of 2005, members of Congress probably cannot be removed from

U.S. senator William Blount of Tennessee was impeached by the House of Representatives in 1797, but no impeachment trial was held, because it was and is unclear whether members of Congress can be impeached. No senator or representative has been impeached since that time. © Bettmann/Corbis.

office by impeachment. The House of Representatives impeached a U.S. senator once, William Blount of Tennessee in 1797. Blount was accused of conspiring to conduct military activities for the king of England. The Senate, however, voted not to conduct an impeachment trial, reasoning that it did not have power under the Constitution to conduct an impeachment trial of a senator. No senator or representative has been impeached since then.

Under Article I, Section 5, of the Constitution, however, each chamber of Congress gets to make its own rules for how to expel its members for misconduct. Under that provision, a two-thirds vote is necessary to expel a member from either the House or Senate. Although declining to hold an impeachment trial, the Senate expelled Senator Blount in 1797.

For More Information

BOOKS

Beard, Charles A. *American Government and Politics.* 10th ed. New York: Macmillan Co., 1949.

Burnham, James. *Congress and the American Tradition.* New Brunswick, NJ: Transaction Publishers, 2003.

Congressional Quarterly Inc. *Guide to the Congress of the United States.* 1st ed. Washington, DC: Congressional Quarterly Service, 1971.

Congressional Quarterly Inc. *Powers of the Presidency.* 2nd ed. Washington, DC: Congressional Quarterly Inc., 1997.

Fisher, Louis. *Constitutional Conflicts between Congress and the President.* 3rd ed., rev. Lawrence: University Press of Kansas, 1991.

Fisher, Louis. *The Politics of Shared Power: Congress and the Executive.* 4th ed. College Station: Texas A&M University Press, 1998.

Janda, Kenneth, Jeffrey M. Berry, and Jerry Goldman. *The Challenge of Democracy.* 5th ed. Boston: Houghton Mifflin Company, 1997.

Kurland, Philip B., and Ralph Lerner. *The Founders' Constitution.* 5 vols. Indianapolis: Liberty Fund, 1987.

Loomis, Burdett A. *The Contemporary Congress.* 3rd ed. Boston: Bedford/St. Martin's, 2000.

McClenaghan, William A. *Magruder's American Government 2003.* Needham, MA: Prentice Hall School Group, 2002.

Nelson, Michael, ed. *The Presidency and the Political System.* 7th ed. Washington, DC: CQ Press, 2003.

Roelofs, H. Mark. *The Poverty of American Politics.* 2nd ed. Philadelphia: Temple University Press, 1998.

Shelley, Mack C., II. *American Government and Politics Today.* 2004–2005 ed. Belmont, CA: Wadsworth Publishing, 2003.

Volkomer, Walter E. *American Government.* 8th ed. Upper Saddle River, NJ: Prentice Hall, 1998.

Wolfensberger, Donald R. *Congress and the People.* Washington, DC, and Baltimore: Woodrow Wilson Center Press and Johns Hopkins University Press, 2000.

Zinn, Howard. *A People's History of the United States.* New York: HarperCollins, 2003.

CASES

INS v. Chadha, 462 U.S. 919 (1983).

United States v. Nixon, 418 U.S. 683 (1974).

WEB SITES

"Bush's Legal Obligation to Tell Congress about $700M for Iraq." *Center for American Progress.* http://www.americanprogress.org/site/pp.asp?c=biJRJ8OVF&b=46962 (accessed on February 24, 2005).

Griffin, Pat. "Working with Congress to Enact an Agenda." In *Mandate for Leadership.* The Heritage Foundation. http://www.heritage.org/Research/Features/Mandate/keys_chapter6.cfm (accessed on March 4, 2005).

Grossman, Joel B. "Impeach Gary Condit?" September 10, 2001. *FindLaw.com.* http://writ.news.findlaw.com/commentary/20010910_grossman.html (accessed on February 17, 2005.)

"Homeland Security Nominee Withdraws." *CNN.com.* December 11, 2004. http://www.cnn.com/2004/ALLPOLITICS/12/10/kerik.withdraws/ (accessed on February 24, 2005).

"Judicial Nominations." *Federalist Society.* http://www.fed-soc.org/judicialnominations.htm (accessed on February 24, 2005).

Sollenberger, Mitchel A. "Congressional Overrides of Presidential Vetoes." CRS Report for Congress, April 7, 2004. *United States House of Representatives.* http://www.senate.gov/reference/resources/pdf/98-157.pdf (accessed on February 14, 2005).

Sollenberger, Mitchel A. "The Presidential Veto and Congressional Procedure." CRS Report for Congress, February 27, 2004. *United States House of Representatives.* http://www.senate.gov/reference/resources/pdf/RS21750.pdf (accessed on February 14, 2005).

United States House of Representatives. http://www.house.gov (accessed on February 17, 2005).

United States Senate. http://www.senate.gov (accessed on February 17, 2005).

"The War Powers Resolution: Thirty Years Later." *CRS Report for Congress.* March 11, 2004. http://www.fas.org/man/crs/RL32267.html (accessed on February 24, 2005).

White House. http://www.whitehouse.gov (accessed on February 17, 2005).

Executive-Judicial Checks and Balances

The U.S. Constitution divides the government into three branches: legislative, executive, and judicial. Generally speaking, the legislative branch, Congress, makes the nation's laws. The executive branch enforces the laws through the president and various executive offices. The judicial branch, made up of the Supreme Court and lower federal courts, decides cases that arise under the laws.

This division of government is called the separation of powers. The separation of powers is supposed to prevent tyranny. Tyranny is arbitrary (random) or unfair government action that can result when one person has all the power to make, enforce, and interpret the laws.

In addition to the broad separation of powers into three branches, the Constitution keeps the executive and judicial branches separate with two specific provisions. Under Article III, Section 1, judges of the Supreme Court and lower federal courts "hold their offices during good behavior." This means the president cannot remove judges from office. Instead, only Congress can remove judges through impeachment and conviction for treason, bribery, and other high crimes and misdemeanors under Article II, section 4. The Constitution defines treason as levying war against America or giving aid and comfort to its enemies. Bribery is an illegal payment to influence official action.

Likewise, the president can be removed from office only through impeachment and conviction by Congress. The Supreme Court and lower federal courts do not hear impeachment cases. This ensures that only Congress, which is accountable for its actions at

Words to Know

checks and balances: The specific powers in one branch of government that allow it to limit the powers of the other branches.

circuit court of appeals: A court in the federal judicial system that handles appeals from the trial courts, called federal district courts. The United States is divided into twelve geographic areas called circuits, and each circuit has one court of appeals that handles appeals from the federal district courts in its circuit. A party who loses in a circuit court of appeals may ask the Supreme Court to review the case.

Constitution of the United States of America: The document written in 1787 that established the federal government under which the United States of America has operated since 1789. Article II covers the executive branch and Article III covers the judicial branch.

federal district courts: The courts in the federal judicial system that handle trials in civil and criminal cases. Each state is divided into one or more federal judicial districts, and each district has one or more federal district courts. A party who loses in a federal district court may appeal to have the case reviewed by a circuit court of appeals.

judicial review: The process by which federal courts review laws to determine whether they violate the U.S. Constitution. If a court finds that a law violates the Constitution, it declares the law unconstitutional, which means the executive branch is not supposed to enforce it anymore. Congress can correct such a defect by passing a new law that does not violate the Constitution.

judiciary: The branch of the federal government that decides cases that arise under the nation's law. The federal judiciary includes the Supreme Court of the United States, circuit courts of appeals, and federal district courts.

president: The highest officer in the executive branch of the federal government, with primary responsibility for enforcing the nation's laws.

separation of powers: Division of the powers of government into different branches to prevent one branch from having too much power.

Supreme Court: The highest court in the federal judiciary. The judiciary is the branch of government responsible for resolving legal disputes and interpreting laws on a case-by-case basis.

election time, can remove a president from office. Supreme Court justices and lower court judges, who are appointed by the president and so are free from popular control, cannot remove a president.

Checks and balances

The men who wrote the Constitution in 1787 wanted each branch's power to be separate, but not absolute. They considered absolute power, even over just a portion of the government, to be dangerous.

To prevent the power of any one branch from being absolute, the Founding Fathers wrote the Constitution to contain a system of checks and balances. These are powers that each branch has for limiting the power of the other branches. Some scholars say the system of checks and balances actually creates a government of shared powers instead of one with separated powers.

The judiciary's main powers over the president are judicial review and judicial interpretation. Judicial review is the power to review executive action to determine if it violates the Constitution. Judicial interpretation is the power to determine the validity and meaning of executive agency regulations. Other judicial checks include the writ (judicial order) of habeas corpus, the writs of mandamus and prohibition, and the chief justice's role in impeachment of the president. A writ of habeas corpus is a procedure that prisoners can use to get released if they are being held in violation of the law. The writ requires a jailer to bring the prisoner before a court, where a judge can set the prisoner free if he or she is being held in violation of constitutional rights. A writ of mandamus is a court order that forces government officials to do their jobs. A writ of prohibition is a court order preventing a government official from doing something prohibited by law.

The executive branch's main powers over the judiciary are the appointment power, executive privilege, and the power to issue pardons and reprieves.

Judicial review

Judicial review is the power to review government action for compliance with the Constitution. The Constitution does not specifically give the federal judiciary this power. Instead, the Supreme Court assumed the power in its decision in *Marbury v. Madison* in 1803.

The case began in 1801, in the waning days of the administration of President John Adams (1735–1826; served 1797–1801). One of the last things Adams did as president was sign commissions, or orders, appointing people to serve as justices of the peace in the District of Columbia. Adams's secretary of state, John Marshall (1755–1835), was supposed to deliver the

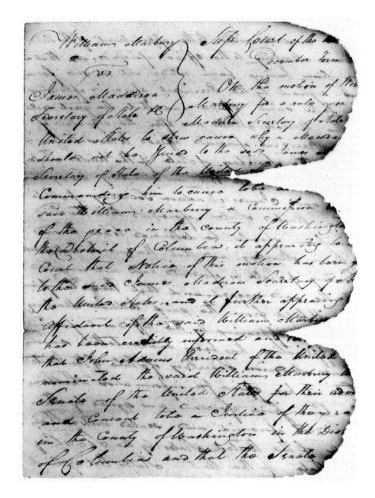

Part of an order served upon Secretary of State James Madison during the Marbury v. Madison *case in 1803. The document was damaged in 1898 during a fire in the U.S. Capitol.* National Archives and Records Administration.

commissions to the appointees. Marshall failed to deliver all of them before Adams left office.

When President Thomas Jefferson (1743–1826; served 1801–9) took office in March 1801, he did not want the people appointed by Adams to take office because they were members of the Federalist Party, the main rival to Jefferson's Democratic-Republican Party. When William Marbury and other appointees asked the new secretary of state, James Madison (1751–1836), to give them their commissions, Madison refused under orders from Jefferson.

Marbury sued Madison in the Supreme Court. The Judiciary Act of 1789 gave the Supreme Court the power to hear cases for writs of mandamus. Marbury wanted the Supreme Court to force Madison to give him his commission.

The Supreme Court did not get to decide the case until 1803. The same John Marshall who had neglected to deliver Marbury's commission in the first place was now chief justice, or leader, of the Supreme Court. (Historians generally agree that if a situation similar to this case came up today, Marshall would disqualify himself due to a clear conflict of interest.) Marshall wrote the court's opinion, saying that Marbury deserved the commission and that Madison should deliver it. The Supreme Court, however, could not issue a writ of mandamus to force Madison to do his job. Marshall said the Judiciary Act of 1789 violated the Constitution because the Constitution does not allow people to sue in the Supreme Court for writs of mandamus. Such cases must begin in a lower federal court and be appealed to the Supreme Court if necessary.

Since *Marbury v. Madison,* the Supreme Court has used judicial review to scrutinize acts of Congress and actions of the executive branch in cases before it. The main limitations on executive power in such cases are the limitations on searches and seizures under the Fourth Amendment and the rights of criminal defendants under the Fifth and Sixth Amendments.

Searches and seizures: the Fourth Amendment America adopted the Fourth Amendment of the Constitution in 1791, three years after adopting the Constitution itself. The Fourth Amendment says:

> The right of the people to be secure in their persons, houses, papers, and effects, against unreasonable searches and seizures, shall not be violated, and no Warrants shall issue, but upon probable cause, supported by Oath or affirmation, and particularly describing the place to be searched, and the persons or things to be seized.

The Fourth Amendment is supposed to restrict the law enforcement activities of the executive branch. Law enforcement agents who investigate crimes often have to search houses, seize possible evidence, and arrest people. The Fourth Amendment says law enforcement must do these things reasonably.

Secretary of State James Madison, a key figure in the Marbury v. Madison *Supreme Court case.*
Library of Congress.

Law enforcement agents often need to get a warrant to conduct a search, seize evidence, or arrest a person. A warrant is a court order authorizing such action. The Fourth Amendment says courts should not issue warrants without testimony or the sworn statement of a witness demonstrating probable cause. Probable cause is a reasonable belief that the search or seizure could produce evidence of a crime. Courts check the power of law enforcement by denying warrant applications when the government does not have enough evidence to support a search, seizure, or arrest.

After law enforcement conducts an investigation, federal prosecutors decide whether to file criminal charges against a suspect. The trial process is another chance for the federal judiciary to check the law enforcement power of the executive branch. Sometimes law enforcement agents collect evidence of a crime by violating the Fourth Amendment. For example, they might search a house or seize evidence without a warrant, or in a manner that violates the terms of the warrant they have.

When law enforcement agents gather evidence by violating the Fourth Amendment, criminal defendants ask the court to enforce the exclusionary rule. The exclusionary rule is a rule created by the U.S. Supreme Court. In general, it prevents the federal government from using evidence at a criminal trial that it got by violating the Fourth Amendment. Enforcement of the exclusionary rule can result in dismissal of criminal charges, even against guilty defendants. In this way, the exclusionary rule encourages law enforcement authorities to obey the Fourth Amendment.

Rights of criminal defendants: the Fifth Amendment Criminal defendants have other rights under the Fifth and Sixth Amendments, also adopted in 1791. The Fifth Amendment says:

> No person shall be held to answer for a capital, or otherwise infamous crime, unless on presentment or indictment of a Grand Jury, except in cases arising in the land or naval forces, or in the Militia, when in actual service in time of War or public danger; nor shall any person be subject for the same offence to be twice put in jeopardy of life or limb; nor shall be compelled in any criminal case to be a witness against himself, nor be deprived of life, liberty, or property, without due process of law. . . .

The federal judiciary checks the law enforcement power of the executive branch by enforcing this amendment in cases against criminal defendants. Under the Grand Jury Clause, the executive branch must use grand juries to charge criminal defendants with capital or infamous crimes. Capital crimes are crimes that may be punishable by death, meaning the death penalty. For example, first degree murder, which means premeditated or preplanned murder, is a capital crime. Infamous crimes are crimes that, under the common law, made a person incapable of testifying in court because of untrustworthiness. Under the common law (judge-made law in English and early-American courts), infamous crimes included treason, felonies, and crimes involving dishonesty, such as

The Steel Seizure Case

In 1950, the communist government of North Korea invaded South Korea in Asia. President Harry S. Truman (1884–1972; served 1945–53) sent American troops to help South Korea. Although Congress has the sole power to declare war, Congress did not give Truman prior approval for his decision.

In 1952, the steel industry was having a dispute with its workers. The United Steel Workers of America (USWA) was a labor union that represented the workers in the dispute. When talks failed to settle the dispute, the USWA decided to support a nationwide labor strike beginning April 9, 1952. A strike is when laborers stop working to protest working terms or conditions.

Truman feared a steel strike would hurt the war effort in South Korea by reducing the production of aircraft, guns, and ammunition. On April 8, the day before the strike was to begin, Truman ordered Secretary of Commerce Charles Sawyer to seize the nation's steel mills so the government could force production to continue.

Truman said the Constitution and laws of the United States gave him the power to seize and operate the steel mills. He relied especially on the portion of the Constitution making him commander in chief of the armed forces. Truman reasoned that in that role, he could seize private steel mills to help the war effort. Indeed, presidents before Truman had seized industries during wartime to avoid labor strikes, sometimes because war legislation from Congress gave them that power.

The Youngstown Sheet and Tube Co. filed a lawsuit against Secretary Sawyer. It argued that President Truman and Secretary Sawyer violated the Constitution by seizing private property without congressional authority. Indeed, when passing the Taft-Hartley Act in 1947, a federal law concerning labor strikes, Congress specifically decided not to give presidents the power to seize industries to stop strikes.

The government conceded that there was no specific congressional law giving Truman the power to seize the steel mills. It argued, however, that Truman implicitly had that power as head of the executive department and commander in chief of the military forces.

The case made it to the U.S. Supreme Court, which announced a decision on June 2, 1952. By a vote of 6–3, the Court said Truman lacked the power to seize the steel mills unless Congress gave him such power. The Court relied heavily on the fact that Congress had declined to give presidents such power in the Taft-Hartley Act. Writing the opinion for the Court, Justice Hugo L. Black (1886–1971) said Truman had to ask Congress for that power if he thought it was necessary.

In a concurring opinion agreeing with the Court's decision, Justice William O. Douglas (1898–1980) wrote, "The emergency did not create power; it merely marked an occasion when power should be exercised. And the fact that it was necessary that measures be taken to keep steel in production does not mean that the president, rather than the Congress, had the constitutional authority to act."

Three justices issued a dissenting opinion written by Chief Justice Frederick M. Vinson (1890–1953), disagreeing with the Court's decision. Vinson wrote, "The broad executive power granted by Article II to perjury. Treason means an act of war against the United States. Felonies refer to the most serious kinds of crime, usually punishable by either death or imprisonment for more than one year.

an officer on duty 365 days a year cannot, it is said, be invoked to avert disaster. Instead, the president must confine himself to sending a message to Congress recommending action. . . . Presidents have been in the past, and any man worthy of the office should be in the future, free to take at least interim [temporary] action necessary to execute legislative programs essential to survival of the Nation."

After the decision, Truman asked Congress to give him the power to seize the steel mills. Congress declined. According to Joan Biskupic and Elder Witt in *The Supreme Court & the Powers of the American Government*, the USWA labor strike started after the Supreme Court's decision and lasted until July 24, 1952. Truman blamed the strike for ammunition shortages that summer and fall.

The Youngstown Sheet & Tube Co. in Youngstown, Ohio. This company filed suit against Secretary of Commerce Charles Sawyer in 1952, claiming that the U.S. government violated the Constitution by seizing private property without congressional authority. © Bettmann/Corbis.

Perjury is lying under oath. A grand jury is a group of citizens who review the evidence against a suspect to make sure there is enough to hold a criminal trial. Federal judges oversee grand jury proceedings to make sure they comply with the law.

The Fifth Amendment's Double Jeopardy Clause says a person may not be tried twice for the same crime. Federal courts enforce this clause against prosecutors. Sometimes a case against a defendant is stopped before the case is finished. In such instances, federal courts must decide whether the first case went far enough to make a second case illegal under the Double Jeopardy Clause.

The Fifth Amendment prevents prosecutors from forcing a criminal defendant to testify at his or her own trial. This is called the privilege against self-incrimination. This privilege also allows criminal suspects to refuse to answer questions during investigations, a practice commonly referred to as "taking the fifth." In criminal cases, federal courts sometimes have to decide whether investigators or prosecutors got evidence from a defendant by violating the privilege against self-incrimination. Under the exclusionary rule, courts are not supposed to allow prosecutors to use such evidence against the person whose privilege was violated.

The Due Process Clause of the Fifth Amendment says the government may not take a person's life, liberty, or property without due process of law. Generally, due process requires a criminal defendant to have notice of the charges against him or her and a chance to present a defense in a fair proceeding. Federal courts check the power of law enforcement by enforcing this clause in criminal prosecutions.

Rights of criminal defendants: the Sixth Amendment The Sixth Amendment says:

> In all criminal prosecutions, the accused shall enjoy a right to a speedy and public trial, by an impartial jury of the State and district wherein the crime shall have been committed, which district shall have been previously ascertained by law, and to be informed of the nature and cause of the accusation; to be confronted with the witnesses against him; to have compulsory [required] process for obtaining witnesses in his favor, and to have the Assistance of Counsel for his defence.

Congress has passed federal laws concerning a defendant's constitutional right to have a speedy public trial by a fair jury in the district where the crime was committed. Federal courts check the power of the executive branch by enforcing these laws in criminal cases. The courts also make sure defendants have fair notice of the charges against them.

Under the Confrontation Clause, a defendant has the right to face the witnesses against him or her. This means that, generally, witnesses have to testify against defendants in open court, and defendants cannot be banned from court during the testimony. Defendants also have the right to force witnesses with favorable evidence to appear in court to testify during criminal trials. Federal courts enforce this right with subpoenas, which are court orders for witnesses to appear in court to give testimony.

Judicial interpretation

Judicial interpretation is the act of deciding what a congressional law or executive regulation means. In theory, judicial interpretation is not supposed to be a check on congressional or executive power. Instead, it is supposed to determine and enforce the will of Congress or the executive branch. In practice, however, interpreting laws and regulations gives courts considerable power to determine what they mean, which can affect the exercise of congressional and executive power.

Judicial interpretation affects the regulatory work of executive agencies. Agencies are executive offices responsible for enforcing specific areas of federal law. The Environmental Protection Agency (EPA), for example, enforces congressional laws that regulate the amount of pollution of air, land, and water.

Executive agencies get their power from such congressional laws. Congress, for instance, has given the EPA the power to enforce the Clean Air Act and the Clean Water Act (among other laws). These laws contain very general standards concerning the pollution of air and water. To enforce them, the EPA writes regulations. Regulations are like congressional laws, but they contain much more detail.

People and businesses in America must obey both congressional laws and executive regulations. If the EPA thinks someone has violated a law or regulation, it can file a civil or criminal case against the offender. The EPA usually resolves such cases by agreements with the offenders or by holding administrative hearings in EPA offices.

Occasionally, however, these cases end up in the federal courts. When they do, federal judges have to interpret the agency's regulations. Interpretation requires the judge to decide whether the agency had the power to adopt the regulation under the relevant congressional law. In this way, interpretation acts as a check on executive power by making sure the agency has not done something Congress did not authorize it to do.

President Richard Nixon signs the Clean Air Act on December 31, 1970. Behind Nixon are (left) William D. Ruckelshaus, head of the Environmental Protection Agency, and Russell Train, chairman of the Council on Environmental Quality. AP/Wide World Photos.

If a regulation was lawfully adopted under congressional law, the judge must decide what the regulation means, and whether the defendant violated it. This process gives the federal judiciary considerable power over the regulatory actions of the executive branch.

Writs of habeas corpus

Federal authorities sometimes arrest, imprison, or convict a person in a way that violates his or her rights under the Constitution or federal law. When this happens, the person can apply to a federal court for a writ of habeas corpus. The writ requires federal authorities to bring the accused to court so he or she can ask the court to decide whether the imprisonment is illegal. If the court agrees with the prisoner, it can order him or her to be released, even if he or she is guilty of a crime.

According to the U.S. Supreme Court, federal courts only have the power to issue writs of habeas corpus if congressional law gives them the power. The court, however, might be wrong about this. Article I, Section 9, of the Constitution says, "The privilege of the writ of habeas corpus shall not be suspended, unless when in cases of rebellion or invasion the public safety may require it." This arguably means Americans have a constitutional right to seek writs of habeas corpus, whether or not Congress authorizes the power. Congressional law, however, has authorized writs of habeas corpus since the federal government began to operate under the Constitution in 1789.

Writs of mandamus and prohibition

A writ of mandamus is a court order forcing a government official to do something required by his or her job. A writ of prohibition is a court order preventing a government official from doing something prohibited by his or her job.

The U.S. Constitution does not mention writs of mandamus and prohibition. Instead, Congress has passed laws giving the federal courts such power. Use of this power acts as a check on the powers of the executive branch.

Courts generally issue writs of mandamus only to compel government officials to do ministerial acts. A ministerial act is one that does not involve discretion, or judgment. Instead, it is action clearly required by the law. An example is issuance of a permit or license to an applicant who qualifies for it.

A discretionary act is an act that requires a government official to exercise judgment. An example is a U.S. attorney's decision whether to prosecute a suspected criminal. Courts generally will not issue writs to compel discretionary conduct because judges are not supposed to substitute their judgment for that of government officials.

In practice, federal judges rarely issue writs of mandamus or prohibition. Instead, if they think a writ is necessary, they write an opinion explaining why and give the government official a chance to correct his or her conduct without being compelled by a writ.

The chief justice's role in presidential impeachments

Under Article II, Section 4, executive officials may only be removed from office by impeachment for and conviction of treason, bribery, and other high crimes and misdemeanors. Under Article I, Congress has the sole authority to conduct the process. The House of Representatives can impeach officials by vote of a simple majority. Impeachment serves as an accusation of misconduct. Once impeached, an official faces trial in the Senate, which can remove the official by vote of at least a two-thirds majority. The federal judiciary plays no role in the process.

There is one small exception to this rule. Normally, the vice president presides over Senate impeachment trials because he is officially the president of the Senate under Article I, Section 3, of the Constitution. When the president faces an impeachment trial in the Senate, however, the chief justice of the Supreme Court presides instead of the vice president. Because the vice president stands to get the job of a president who is removed from office, it would not be fair to let him or her preside over the trial. In this way, the chief justice serves as a check on the vice president's senatorial power and, therefore, a check on the legislative branch as well.

The chief justice, who is the leader of the Supreme Court, has a limited role in presidential impeachment trials. He or she does not get to vote whether to convict and remove the president. The chief justice mainly interprets and enforces the Senate's rules for conducting the trial. Under the rules, the Senate can overrule an interpretation or decision by the chief justice. The chief justice's presence, however, lends an air of credibility and authority to the controversial business of trying to remove a president from office. In American history, there have been only two times that a president has been impeached: Andrew Johnson (1808–1875; served 1865–69) in 1868 and Bill Clinton (1946–; served 1993–2001) in 1998. Neither was removed from office, though Johnson retained his position by only a single vote.

Appointment power

Under Article II, Section 2, of the Constitution, presidents have the power to nominate people to serve on the Supreme Court and lower federal courts. The Senate gets to vote whether to approve or reject these nominations. A simple majority is all that is required to approve the president's choices.

Supreme Court justices and lower federal judges serve as long as they want unless impeached and convicted by Congress for treason, bribery, or other high crimes and misdemeanors. This means presidents cannot remove them from office. Presidents get to appoint new justices and judges only when one retires or when Congress creates a new seat on a court.

The power to appoint justices and judges to the Supreme and lower courts, however, acts as a check on the power of the Court. This is especially true when the president's political philosophy differs greatly from those of the Supreme Court justices. When justices retire, the president can affect the Supreme Court's decisions for years or decades into the future by nominating justices who agree with his philosophies, as long as the Senate approves the nominations.

Executive privilege

The executive branch often faces demands that it produce information about its conduct. Congress might ask for information on how an executive agency is functioning under federal law. A special prosecutor might demand information on whether a president or other executive official has violated the law. Citizens can request information under a law called the Freedom of Information Act (FOIA). When a government office gets a FOIA request from a citizen, it must respond to the request in a certain amount of time. Much of the time, the office has to release the information requested. The FOIA law, however, allows the government to keep certain kinds of information secret. Examples include information relating to national security, and private business information of individual companies. Citizens and the government frequently end up in lawsuits over whether the government must release information requested under the FOIA.

If an executive official resists a demand for information, the person seeking the information can sue for it. Federal courts can force an official to produce information if production is required or allowed under the applicable law. Serving in this role, federal courts act as a check on the secret exercise of executive power.

Roosevelt's Court-packing Plan

The president of the United States gets to appoint people to serve on the U.S. Supreme Court and lower federal courts. In 1937, President Franklin D. Roosevelt (1882–1945; served 1933–45) tried to use the power to change the philosophical makeup of the Supreme Court.

Roosevelt had entered office in 1933, when the country was in the middle of the Great Depression (1929–41). The Great Depression was a period in the 1930s when the U.S. economy reached an extreme low point. By 1933, industrial production had fallen to half of 1929 levels, leaving one out of every three or four working Americans without a job.

Roosevelt wanted to revive the American economy with a program he called the New Deal. The New Deal was a series of bills designed to pump government money into the economy, raise commodity prices, provide relief to debtors, and regulate wages and trade practices, all to improve the economy. Beginning in March 1933, Congress passed and Roosevelt signed dozens of New Deal bills into law.

People and businesses who were harmed by the New Deal filed lawsuits challenging the laws, and many of the cases reached the U.S. Supreme Court. According to Joan Biskupic and Elder Witt in *The Supreme Court & the Powers of American Government*, the court struck down eight major New Deal statutes between January 1935 and June 1936. The nine-person court often voted 5–4 or 6–3 in these close cases.

In 1936, the country reelected Roosevelt to his second term. The results were overwhelming, with Roosevelt winning the popular vote in every state except Maine and Vermont. Roosevelt took this as a sign of support for his New Deal program.

On February 5, 1937, Roosevelt sent Congress a message. He asked Congress to increase the number of seats on the Supreme Court from nine to fifteen, and to allow Roosevelt to fill the new seats whenever a justice over seventy years of age did not resign. Four justices who regularly voted against the New Deal, including James C. McReynolds (1862–1946), Willis Van Devanter (1859–1941), George Sutherland (1862–1942), and Pierce Butler (1866–1939), were already

When executive officials defend such cases, they have two main strategies. First, they often argue that the applicable law does not require them to produce the desired information. Second, they sometimes argue that they have a privilege, called executive privilege, that allows them to keep the information secret.

The executive privilege is a right to keep information secret for national safety or the public good. The Constitution does not give the executive branch an executive privilege. Instead, presidents have created it themselves, and the Supreme Court has approved it. When an executive official successfully keeps information secret, he or she checks the power of Congress, the courts, and the citizens to require access to governmental information. Some scholars and citizens consider such secrecy to be an abuse of executive power.

over seventy. Roosevelt's theory was that by appointing new justices to a fifteen-member court, he would be able to change the philosophy of the court to support his New Deal.

Roosevelt's plan was controversial. Many Democrats in Congress sided with Republicans against the plan. According to Biskupic and Witt, Secretary of the Interior Harold Ickes said, "The president has a first class fight on his hands. Practically all of the newspapers are against him."

Developments in the months after Roosevelt's proposal made the proposal unnecessary. In five cases from March to May 1937, the Supreme Court approved New Deal legislation. On May 18, Justice Van Devanter announced he would resign at the end of the Supreme Court's term.

Between 1937 and 1940, Roosevelt appointed four new justices to the Supreme Court. His proposal to add more judges, or "pack" the court, however, cost him support from moderate Democrats. Many of them joined with Republicans to prevent new New Deal legislation from passing Congress after the court-packing plan was over.

Editorial cartoon shows President Franklin D. Roosevelt suggesting to Secretary of the Interior Harold Ickes that the only way to increase the total number of Supreme Court justices is for the Supreme Court building itself to be enlarged. Ickes was also in charge of the Public Works Administration (PWA), which was involved at the time in a huge public building program. Pen and ink drawing by Clifford Berryman. Library of Congress.

Former secretary of defense Caspar Weinberger was pardoned by President George Bush for any offenses he may have committed during the Reagan administration's Iran-Contra Affair.
Getty Images.

Others think it is necessary for the executive branch to handle important government matters. Richard Nixon (1913–1994; served 1969–74), for instance, unsuccessfully tried to use executive privilege amidst the Watergate scandal. His participation in the cover-up of a burglary of the Democratic National Committee headquarters in 1972 led to his resignation in 1974.

Pardons and reprieves

Article II, Section 2, gives the president the power to grant pardons and reprieves for offenses against the United States. A pardon is complete forgiveness for a crime. It prevents the criminal from being punished by the law. A reprieve suspends a sentence, or punishment, to give a criminal time to ask the court to change the sentence. The pardon power checks the power of the courts by allowing a president to forgive a criminal if he thinks the court's sentence was unfair. On December 24, 1992, outgoing president George Bush (1924–; served 1989–93) pardoned six members of the administration of Ronald Reagan (1911–2004; served 1981–89) who were involved in the Iran-Contra arms-for-hostages investigation, including former defense secretary Caspar Weinberger (1917–). According to U.S. Information Agency writer Dian McDonald, Bush pardoned the men, who had not gone to trial, because the "common denominator of their motivation—whether their actions were right or wrong—was patriotism."

For More Information

BOOKS

Beard, Charles A. *American Government and Politics.* 10th ed. New York: Macmillan Co., 1949.

Biskupic, Joan, and Elder Witt. *The Supreme Court & the Powers of the American Government.* Washington, DC: Congressional Quarterly Inc., 1997.

Congressional Quarterly Inc. *Powers of the Presidency.* 2nd ed. Washington, DC: Congressional Quarterly Inc., 1997.

Dougherty, J. Hampden. *Power of Federal Judiciary over Legislation.* New York: Putnam's Sons, 1912. Reprint, Clark, NJ: Lawbook Exchange, 2004.

Janda, Kenneth, Jeffrey M. Berry, and Jerry Goldman. *The Challenge of Democracy.* 5th ed. Boston: Houghton Mifflin Company, 1997.

McClenaghan, William A. *Magruder's American Government 2003.* Needham, MA: Prentice Hall School Group, 2002.

Nelson, Michael, ed. *The Presidency and the Political System.* 7th ed. Washington, DC: CQ Press, 2003.

Parenti, Michael. *Democracy for the Few.* 6th ed. New York: St. Martin's Press, 1995.

Roelofs, H. Mark. *The Poverty of American Politics.* 2nd ed. Philadelphia: Temple University Press, 1998.

Shelley, Mack C., II. *American Government and Politics Today.* 2004–2005 ed. Belmont, CA: Wadsworth Publishing, 2003.

Volkomer, Walter E. *American Government.* 8th ed. Upper Saddle River, NJ: Prentice Hall, 1998.

CD-ROM

21st Century Complete Guide to U.S. Courts. Progressive Management, 2003.

CASES

Marbury v. Madison, 1 Cranch 137 (1803).

Youngstown Sheet and Tube Co. v. Sawyer, 343 U.S. 579 (1952).

WEB SITES

McDonald, Dian. "Bush Pardons Weinberger, Five Others Tied to Iran-Contra." *Federation of American Scientists.* http://www. fas.org/news/iran/1992/921224-260039.htm (accessed on February 23, 2005).

Sabato, Larry J. "Feeding Frenzy: Judge Douglas Ginsburg's Marijuana Use—1987." *Washington Post.* http://www.washingtonpost.com/ wp-srv/politics/special/clinton/frenzy/ginsburg.htm (accessed on February 18, 2005).

Supreme Court of the United States. http://www.supremecourtus.gov (accessed on February 18, 2005).

U.S. Courts: Federal Judiciary. http://www.uscourts.gov (accessed on February 18, 2005).

White House. http://www.whitehouse.gov (accessed on February 16, 2005).

Appendix

THE CONSTITUTION OF THE UNITED STATES OF AMERICA

We the People of the United States, in Order to form a more perfect Union, establish Justice, insure domestic Tranquility, provide for the common defence, promote the general Welfare, and secure the Blessings of Liberty to ourselves and our Posterity, do ordain and establish this Constitution for the United States of America.

Article I.

SECTION 1. All legislative Powers herein granted shall be vested in a Congress of the United States, which shall consist of a Senate and House of Representatives.

SECTION 2. The House of Representatives shall be composed of Members chosen every second Year by the People of the several States, and the Electors in each State shall have the Qualifications requisite for Electors of the most numerous Branch of the State Legislature. No Person shall be a Representative who shall not have attained to the Age of twenty five Years, and been seven Years a Citizen of the United States, and who shall not, when elected, be an Inhabitant of that State in which he shall be chosen.

Representatives and direct Taxes shall be apportioned among the several States which may be included within this Union, according to their respective Numbers, which shall be determined by adding to the whole Number of free Persons, including those bound to Service for a Term of Years, and excluding Indians not taxed, three fifths of all other Persons. The actual Enumeration shall be made within three Years after the first Meeting of the Congress of the United States, and within every subsequent Term of ten Years, in such Manner as they shall by Law direct. The Number of Representatives shall not exceed one for every thirty Thousand, but each State shall have at Least one Representative; and until such enumeration shall be made, the State of New Hampshire shall be entitled to chuse three, Massachusetts eight, Rhode-Island and Providence Plantations one, Connecticut five, New-York six, New Jersey four, Pennsylvania eight, Delaware one, Maryland six, Virginia ten, North Carolina five, South Carolina five, and Georgia three.

When vacancies happen in the Representation from any State, the Executive Authority thereof shall issue Writs of Election to fill such Vacancies.

The House of Representatives shall chuse their Speaker and other Officers; and shall have the sole Power of Impeachment.

SECTION 3. The Senate of the United States shall be composed of two Senators from each State, chosen by the Legislature thereof, for six Years; and each Senator shall have one Vote.

Immediately after they shall be assembled in Consequence of the first Election, they shall be divided as equally as may be into three Classes. The Seats of the Senators of the first Class shall be vacated at the Expiration of the second Year, of the second Class at the Expiration of the fourth Year, and of the third Class at the Expiration of the sixth Year, so that one third may be chosen every second Year; and if Vacancies happen by Resignation, or otherwise, during the Recess of the Legislature of any State, the Executive thereof may make temporary Appointments until the next Meeting of the Legislature, which shall then fill such Vacancies.

No Person shall be a Senator who shall not have attained to the Age of thirty Years, and been nine Years a Citizen of the United States, and who shall not, when elected, be an Inhabitant of that State for which he shall be chosen.

The Vice President of the United States shall be President of the Senate, but shall have no Vote, unless they be equally divided.

The Senate shall chuse their other Officers, and also a President pro tempore, in the Absence of the Vice President, or when he shall exercise the Office of President of the United States. The Senate shall have the sole Power to try all Impeachments. When sitting for that Purpose, they shall be on Oath or Affirmation. When the President of the United States is tried, the Chief Justice shall preside: And no Person shall be convicted without the Concurrence of two thirds of the Members present.

Judgment in Cases of Impeachment shall not extend further than to removal from Office, and disqualification to hold and enjoy any Office of honor, Trust or Profit under the United States: but the Party convicted shall nevertheless be liable and subject to Indictment, Trial, Judgment and Punishment, according to Law.

SECTION 4. The Times, Places and Manner of holding Elections for Senators and Representatives, shall be prescribed in each State by the Legislature thereof; but the Congress may at any time by Law make or alter such Regulations, except as to the Places of chusing Senators. The Congress shall assemble at least once in every Year, and such Meeting shall be on the first Monday in December, unless they shall by Law appoint a different Day.

SECTION 5. Each House shall be the Judge of the Elections, Returns and Qualifications of its own Members, and a Majority of each shall constitute a Quorum to do Business; but a smaller Number may adjourn from day to day, and may be authorized to compel the Attendance of absent Members, in such Manner, and under such Penalties as each House may provide. Each House may determine the Rules of its Proceedings, punish its Members for disorderly Behaviour, and, with the Concurrence of two thirds, expel a Member. Each House shall keep a Journal of its Proceedings, and from time to time publish the same, excepting such Parts as may in their Judgment require Secrecy; and the Yeas and Nays of the Members of either House on any question shall, at the Desire of one fifth of those Present, be entered on the Journal.

Neither House, during the Session of Congress, shall, without the Consent of the other, adjourn for more than three days, nor to any other Place than that in which the two Houses shall be sitting.

SECTION 6. The Senators and Representatives shall receive a Compensation for their Services, to be ascertained by Law, and paid out of the Treasury of the United States. They shall in all Cases, except Treason, Felony and Breach of the Peace, be privileged from Arrest during their Attendance at the Session of their respective Houses, and in going to and returning from the same; and for any Speech or Debate in either House, they shall not be questioned in any other Place.

No Senator or Representative shall, during the Time for which he was elected, be appointed to any civil Office under the Authority of the United States, which shall have been created, or the Emoluments whereof shall have been encreased during such time; and no Person holding any Office under the United States, shall be a Member of either House during his Continuance in Office.

SECTION 7. All Bills for raising Revenue shall originate in the House of Representatives; but the Senate may propose or concur with Amendments as on other Bills.

Every Bill which shall have passed the House of Representatives and the Senate, shall, before it become a Law, be presented to the President of the United States: If he approve he shall sign it, but if not he shall return it, with his Objections to that House in which it shall have originated, who shall enter the Objections at large on their Journal, and proceed to reconsider it. If after such Reconsideration two thirds of that House shall agree to pass the Bill, it shall be sent, together with the Objections, to the other House, by which it shall likewise be reconsidered, and if approved by two thirds of that House, it shall become a Law. But in all such Cases the Votes of both Houses shall be determined by yeas and Nays, and the Names of the Persons voting for and against the Bill shall be entered on the Journal of each House respectively. If any Bill shall not be returned by the President within ten Days (Sundays excepted) after it shall have been presented to him, the Same shall be a Law, in like Manner as if he had signed it, unless the Congress by their Adjournment prevent its Return, in which Case it shall not be a Law.

Every Order, Resolution, or Vote to which the Concurrence of the Senate and House of Representatives may be necessary (except on a question of Adjournment) shall be presented to the President of the United States; and before the Same shall take Effect, shall be approved by him, or being disapproved by him, shall be repassed by two thirds of the Senate and House of Representatives, according to the Rules and Limitations prescribed in the Case of a Bill.

SECTION 8. The Congress shall have Power To lay and collect Taxes, Duties, Imposts and Excises, to pay the Debts and provide for the common Defence and general Welfare of the United

States; but all Duties, Imposts and Excises shall be uniform throughout the United States;

To borrow Money on the credit of the United States;

To regulate Commerce with foreign Nations, and among the several States, and with the Indian Tribes;

To establish an uniform Rule of Naturalization, and uniform Laws on the subject of Bankruptcies throughout the United States;

To coin Money, regulate the Value thereof, and of foreign Coin, and fix the Standard of Weights and Measures;

To provide for the Punishment of counterfeiting the Securities and current Coin of the United States;

To establish Post Offices and post Roads;

To promote the Progress of Science and useful Arts, by securing for limited Times to Authors and Inventors the exclusive Right to their respective Writings and Discoveries;

To constitute Tribunals inferior to the Supreme Court;

To define and punish Piracies and Felonies committed on the high Seas, and Offences against the Law of Nations;

To declare War, grant Letters of Marque and Reprisal, and make Rules concerning Captures on Land and Water;

To raise and support Armies, but no Appropriation of Money to that Use shall be for a longer Term than two Years;

To provide and maintain a Navy;

To make Rules for the Government and Regulation of the land and naval Forces;

To provide for calling forth the Militia to execute the Laws of the Union, suppress Insurrections and repel Invasions;

To provide for organizing, arming, and disciplining, the Militia, and for governing such Part of them as may be employed in the Service of the United States, reserving to the States respectively, the Appointment of the Officers, and the Authority of training the Militia according to the discipline prescribed by Congress;

To exercise exclusive Legislation in all Cases whatsoever, over such District (not exceeding ten Miles square) as may, by Cession of particular States, and the Acceptance of Congress, become the Seat of the Government of the United States, and to exercise like Authority over all Places purchased by the

Consent of the Legislature of the State in which the Same shall be, for the Erection of Forts, Magazines, Arsenals, dock-Yards, and other needful Buildings; –And

To make all Laws which shall be necessary and proper for carrying into Execution the foregoing Powers, and all other Powers vested by this Constitution in the Government of the United States, or in any Department or Officer thereof.

SECTION 9. The Migration or Importation of such Persons as any of the States now existing shall think proper to admit, shall not be prohibited by the Congress prior to the Year one thousand eight hundred and eight, but a Tax or duty may be imposed on such Importation, not exceeding ten dollars for each Person.

The Privilege of the Writ of Habeas Corpus shall not be suspended, unless when in Cases of Rebellion or Invasion the public Safety may require it.

No Bill of Attainder or ex post facto Law shall be passed.

No Capitation, or other direct, Tax shall be laid, unless in Proportion to the Census or Enumeration herein before directed to be taken.

No Tax or Duty shall be laid on Articles exported from any State.

No Preference shall be given by any Regulation of Commerce or Revenue to the Ports of one State over those of another; nor shall Vessels bound to, or from, one State, be obliged to enter, clear, or pay Duties in another.

No Money shall be drawn from the Treasury, but in Consequence of Appropriations made by Law; and a regular Statement and Account of the Receipts and Expenditures of all public Money shall be published from time to time.

No Title of Nobility shall be granted by the United States: And no Person holding any Office of Profit or Trust under them, shall, without the Consent of the Congress, accept of any present, Emolument, Office, or Title, of any kind whatever, from any King, Prince, or foreign State.

SECTION 10. No State shall enter into any Treaty, Alliance, or Confederation; grant Letters of Marque and Reprisal; coin Money; emit Bills of Credit; make any Thing but gold and silver Coin a Tender in Payment of Debts; pass any Bill of

Attainder, ex post facto Law, or Law impairing the Obligation of Contracts, or grant any Title of Nobility.

No State shall, without the Consent of the Congress, lay any Imposts or Duties on Imports or Exports, except what may be absolutely necessary for executing it's [sic] inspection Laws; and the net Produce of all Duties and Imposts, laid by any State on Imports or Exports, shall be for the Use of the Treasury of the United States; and all such Laws shall be subject to the Revision and Controul of the Congress.

No State shall, without the Consent of Congress, lay any Duty of Tonnage, keep Troops, or Ships of War in time of Peace, enter into any Agreement or Compact with another State, or with a foreign Power, or engage in War, unless actually invaded, or in such imminent Danger as will not admit of delay.

Article II.

SECTION 1. The executive Power shall be vested in a President of the United States of America. He shall hold his Office during the Term of four Years, and, together with the Vice President, chosen for the same Term, be elected, as follows:

Each State shall appoint, in such Manner as the Legislature thereof may direct, a Number of Electors, equal to the whole Number of Senators and Representatives to which the State may be entitled in the Congress: but no Senator or Representative, or Person holding an Office of Trust or Profit under the United States, shall be appointed an Elector.

The Electors shall meet in their respective States, and vote by Ballot for two Persons, of whom one at least shall not be an Inhabitant of the same State with themselves. And they shall make a List of all the Persons voted for, and of the Number of Votes for each; which List they shall sign and certify, and transmit sealed to the Seat of the Government of the United States, directed to the President of the Senate. The President of the Senate shall, in the Presence of the Senate and House of Representatives, open all the Certificates, and the Votes shall then be counted. The Person having the greatest Number of Votes shall be the President, if such Number be a Majority of the whole Number of Electors appointed; and if there be more than one who have such Majority, and have an equal Number of Votes, then the House of Representatives shall immediately chuse by

Ballot one of them for President; and if no Person have a Majority, then from the five highest on the List the said House shall in like Manner chuse the President. But in chusing the President, the Votes shall be taken by States, the Representation from each State having one Vote; a quorum for this Purpose shall consist of a Member or Members from two thirds of the States, and a Majority of all the States shall be necessary to a Choice. In every Case, after the Choice of the President, the Person having the greatest Number of Votes of the Electors shall be the Vice President. But if there should remain two or more who have equal Votes, the Senate shall chuse from them by Ballot the Vice President.

The Congress may determine the Time of chusing the Electors, and the Day on which they shall give their Votes; which Day shall be the same throughout the United States.

No Person except a natural born Citizen, or a Citizen of the United States, at the time of the Adoption of this Constitution, shall be eligible to the Office of President; neither shall any Person be eligible to that Office who shall not have attained to the Age of thirty five Years, and been fourteen Years a Resident within the United States.

In Case of the Removal of the President from Office, or of his Death, Resignation, or Inability to discharge the Powers and Duties of the said Office, the Same shall devolve on the Vice President, and the Congress may by Law provide for the Case of Removal, Death, Resignation or Inability, both of the President and Vice President, declaring what Officer shall then act as President, and such Officer shall act accordingly, until the Disability be removed, or a President shall be elected.

The President shall, at stated Times, receive for his Services, a Compensation, which shall neither be increased nor diminished during the Period for which he shall have been elected, and he shall not receive within that Period any other Emolument from the United States, or any of them.

Before he enter on the Execution of his Office, he shall take the following Oath or Affirmation: "I do solemnly swear (or affirm) that I will faithfully execute the Office of President of the United States, and will to the best of my Ability, preserve, protect and defend the Constitution of the United States."

SECTION 2. The President shall be Commander in Chief of the Army and Navy of the United States, and of the Militia of the several States, when called into the actual Service of the United States; he may require the Opinion, in writing, of the principal Officer in each of the executive Departments, upon any Subject relating to the Duties of their respective Offices, and he shall have Power to grant Reprieves and Pardons for Offences against the United States, except in Cases of Impeachment.

He shall have Power, by and with the Advice and Consent of the Senate, to make Treaties, provided two thirds of the Senators present concur; and he shall nominate, and by and with the Advice and Consent of the Senate, shall appoint Ambassadors, other public Ministers and Consuls, Judges of the Supreme Court, and all other Officers of the United States, whose Appointments are not herein otherwise provided for, and which shall be established by Law: but the Congress may by Law vest the Appointment of such inferior Officers, as they think proper, in the President alone, in the Courts of Law, or in the Heads of Departments.

The President shall have Power to fill up all Vacancies that may happen during the Recess of the Senate, by granting Commissions which shall expire at the End of their next Session.

SECTION 3. He shall from time to time give to the Congress Information of the State of the Union, and recommend to their Consideration such Measures as he shall judge necessary and expedient; he may, on extraordinary Occasions, convene both Houses, or either of them, and in Case of Disagreement between them, with Respect to the Time of Adjournment, he may adjourn them to such Time as he shall think proper; he shall receive Ambassadors and other public Ministers; he shall take Care that the Laws be faithfully executed, and shall Commission all the Officers of the United States.

SECTION 4. The President, Vice President and all civil Officers of the United States, shall be removed from Office on Impeachment for, and Conviction of, Treason, Bribery, or other high Crimes and Misdemeanors.

Article III.

SECTION 1. The judicial Power of the United States shall be vested in one Supreme Court, and in such inferior Courts as the Congress may from time to time ordain and establish. The Judges, both of the supreme and inferior Courts, shall hold their Offices during good Behaviour, and shall, at stated Times, receive for their Services a Compensation, which shall not be diminished during their Continuance in Office.

SECTION 2. The judicial Power shall extend to all Cases, in Law and Equity, arising under this Constitution, the Laws of the United States, and Treaties made, or which shall be made, under their Authority; –to all Cases affecting Ambassadors, other public Ministers and Consuls; –to all Cases of admiralty and maritime Jurisdiction; –to Controversies to which the United States shall be a Party; –to Controversies between two or more States; – between a State and Citizens of another State; –between Citizens of different States; –between Citizens of the same State claiming Lands under Grants of different States, and between a State, or the Citizens thereof, and foreign States, Citizens or Subjects.

In all Cases affecting Ambassadors, other public Ministers and Consuls, and those in which a State shall be Party, the Supreme Court shall have original Jurisdiction. In all the other Cases before mentioned, the Supreme Court shall have appellate Jurisdiction, both as to Law and Fact, with such Exceptions, and under such Regulations as the Congress shall make.

The Trial of all Crimes, except in Cases of Impeachment, shall be by Jury; and such Trial shall be held in the State where the said Crimes shall have been committed; but when not committed within any State, the Trial shall be at such Place or Places as the Congress may by Law have directed.

SECTION 3. Treason against the United States shall consist only in levying War against them, or in adhering to their Enemies, giving them Aid and Comfort. No Person shall be convicted of Treason unless on the Testimony of two Witnesses to the same overt Act, or on Confession in open Court.

The Congress shall have Power to declare the Punishment of Treason, but no Attainder of Treason shall work Corruption of Blood, or Forfeiture except during the Life of the Person attainted.

Article IV.

SECTION 1. Full Faith and Credit shall be given in each State to the public Acts, Records, and judicial Proceedings of every other State. And the Congress may by general Laws prescribe the

Manner in which such Acts, Records and Proceedings shall be proved, and the Effect thereof.

SECTION 2. The Citizens of each State shall be entitled to all Privileges and Immunities of Citizens in the several States.

A Person charged in any State with Treason, Felony, or other Crime, who shall flee from Justice, and be found in another State, shall on Demand of the executive Authority of the State from which he fled, be delivered up, to be removed to the State having Jurisdiction of the Crime.

No Person held to Service or Labour in one State, under the Laws thereof, escaping into another, shall, in Consequence of any Law or Regulation therein, be discharged from such Service or Labour, but shall be delivered up on Claim of the Party to whom such Service or Labour may be due.

SECTION 3. New States may be admitted by the Congress into this Union; but no new State shall be formed or erected within the Jurisdiction of any other State; nor any State be formed by the Junction of two or more States, or Parts of States, without the Consent of the Legislatures of the States concerned as well as of the Congress.

The Congress shall have Power to dispose of and make all needful Rules and Regulations respecting the Territory or other Property belonging to the United States; and nothing in this Constitution shall be so construed as to Prejudice any Claims of the United States, or of any particular State.

SECTION 4. The United States shall guarantee to every State in this Union a Republican Form of Government, and shall protect each of them against Invasion; and on Application of the Legislature, or of the Executive (when the Legislature cannot be convened), against domestic Violence.

Article V.

The Congress, whenever two thirds of both Houses shall deem it necessary, shall propose Amendments to this Constitution, or, on the Application of the Legislatures of two thirds of the several States, shall call a Convention for proposing Amendments, which, in either Case, shall be valid to all Intents and Purposes, as Part of this Constitution, when ratified by the Legislatures of three fourths of the several States, or by

Conventions in three fourths thereof, as the one or the other Mode of Ratification may be proposed by the Congress; Provided that no Amendment which may be made prior to the Year One thousand eight hundred and eight shall in any Manner affect the first and fourth Clauses in the Ninth Section of the first Article; and that no State, without its Consent, shall be deprived of its equal Suffrage in the Senate.

Article VI.

All Debts contracted and Engagements entered into, before the Adoption of this Constitution, shall be as valid against the United States under this Constitution, as under the Confederation.

This Constitution, and the Laws of the United States which shall be made in Pursuance thereof; and all Treaties made, or which shall be made, under the Authority of the United States, shall be the supreme Law of the Land; and the Judges in every State shall be bound thereby, any Thing in the Constitution or Laws of any State to the Contrary notwithstanding.

The Senators and Representatives before mentioned, and the Members of the several State Legislatures, and all executive and judicial Officers, both of the United States and of the several States, shall be bound by Oath or Affirmation, to support this Constitution; but no religious Test shall ever be required as a Qualification to any Office or public Trust under the United States.

Article VII.

The Ratification of the Conventions of nine States, shall be sufficient for the Establishment of this Constitution between the States so ratifying the Same.

The Word, "the," being interlined between the seventh and eighth Lines of the first Page, The Word "Thirty" being partly written on an Erazure in the fifteenth Line of the first Page, The Words "is tried" being interlined between the thirty second and thirty third Lines of the first Page and the Word "the" being interlined between the forty third and forty fourth Lines of the second Page.

Attest William Jackson Secretary

done in Convention by the Unanimous Consent of the States present the Seventeenth Day of September in the Year of our Lord one thousand seven hundred and Eighty seven and of the Independence of the United States of America the Twelfth In witness whereof We have hereunto subscribed our Names,

Go. WASHINGTON, Presidt. and deputy from Virginia

NEW HAMPSHIRE: John Langdon, Nicholas Gilman

MASSACHUSETTS: Nathaniel Gorham, Rufus King

CONNECTICUT: Wm. Saml. Johnson, Roger Sherman

NEW YORK: Alexander Hamilton

NEW JERSEY: Wil. Livingston, David Brearley, Wm. Paterson, Jona. Dayton

PENSYLVANIA [sic]: B. Franklin, Thomas Mifflin, Robt. Morris, Geo. Clymer, Thos. FitzSimons, Jared Ingersoll, James Wilson, Gouv. Morris

DELAWARE: Geo. Read, Gunning Bedford jun., John Dickinson, Richard Bassett, Jaco. Broom

MARYLAND: James McHenry, Dan of St. Thos. Jenifer, Danl. Carroll

VIRGINIA: John Blair, James Madison Jr.

NORTH CAROLINA: Wm. Blount, Richd. Dobbs Spaight, Hu. Williamson

SOUTH CAROLINA: J. Rutledge, Charles Cotesworth Pinckney, Charles Pinckney, Pierce Butler

GEORGIA: William Few, Abr. Baldwin

Attest: William Jackson, Secretary.

In Convention Monday, September 17th, 1787. Present The States of New Hampshire, Massachusetts, Connecticut, MR. Hamilton from New York, New Jersey, Pennsylvania, Delaware, Maryland, Virginia, North Carolina, South Carolina and Georgia.

Resolved,

That the preceeding Constitution be laid before the United States in Congress assembled, and that it is the Opinion of this Convention, that it should afterwards be submitted to a Convention of Delegates, chosen in each State by the People thereof, under the Recommendation of its Legislature, for their Assent and Ratification; and that each Convention assenting to, and ratifying the Same, should give Notice thereof to the United States in Congress assembled.

Resolved, That it is the Opinion of this Convention, that as soon as the Conventions of nine States shall have ratified this Constitution, the United States in Congress assembled should fix a Day on which Electors should be appointed by the States which have ratified the same, and a Day on which the Electors should assemble to vote for the President, and the Time and Place for commencing Proceedings under this Constitution. That after such Publication the Electors should be appointed, and the Senators and Representatives elected: That the Electors should meet on the Day fixed for the Election of the President, and should transmit their Votes certified, signed, sealed and directed, as the Constitution requires, to the Secretary of the United States in Congress assembled, that the Senators and Representatives should convene at the Time and Place assigned; that the Senators should appoint a President of the Senate, for the sole purpose of receiving, opening and counting the Votes for President; and, that after he shall be chosen, the Congress, together with the President, should, without Delay, proceed to execute this Constitution.

By the Unanimous Order of the Convention

Go. WASHINGTON–Presidt. W. JACKSON Secretary.

AMENDMENTS

Articles in Addition to, and Amendment of, the Constitution of the United States of America, Proposed by Congress, and Ratified by the Legislatures of the Several States, Pursuant to the Fifth Article of the Original Constitution.

Article I.

Congress shall make no law respecting an establishment of religion, or prohibiting the free exercise thereof; or abridging the freedom of speech, or of the press, or the right of the people peaceably to assemble, and to petition the Government for a redress of grievances.

Article II.

A well regulated Militia, being necessary to the security of a free State, the right of the people to keep and bear Arms, shall not be infringed.

Article III.

No Soldier shall, in time of peace be quartered in any house, without the consent of the Owner, nor in time of war, but in a manner to be prescribed by law.

Article IV.

The right of the people to be secure in their persons, houses, papers, and effects, against unreasonable searches and seizures, shall not be violated, and no Warrants shall issue, but upon probable cause, supported by Oath or affirmation, and particularly describing the place to be searched, and the persons or things to be seized.

Article V.

No person shall be held to answer for a capital, or otherwise infamous crime, unless on a presentment or indictment of a Grand Jury, except in cases arising in the land or naval forces, or in the Militia, when in actual service in time of War or public danger; nor shall any person be subject for the same offence to be twice put in jeopardy of life or limb, nor shall be compelled in any criminal case to be a witness against himself, nor be deprived of life, liberty, or property, without due process of law; nor shall private property be taken for public use without just compensation.

Article VI.

In all criminal prosecutions, the accused shall enjoy the right to a speedy and public trial, by an impartial jury of the State and district wherein the crime shall have been committed; which district shall have been previously ascertained by law, and to be informed of the nature and cause of the accusation; to be confronted with the witnesses against him; to have compulsory process for obtaining witnesses in his favor, and to have the assistance of counsel for his defence.

Article VII.

In Suits at common law, where the value in controversy shall exceed twenty dollars, the right of trial by jury shall be preserved, and no fact tried by a jury shall be otherwise re-examined in any Court of the United States, than according to the rules of the common law.

Article VIII.

Excessive bail shall not be required, nor excessive fines imposed, nor cruel and unusual punishments inflicted.

Article IX.

The enumeration in the Constitution of certain rights shall not be construed to deny or disparage others retained by the people.

Article X.

The powers not delegated to the United States by the Constitution, nor prohibited by it to the States, are reserved to the States respectively, or to the people.

Article XI.

The Judicial power of the United States shall not be construed to extend to any suit in law or equity, commenced or prosecuted against one of the United States by Citizens of another State, or by Citizens or Subjects of any Foreign State.

Article XII.

The Electors shall meet in their respective states, and vote by ballot for President and Vice President, one of whom, at least, shall not be an inhabitant of the same state with themselves; they shall name in their ballots the person voted for as President, and in distinct ballots the person voted for as Vice-President, and they shall make distinct lists of all persons voted for as President, and of all persons voted for as Vice-President, and of the number of votes for each, which lists they shall sign and certify, and transmit sealed to the seat of the government of the United States, directed to the President of the Senate;

The President of the Senate shall, in the presence of the Senate and House of Representatives, open all the certificates and the votes shall then be counted;

The person having the greatest number of votes for President, shall be the President, if such number be a majority of the whole number of Electors appointed; and if no person have such majority, then from the persons having the highest numbers not exceeding three on the list of those voted for as President, the House of Representatives shall choose immediately, by ballot, the President. But in choosing the President, the votes shall be taken by states, the representation from each state having one vote; a quorum for this purpose shall consist of a member or members from two-thirds of the states, and a majority of all the states shall be necessary to a choice.

And if the House of Representatives shall not choose a President whenever the right of choice shall devolve upon them, before the fourth day of March next following, then the Vice-President shall act as President, as in the case of the death or other constitutional disability of the President. The person having the greatest number of votes as Vice-President, shall be the Vice-President, if such number be a majority of the whole number of Electors appointed, and if no person have a majority, then from the two highest numbers on the list, the Senate shall choose the Vice-President; a quorum for the purpose shall consist of two-thirds of the whole number of Senators, and a majority of the whole number shall be necessary to a choice. But no person constitutionally ineligible to the office of President shall be eligible to that of Vice-President of the United States.

Article XIII.

SECTION 1. Neither slavery nor involuntary servitude, except as a punishment for crime whereof the party shall have been duly convicted, shall exist within the United States, or any place subject to their jurisdiction.

SECTION 2. Congress shall have power to enforce this article by appropriate legislation.

Article XIV.

SECTION 1. All persons born or naturalized in the United States and subject to the jurisdiction thereof, are citizens of the United

States and of the State wherein they reside. No State shall make or enforce any law which shall abridge the privileges or immunities of citizens of the United States; nor shall any State deprive any person of life, liberty, or property, without due process of law; nor deny to any person within its jurisdiction the equal protection of the laws.

SECTION 2. Representatives shall be apportioned among the several States according to their respective numbers, counting the whole number of persons in each State, excluding Indians not taxed. But when the right to vote at any election for the choice of electors for President and Vice President of the United States, Representatives in Congress, the Executive and Judicial officers of a State, or the members of the Legislature thereof, is denied to any of the male inhabitants of such State, being twenty-one years of age, and citizens of the United States, or in any way abridged, except for participation in rebellion, or other crime, the basis of representation therein shall be reduced in the proportion which the number of such male citizens shall bear to the whole number of male citizens twenty-one years of age in such State.

SECTION 3. No person shall be a Senator or Representative in Congress, or elector of President and Vice President, or hold any office, civil or military, under the United States, or under any State, who, having previously taken an oath, as a member of Congress, or as an officer of the United States, or as a member of any State legislature, or as an executive or judicial officer of any State, to support the Constitution of the United States, shall have engaged in insurrection or rebellion against the same, or given aid or comfort to the enemies thereof. But Congress may by a vote of two-thirds of each House, remove such disability.

SECTION 4. The validity of the public debt of the United States, authorized by law, including debts incurred for payment of pensions and bounties for services in suppressing insurrection or rebellion, shall not be questioned. But neither the United States nor any State shall assume or pay any debt or obligation incurred in aid of insurrection or rebellion against the United States, or any claim for the loss or emancipation of any slave; but all such debts, obligations and claims shall be held illegal and void.

SECTION 5. The Congress shall have power to enforce, by appropriate legislation, the provisions of this article.

Article XV.

SECTION 1. The right of citizens of the United States to vote shall not be denied or abridged by the United States or by any State on account of race, color, or previous condition of servitude.

SECTION 2. The Congress shall have power to enforce this article by appropriate legislation.

Article XVI.

The Congress shall have power to lay and collect taxes on incomes, from whatever source derived, without apportionment among the several States, and without regard to any census or enumeration.

Article XVII.

The Senate of the United States shall be composed of two Senators from each State, elected by the people thereof, for six years; and each Senator shall have one vote. The electors in each State shall have the qualifications requisite for electors of the most numerous branch of the State legislatures.

When vacancies happen in the representation of any State in the Senate, the executive authority of such State shall issue writs of election to fill such vacancies: Provided, That the legislature of any State may empower the executive thereof to make temporary appointments until the people fill the vacancies by election as the legislature may direct.

This amendment shall not be so construed as to affect the election or term of any Senator chosen before it becomes valid as part of the Constitution.

Article XVIII.

SECTION 1. After one year from the ratification of this article the manufacture, sale, or transportation of intoxicating liquors within, the importation thereof into, or the exportation thereof from the United States and all territory subject to the jurisdiction thereof for beverage purposes is hereby prohibited.

SECTION 2. The Congress and the several States shall have concurrent power to enforce this article by appropriate legislation.

SECTION 3. This article shall be inoperative unless it shall have been ratified as an amendment to the Constitution by the legislatures of the several States, as provided in the Constitution, within seven years from the date of the submission hereof to the States by the Congress.

Article XIX.

The right of citizens of the United States to vote shall not be denied or abridged by the United States or by any State on account of sex.

Congress shall have power to enforce this article by appropriate legislation.

Article XX.

SECTION 1. The terms of the President and Vice President shall end at noon the 20th day of January, and the terms of Senators and Representatives at noon on the 3d day of January, of the years in which such terms would have ended if this article had not been ratified; and the terms of their successors shall then begin.

SECTION 2. The Congress shall assemble at least once in every year, and such meeting shall begin at noon on the 3d day of January, unless they shall by law appoint a different day.

SECTION 3. If, at the time fixed for the beginning of the term of the President, the President elect shall have died, the Vice President elect shall become President. If a President shall not have been chosen before the time fixed for the beginning of his term, or if the President elect shall have failed to qualify, then the Vice President elect shall act as President until a President shall have qualified; and the Congress may by law provide for the case wherein neither a President elect nor a Vice President elect shall have qualified, declaring who shall then act as President, or the manner in which one who is to act shall be selected, and such person shall act accordingly until a President or Vice President shall have qualified.

SECTION 4. The Congress may by law provide for the case of the death of any of the persons from whom the House of Representatives may choose a President whenever the right of choice shall have devolved upon them, and for the case of the death of any of the persons from whom the Senate may choose a Vice President whenever the right of choice shall have devolved upon them.

SECTION 5. Sections 1 and 2 shall take effect on the 15th day of October following the ratification of this article.

SECTION 6. This article shall be inoperative unless it shall have been ratified as an amendment to the Constitution by the legislatures of three-fourths of the several States within seven years from the date of its submission.

Article XXI.

SECTION 1. The eighteenth article of amendment to the Constitution of the United States is hereby repealed.

SECTION 2. The transportation or importation into any State, Territory, or possession of the United States for delivery or use therein of intoxicating liquors, in violation of the laws thereof, is hereby prohibited.

SECTION 3. This article shall be inoperative unless it shall have been ratified as an amendment to the Constitution by conventions in the several States, as provided in the Constitution, within seven years from the date of the submission hereof to the States by the Congress.

Article XXII.

SECTION 1. No person shall be elected to the office of the President more than twice, and no person who has held the office of President, or acted as President, for more than two years of a term to which some other person was elected President shall be elected to the office of President more than once. But this Article shall not apply to any person holding the office of President when this Article was proposed by the Congress, and shall not prevent any person who may be holding the office of President, or acting as President, during the term within which this Article becomes operative from holding the office of President or acting as President during the remainder of such term.

SECTION 2. This article shall be inoperative unless it shall have been ratified as an amendment to the Constitution by the legislatures of three-fourths of the several States within seven years from the date of its submission to the States by the Congress.

Article XXIII.

SECTION 1. The District constituting the seat of Government of the United States shall appoint in such manner as the Congress may direct:

A number of electors of President and Vice President equal to the whole number of Senators and Representatives in Congress to which the District would be entitled if it were a State, but in no event more than the least populous State; they shall be in addition to those appointed by the States, but they shall be considered, for the purposes of the election of President and Vice President, to be electors appointed by a State; and they shall meet in the District and perform such duties as provided by the twelfth article of amendment.

SECTION 2. The Congress shall have power to enforce this article by appropriate legislation.

Article XXIV.

SECTION 1. The right of citizens of the United States to vote in any primary or other election for President or Vice President, for electors for President or Vice President, or for Senator or Representative in Congress, shall not be denied or abridged by the United States or any State by reason of failure to pay any poll tax or other tax.

SECTION 2. The Congress shall have power to enforce this article by appropriate legislation.

Article XXV.

SECTION 1. In case of the removal of the President from office or of his death or resignation, the Vice President shall become President.

SECTION 2. Whenever there is a vacancy in the office of the Vice President, the President shall nominate a Vice President who shall take office upon confirmation by a majority vote of both Houses of Congress.

SECTION 3. Whenever the President transmits to the President pro tempore of the Senate and the Speaker of the House of Representatives his written declaration that he is unable to discharge the powers and duties of his office, and until he transmits to them a written declaration to the contrary, such powers and duties shall be discharged by the Vice President as Acting President.

SECTION 4. Whenever the Vice President and a majority of either the principal officers of the executive departments or of such other body as Congress may by law provide, transmit to the President pro tempore of the Senate and the Speaker of the House of Representatives their written declaration that the President is unable to discharge the powers and duties of his office, the Vice President shall immediately assume the powers and duties of the office as Acting President.

Thereafter, when the President transmits to the President pro tempore of the Senate and the Speaker of the House of Representatives his written declaration that no inability exists, he shall resume the powers and duties of his office unless the Vice President and a majority of either the principal officers of the executive department or of such other body as Congress may by law provide, transmit within four days to the President pro tempore of the Senate and the Speaker of the House of Representatives their written declaration that the President is unable to discharge the powers and duties of his office. Thereupon Congress shall decide the issue, assembling within forty-eight hours for that purpose if not in session. If the Congress, within twenty-one days after receipt of the latter written declaration, or, if Congress is not in session, within twenty-one days after Congress is required to assemble, determines by two-thirds vote of both Houses that the President is unable to discharge the powers and duties of his office, the Vice President shall continue to discharge the same as Acting President; otherwise, the President shall resume the powers and duties of his office.

Article XXVI.

SECTION 1. The right of citizens of the United States, who are eighteen years of age or older, to vote shall not be denied or abridged by the United States or by any State on account of age.

SECTION 2. The Congress shall have power to enforce this article by appropriate legislation.

Article XXVII.

No law, varying the compensation for the services of the Senators and Representatives, shall take effect, until an election of Representatives shall have intervened.

Where to Learn More

Books

Abraham, Henry J. *Justices, Presidents, and Senators.* Lanham, MD: Rowman & Littlefield Publishers, 1999.

Baum, Lawrence. *The Supreme Court.* Washington, DC: Congressional Quarterly Inc., 1998.

Beard, Charles A. *American Government and Politics.* 10th ed. New York: Macmillan Co., 1949.

Beard, Charles A. *An Economic Interpretation of the Constitution of the United States.* New York: Macmillan, 1935.

Biskupic, Joan, and Elder Witt. *The Supreme Court & the Powers of the American Government.* Washington, DC: Congressional Quarterly Inc., 1997.

Biskupic, Joan, and Elder Witt. *The Supreme Court at Work.* Washington, DC: Congressional Quarterly Inc., 1997.

Brannen, Daniel E., and Richard Clay Hanes. *Supreme Court Drama: Cases That Changed America.* Detroit: UXL, 2001.

Burnham, James. *Congress and the American Tradition.* New Brunswick, NJ: Transaction Publishers, 2003.

Carp, Robert A., and Ronald Stidham. *The Federal Courts.* 2nd ed. Washington, DC: Congressional Quarterly Inc., 1991.

Charleton, James H., Robert G. Ferris, and Mary C. Ryan, eds. *Framers of the Constitution.* Washington, DC: National Archives and Records Administration, 1976.

Choper, Jesse H., ed. *The Supreme Court and Its Justices.* 2nd ed. Chicago: American Bar Association, 2001.

Clark, J. C. D. *The Language of Liberty, 1660–1832.* Cambridge, Eng.: Cambridge University Press, 1994.

Congressional Quarterly Inc. *Guide to the Congress of the United States.* 1st ed. Washington, DC: Congressional Quarterly Service, 1971.

Congressional Quarterly Inc. *Powers of the Presidency.* 2nd ed. Washington, DC: Congressional Quarterly Inc., 1997.

Cronin, Thomas E. *Inventing the American Presidency.* Lawrence: University Press of Kansas, 1989.

DiClerico, Robert E. *The American President.* 5th ed. Upper Saddle River, NJ: Prentice Hall, 2000.

Dougherty, J. Hampden. *Power of Federal Judiciary over Legislation.* New York: Putnam's Sons, 1912. Reprint, Clark, NJ: Lawbook Exchange, 2004.

Fisher, Louis. *Constitutional Conflicts between Congress and the President.* 3rd ed. Lawrence: University Press of Kansas, 1991.

Fisher, Louis. *The Politics of Shared Power: Congress and the Executive.* 4th ed. College Station: Texas A&M University Press, 1998.

Goebel, Julius, Jr. *Antecedents and Beginnings to 1801.* Vol. I. New York: Macmillan, 1971.

Green, Mark. *Who Runs Congress?* 3rd ed. New York: The Viking Press, 1979.

Hart, John. *The Presidential Branch.* 2nd ed. Chatham, NJ: Chatham House Publishers, 1995.

Irons, Peter. *A People's History of the Supreme Court.* New York: Penguin Books, 1999.

Janda, Kenneth, Jeffrey M. Berry, and Jerry Goldman. *The Challenge of Democracy.* 5th ed. Boston: Houghton Mifflin Company, 1997.

Kelly, Alfred H., and Winfred A. Harbison. *The American Constitution: Its Origins and Development.* 5th ed. New York: W. W. Norton & Co., 1976.

Kurland, Philip B., and Ralph Lerner. *The Founders' Constitution.* 5 vols. Indianapolis: Liberty Fund, 1987.

Lazarus, Edward P. *Closed Chambers.* New York: Times Books, 1998.

Levy, Leonard W. *Original Intent and the Framers' Constitution.* New York: Macmillan, 1988.

Lintcott, Andrew. *The Constitution of the Roman Republic.* Oxford: Clarendon Press, 1999.

Loomis, Burdett A. *The Contemporary Congress.* 3rd ed. Boston: Bedford/St. Martin's, 2000.

MacNeil, Neil. *Forge of Democracy: The House of Representatives.* New York: David MacKay Co., 1963.

McClenaghan, William A. *Magruder's American Government 2003.* Needham, MA: Prentice Hall School Group, 2002.

McDonald, Forrest. *The American Presidency.* Lawrence: University Press of Kansas, 1994.

Milkis, Sidney M., and Michael Nelson. *The American Presidency: Origins & Development.* 3rd ed. Washington, DC: Congressional Quarterly Inc., 1999.

Millar, Fergus. *The Roman Republic in Political Thought.* Hanover and London: Brandeis University Press and Historical Society of Israel, 2002.

Moran, Thomas Francis. *The Rise and Development of the Bicameral System in America.* Baltimore: The Johns Hopkins Press, 1895.

Nelson, Michael, ed. *The Evolving Presidency.* Washington, DC: Congressional Quarterly Inc., 1999.

Nelson, Michael, ed. *The Presidency and the Political System.* 7th ed. Washington, DC: CQ Press, 2003.

Parenti, Michael. *Democracy for the Few.* 6th ed. New York: St. Martin's Press, 1995.

Pole, J. R. *Political Representation in England and the Origins of the American Republic.* London: Macmillan, 1966.

Ripley, Randall B. *Party Leaders in the House of Representatives.* Washington, DC: Brookings Institution, 1967.

Roelofs, H. Mark. *The Poverty of American Politics.* 2nd ed. Philadelphia: Temple University Press, 1998.

Rozell, Mark J. *Executive Privilege.* Lawrence: University Press of Kansas, 2002.

Rozell, Mark J., William D. Pederson, and Frank J. Williams. *George Washington and the Origins of the American Presidency.* Westport, CT: Praeger, 2000.

Schwartz, Bernard. *A History of the Supreme Court.* New York: Oxford University Press, 1993.

Shelley, Mack C., II. *American Government and Politics Today.* 2004–2005 ed. Belmont, CA: Wadsworth Publishing, 2003.

Surrency, Erwin C. *History of the Federal Courts.* 2nd ed. Dobbs Ferry, NY: Oceana Publications, 2002.

Volkomer, Walter E. *American Government.* 8th ed. Upper Saddle River, NJ: Prentice Hall, 1998.

Wasby, Stephen L. *The Supreme Court in the Federal Judicial System.* 2nd ed. New York: Holt, Rinehart and Winston, 1984.

Wheeler, Russell R., and Cynthia Harrison. *Creating the Federal Judicial System.* Washington, DC: Federal Judicial Center, 1994.

Wilson, Woodrow. *Congressional Government.* Houghton Mifflin Co., 1885. Reprint, New Brunswick, NJ: Transaction Publishers, 2002.

Wolfensberger, Donald R. *Congress and the People.* Washington, DC, and Baltimore: Woodrow Wilson Center Press and Johns Hopkins University Press, 2000.

Woll, Peter. *American Government: Readings and Cases.* 15th ed. New York: Longman, 2003.

Young, Roland. *American Law and Politics: The Creation of Public Order.* New York: Harper & Row, 1967.

Zinn, Howard. *A People's History of the United States.* New York: HarperCollins, 2003.

CD-ROMs

21st Century Complete Guide to U.S. Courts. Progressive Management, 2003.

Web Sites

Federal Judicial Center. http://www.fjc.gov/ (accessed on March 31, 2005).

Federal Judiciary. http://www.uscourts.gov (accessed on February 18, 2005).

Library of Congress. http://www.loc.gov (accessed on March 15, 2005).

O'Hara, James B. "Court History Quizzes." *Supreme Court Historical Society.* http://www.supremecourthistory.org/02_history/ subs_
history/02_f.html (accessed on March 30, 2005).

Supreme Court of the United States. http://www.supremecourtus.gov (accessed on February 18, 2005).

United States Department of Justice. http://www.usdoj.gov/ (accessed on February 12, 2005).

United States House of Representatives. http://www.house.gov (accessed on March 14, 2005).

United States Senate. http://www.senate.gov (accessed on March 14, 2005).

U.S. Census Bureau. http://www.census.gov (accessed on February 16, 2005).

U.S. Courts: The Federal Judiciary. http://www.uscourts.gov (accessed on March 23, 2005).

U.S. Term Limits. http://www.termlimits.org/ (accessed on March 11, 2005).

The White House. http://www.whitehouse.gov (accessed on February 16, 2005).

Index

C

d

★ j